THE CONSEQUENCE OF FALLING

NEW YORK TIMES BESTSELLING AUTHOR

CLAIRE CONTRERAS

ONE

PRESLEY

MAYBE I WAS BEING OVERLY dramatic and petty, but I was having the worst day imaginable. First, I lost the photography contest to Jamie, which meant she was going on an all-expenses-paid trip to China while I spent the summer at home pretending to breeze through my summer reading list. Actually, I'd just buy the CliffsNotes and pay someone to do my report for me. Then, my parents told me they were getting a divorce. Actually, the word they used was *separating*, but everyone knew that was a nice way of saying they hated each other and wanted to eventually divorce—eventually meaning when Dad figured out a way to keep Mom from taking all his money. Lastly, I was getting soaked while I waited for one of them to pick me up from cheerleading practice. It was ridiculous, really. They'd picked me up after school, and in the break I had from getting drilled by teachers and then by my cheerleading coach because I was off my game, they laid the news on me. And now, they were late to pick me up.

This was exactly how kids ended up traumatized by divorce. It resulted in splitting their time between two houses and being forgotten all the time. If our parents couldn't be trusted to

1

make something as big as marriage work, how could they figure out how to schedule their lives around their children? I was already seething, but that thought made me rage. How could they just decide to not be together? It was May. We were only a month away from our annual family trip to Europe. Dad had chosen San Sebastian as this year's excursion after I'd traced our genealogy back there to the Basques and connected with second cousins. We couldn't not go. We'd been looking forward to it all year. Instead of going back inside or trying to find cover from the rain, I walked forward and sat on the steps, letting the storm consume me. I wanted them to see the effects of their selfishness. If I got sick, it would be a bonus. Maybe I could skip the stupid end of school year dance this weekend and the field day performance while I was at it. Suddenly, being captain of the cheerleading squad just seemed stupid. All of this was stupid.

The sound of a car approaching made my head snap up. It was Dad's tinted black Mercedes. I ground my teeth together as I stood, pulling my now-soaked backpack with me. I hoped everything in it was water damaged. My entire body shook as I stomped to the car and pulled the door open, letting the backpack drop in the feet compartment of the passenger seat and sitting down as heavily as my body allowed. That was when I saw the person in the driver's seat was not my father, and my anger was replaced by panic.

"Who the hell are you?" I reached for the door handle.

I'd seen enough suspense movies to know a kidnapper when I saw one, and even though this guy was younger than I would've imagined a kidnapper being, and a hell of a lot cuter, I jumped out of the car and ran back to the front of the school.

"Presley." He called my name as I tried to open the front door, which was locked. Of course they fucking locked it.

"I need to go back inside." I pulled the handles with both hands and shook the door.

"Your dad sent me."

"Yeah right. I've heard that one before." I slapped my hand on the glass as I looked inside. "Help!"

I heard his footsteps behind me and froze, grabbing the handles even tighter. I wasn't going down without a fight, that was for sure.

"Your father sent me to pick you up," he said. He was literally right behind me. Panic crept into my throat, blocking out the yell I wanted to produce.

"Stay the fuck away from me."

"I'm not going to hurt you." He chuckled, then that chuckle turned into a full-on laugh. "You look crazy, you know that?"

"I don't care about how I look. I've heard of people getting kidnapped for ransom, and I've had a really bad day already and refuse to succumb to your bullshit."

"I'm not going to kidnap you." He put his hands on my shoulders and squeezed, not roughly, but not lightly either. "I'll get your father on the phone."

"You have his car." I shot a narrowed look over my shoulder. He dropped his hands. "You could've kidnapped him first. Call the police and have them send an escort."

"Wha . . . I . . . do they do that?" His brows furrowed. His genuine shock made me loosen the grip on the handles. That and my hands hurt.

"Call them."

His eyes widened. He looked unsure of what to do. I could practically see his thoughts ping-ponging back and forth— would he call or not? After what felt like an eternity, he pulled a cell phone out of his pocket and dialed. I knew from the way his back straightened and the way he was talking that he'd called my father. I didn't know this guy, but I knew that much, because it was what they all did when my dad was on the line. I rolled my eyes as he stepped forward and pressed the phone to my ear.

"Hello?"

"Presley Carina Rose, I swear to all that's holy that if you don't get your ass in that car right this second, I'm going to ground you for a month." He was fuming. I felt my eyes narrow as I let go of the door and yanked the phone out of the driver's hand, stomping toward the car.

"You know what? Fucking ground me. Send me away to boarding school. Send me to live with Aunt—"

"Did you just curse at me?"

I stopped walking and slapped a hand over my mouth. I'd just cursed at him. I never did that. I opened my mouth to apologize, to say something, anything. Instead, I hung up the call and closed the car door. The guy slid into the driver's seat. I didn't turn to acknowledge him, but I heard the click of his seat belt before he started driving. I hated—no, loathed—when my parents hired people to drive me around or watch over me when they went out of town as if I was a child. Technically, at fifteen years old, I was, but I hated being treated as such.

"He means well . . . your dad," the driver said.

My arms, crossed over my chest, tightened. "What do you know about him? You just met him."

"I know a lot more about him than you think," he said. "And I didn't just meet him."

My eyes widened. I glanced at him. "You're not like, my half-brother or something, are you?"

"What? No." He made a face like he had a million sour things in his mouth. "Are you seeing a therapist? Because you should. You jump to crazy conclusions about perfectly normal situations."

"I don't need a therapist. I need the people in my life to get their shit together." I looked out the window. "And for the record, you don't know me or what conclusions I jump to on a regular day, which this is not, so I'd appreciate it if you kept your preconceived judgments to yourself."

"Preconceived? You jumped out of this car saying I was trying to kidnap you. You wanted me to call the cops to escort us to your house, which I'm still not certain they'd do." He shot me a stern glance. I looked at his mouth. I don't know why I did that, but I did. His lips were plump and soft looking. It was hard *not* to look at his mouth. He didn't notice. "You were also sitting in the rain when I got here. Who the hell does that?"

"Someone who's trying to make a point."

"By catching pneumonia?"

"Maybe." I tilted my chin upward as if I'd made a great point, but it really did sound stupid now that I was playing it back. "Anyway, he didn't tell me he hired a new driver and you look too young to be employed by him."

"I've been employed by him for years."

My face twisted. "How old are you?"

"Eighteen."

"And what the hell could you have possibly doing 'for years'?"

"His dry cleaning." He caught me staring at him, waiting for him to expand on that, so he did. "My uncle owns a dry cleaning business."

"Oh."

"Would it kill you to be a little more grateful for everything you have? Your parents work hard to maintain the idyllic lifestyle you have. Some people would kill to trade places with you."

"You don't know what you're talking about, and I'd appreciate it if we keep this conversation to a minimum until you drop me off. I don't need to be reprimanded by one of Dad's employees, and I definitely don't need to explain my gratitude to you."

"I'm just saying, you may want to ease up on him. He's going through a hard time right now."

"Let's make something clear." I turned my glare toward him.

Thankfully, we were turning into my driveway and this little conversation would soon be over. "You don't know me and despite what you think, you'll never know him either. Whatever façade he's showing you is just that." I reached for the door handle and grabbed my backpack when the car came to a full stop. "And next time he sends you to pick me up, ignore him. I'll gladly walk home."

I opened the door and slammed it behind me. I ignored my mother's voice when I heard her calling from the kitchen and stomped upstairs. I needed to shower and get rid of the stench of the day. What I wanted to do was punch something, no, *someone*. I wanted to punch that stupid driver. I didn't even get his name, and I didn't want to know what it was anyway. I would forever associate *him* with my most fucked-up day of the century.

TWO

TWO YEARS LATER

"OH, HELL NO." I stood completely still in front of the driver. "This has to be some kind of joke."

I hadn't seen him since he'd taken me home *that* day years ago, but I had learned his name and a few things about him: Nathaniel Bradley, my father's favorite pet. He was currently putting himself through business school at NYU, which I'd admit was impressive. What wasn't impressive was hearing my father talk about him all the time. That was unbearably annoying. It was surprising that when I went to visit my father, Nathaniel wasn't sitting on his damn lap like a dog enjoying being pet or something.

Seeing him now, I realized he couldn't possibly fit on Dad's lap. He'd clearly filled out his formerly bony frame and morphed into someone who looked like he belonged in cleats, shoulder pads, and smack in the center of every woman's fantasies. He grinned as I gaped at him, and I snapped out of my stupid thoughts. Yes, he was devastatingly handsome. No, I didn't want him, and I definitely didn't want him to think I wanted him.

"I'm here to drive you to prom."

"I'd rather walk."

"In those heels?" His eyes traveled slowly down my body until they reached my shoes. I fought the urge to cover myself. It wasn't like he was looking at me in a creepy *I-want-you* way or anything, but this guy, as annoying as he was, was really damn good-looking and the whole thing was weird. Why had my father hired hot guys to drive me around anyway? Not *guys* plural, because I highly doubted there were very many who looked like this. I took in the amused expression on his face and remembered how obnoxious he was last time and shook off the attraction, meeting his gaze full-on.

"I'll take them off if I have to."

"You?" he scoffed. "Have you ever walked barefoot in your life, princess?"

"Don't call me that." I rolled my eyes and walked past him, letting myself into the back seat of the car.

If he was going to drive me, there would be a clear line between us. He was my father's employee, which meant he was sort of my employee too, and I didn't have to answer to him. In truth, most of Dad's employees were family, and even the ones who weren't treated me like I was one of their own, so I'd never thought to draw a line between us. I wouldn't dare. It was this guy who brought out the ugly in me, with his untamed dark hair and his chiseled jaw and that stupid arrogance his blue eyes gleamed with.

"Isn't it customary for the guy to pick up the girl for prom?"

I bit my lip to keep quiet. I wouldn't respond. I wouldn't respond. I wouldn't respond. Truth was, Ben and I had broken up last week but decided to go together anyway and the prom was happening in his building, so it seemed like a waste of time for him to collect me from my house across town. He was a self-absorbed asshole, who felt like if he wasn't getting something out of the exchange, he'd rather not make an effort. Not that I would say any of that to Nathaniel Bradley. He'd probably side with Ben anyway.

"Cat got your tongue, Presley?"

"Why aren't you at some college party or something? Don't you have anything better to do on a Saturday night?"

"Sure I do, but I'm having so much fun driving a little over-privileged brat around." His eyes twinkled as he looked at me through the rearview.

My fists clenched so hard my nails dug into my palms. "You know what would make this night a whole lot better? If you weren't in it, so can you just shut up for the rest of the night?"

"I'll think about it."

"HE'S NOT GOOD FOR YOU."

Those were the first words Nathaniel Bradley said to me when I got back in the car at the end of the night. I sat in the front seat this time and instantly regretted my move when he spoke the words.

"You literally dropped me off here. How would you possibly know whether or not he's good for me?" I rolled my eyes and shook my head as he drove away from the Ritz, where the prom had taken place, and Ben's parents had a penthouse apartment.

"He didn't even walk you to the car."

"Because he lives in the building."

"He should've still walked you to the car."

"Maybe he wanted me to stay."

That shut him up for all of ten seconds. He cleared his throat. "Why didn't you? Isn't that what people do on prom night?"

"What year do you live in?" I made a face. "People don't wait for prom night to fuck anymore."

9

"I don't think they ever did." He glanced at me. "I meant, why didn't you stay out later? It's not even midnight."

I shrugged. "I was bored."

"Bored at your boyfriend's house?"

I sighed heavily. "Can you just drive me home in silence?"

My night hadn't gone as planned. For starters, Nathaniel wasn't wrong. I should've still been in that building, preferably upstairs in Ben's room, naked. Instead, I'd left the minute things started getting hot and heavy. Everything felt off. One minute I wanted him to rip my dress off, as usual, and the next I felt cold as stone and wanted to get the hell out of there as fast as my heels would allow it. He hadn't done anything wrong, but something was definitely wrong with me. It'd been that way since my parents finalized their divorce last year.

My emotions had been all over the place. My therapist said it was normal. She said I had to give myself time to heal. I'd felt like I'd been sucker-punched with the news of the divorce though and everything that followed was a bit of a blur. I'd done everything I could to cope with the heavy guilt I felt in a healthy way. I knew deep down that it wasn't my fault that Mom decided to step out on her marriage. It wasn't my fault that she seemed to be looking for happiness in someone else's house instead of ours. It wasn't my fault, yet I felt like maybe something I'd done was the cause of all of this. Maybe it was because I'd heard her say that kids ruined everything in her relationships. Kids meaning me, since I was an only child. Whatever the reason for this feeling, I wanted to numb it. Those were the times I got myself into things that made me feel like I was in over my head. Tonight would have been another one of those nights if I hadn't bailed on Ben. I pressed the back of my head on the headrest and turned my face to look out the window. It was definitely for the best that I left when I did. I was so lost in thought that I nearly jumped out of my seat when Nathaniel spoke again.

"What are you going to do now that you're graduating?"

"Go to college." I snuck a glance in his direction. "Duh."

The side of his mouth twitched and I decided I'd pay good money to see his full smile. "What college? What are you going to study?"

"Business," I said slowly, wondering if there was a catch to him being nice to me. "NYU, actually. Dad said that's where you are now, but if we run into each other there, you can just pretend you don't know me."

He chuckled, a deep sound that made my pulse kick. "Not a problem, princess. I wouldn't be caught dead hanging around with a lowly freshman anyway."

"I'm surprised you have anyone to hang out with at all." I glanced at him at the same time that he looked at me, and our eyes locked. For a second, as I looked into his eyes, I forgot what I was going to say. I blinked away when I remembered who he was and why he was even here to begin with. I cleared my throat and added, "Don't call me princess."

"Is your boyfriend also going to NYU?"

"Columbia."

"Fancy."

"Not really." I made a face.

Most of our classmates were going to Ivy League schools. I had a really bad junior year, so I had no chance at that. My senior year hadn't been any better, if I'm honest, which I wouldn't be with Nathaniel. He didn't need to know that I'd been skipping school and had let myself go from potential vale-dictorian to "only had a chance at a public university because her dad was a major donor there" status.

"Are you planning on working for your dad at some point?"

"I guess that's what I'm supposed to do."

He pulled up to the curb outside of my dad's building and looked at me as he set the gear in park, leaving the car running. I met his gaze only because I was confused why he wasn't turning it off, and found him staring at me. If I wasn't in such an awful mood all the time, I knew I would have appreciated this guy paying attention to me, employee or not, but I was in a mood all the time, therefore, I snapped.

"What?"

"What do you want to do with your life?"

I opened my mouth and closed it, frowning. No one had ever asked me that before. Not even the school college counselor had asked me that. Everyone assumed I'd take over my dad's business. It wasn't like I could explain to people that I wanted nothing to do with the brewery. Because of White Oak Brewery, I'd been afforded an incredible life. People would think I was a complete idiot if I didn't take over one day. It'd been my grandfather's, handed down to my father, and it was assumed it would be handed down to me. Even Dad didn't ask me whether or not I wanted to be part of it, because he knew I felt like I had no choice and he liked it that way.

I always tried to tell myself that if he owned something cooler, I'd be okay with working there for the rest of my life, but beer? I hated beer. I'd never say those words aloud, but I hated it. If I had a choice, I'd do something a little more meaningful with my life. I'd said that to my mother once and she'd assured me I could do both. I knew I could, but I really didn't want to be stuck with the brewery.

"Presley?" Nathaniel's voice brought me back to the moment.

"I want to work for my father. It's what I'm supposed to do." I smiled. I'd never smiled at him before, so I knew he'd be surprised. It didn't matter that my smile was fake.

It was the only one I had to offer. No one cared it wasn't genuine, because no one looked closely enough to know the truth. *Why bother?*

THREE

THREE YEARS LATER

"YOU KNOW that whole hoes before bros rule only works if there are bros to brush off in the picture," Jamie said from the bathroom.

"Please," I scoffed as I applied my makeup. "You're the one in the relationship. I've been brushing them off like it's my job."

Jamie laughed. We were getting dressed for a Halloween party. We were both going as pink ladies—the bad-girl versions —with skin-tight black jeans, black bodysuits, and killer heels. I had a feeling my mother, who was a huge fan of *Grease*, would be proud. If I were on speaking terms with her right now, I'd send a picture. Not that she'd receive the picture given she was sailing around the world with her new boyfriend. I felt my excitement dwindle as I thought of her. I set my makeup brush down and walked to the kitchen, picking up one of the orange and green Jell-O shots we'd made for the occasion. After two years of partying hard, Jamie and I had decided that this year we'd tone it down and be good girls, the kind who focused on school. So far, we'd succeeded, but tonight was looking a little bit like the former years.

"Jamie, did you already take a shot?" I counted the little

cups. There had been fifteen and we were down to ten. "Or five?"

She laughed, walking toward me. "I couldn't taste the alcohol in the first two."

"So you took three more to make sure?" I raised an eyebrow and turned to her. She shrugged, plucking another one from the counter and squishing it into her mouth.

"Tonight's about having fun."

I lifted a little cup in the air. "To having fun."

TWO HOURS LATER, we were in the Meatpacking District with Jamie's boyfriend and a few of his friends and their girl-friends. I would've felt like the sixth wheel had it not been for Adam, whom I'd just met and who had kept me laughing the entire time. He definitely seemed like the kind of guy I could settle down with. A nice, good-looking man with big aspirations.

"Why in the world would you want to become a politician?" I asked. It was the only downfall I could see affecting this potential thing between us.

Adam shrugged, smiling. "I want to change the world."

"I've known a lot of politicians," I said. "My father included, though he only did it for a short time, and the only thing it changes is your morals."

"I'm up for the challenge."

The way he said it, with a warm gleam in his eyes, made me feel like maybe he'd be the one to survive politics. Maybe he'd be the one to change the world. Who knew? When he smiled at me, I felt like genuinely smiling back.

"I guess I'll be on the lookout. Maybe I'll vote for you if you get on a ballot. If I feel you're a good fit, of course."

"Maybe I should take you out and prove I'm the perfect fit." His eyes twinkled as he said that, and I smiled wider.

"Maybe you should."

Two of the guys and their girlfriends stood up and one walked over and clapped Adam on the shoulder. "We should head out."

Adam nodded and looked at me. "You should give me your number so we can set something up next weekend."

I tapped my number into his phone and waved goodbye as Jamie saddled up in the seat beside me.

"Well, well, well," she said.

I rolled my eyes. "Don't start."

"I won't." She laughed. "I knew you guys would get along though. He's one of the good ones." She turned to her boyfriend, Mark. "Right?"

Mark nodded, taking a sip of his beer. "He's the only guy I'd trust to date my sister."

"Did he?" I asked. "Date your sister?"

"No." Mark laughed. "I just meant, he's that good."

"Well, I don't even know if he'll call or if we'll go on a date and if we do, if we'll hit it off." I shrugged, sliding my drink toward me. "I'm going to take it one day at a time."

"He'll call," Mark said.

"And you've already hit it off," Jamie added, raising an eyebrow.

We were sitting near the bathroom but had a clear view of the front door, which I was still looking at since Adam left. When it opened again and a new wave of guys came inside, my stomach clenched the way it always did when I saw him. *Nathaniel*. It was built-in annoyance. At least, that's what I told myself. I'd seen him around campus and at parties for the last two years. He'd graduated with his degree my freshman year, but he'd been working on his master's, something I knew my father was proud of and also paying half of. Dad saw Nathaniel as an investment, as someone he could groom into a shrewd and successful businessman. Dad didn't seem to see his tattoos and bad-boy image, although if he did, he didn't mind it.

"Holy cow. He looks so fucking good with that haircut," Jamie commented.

I blinked away from Nathaniel and looked at her. "Who?"

"You know who." She shot me a look. "I don't know why you insist on being so mean to him."

"First of all, he's mean to me first and then I can't seem to help myself. I fire back."

"He likes you. It's classic boy-likes-girl, therefore boy is mean to girl elementary shit."

"No." I glanced over at Nathaniel again.

He seemed to command the room everywhere he went. He wasn't even the best-looking guy in his group of friends, but that didn't matter. His arrogance and the way he carried himself spoke for itself. He was the epitome of "fake it till you make it" and he'd definitely made it all right. He'd made it and earned all the love from my father that I only hoped one day could be for me. Maybe when I started answering his phone calls and visiting him. I lifted my drink and took a big gulp, hoping to wash away the guilt I felt seeping into me.

"I can't believe you don't see it," Jamie said. "I bet you if you made a move on him, he'd break down and tell you he's in love with you."

I scoffed. "He's too full of himself to be in love with anyone other than himself."

As if hearing my words, which was impossible given the loud music playing in the restaurant-slash bar, he looked up and saw me. As our eyes locked, I felt my heart pound harder. He lifted his glass to me, and I did the same in a faraway cheer before taking a sip and tearing my eyes from his. By the time the restaurant shut down and the DJ got louder, more friends had joined us, and I was too busy talking to Danika about her

Russian upbringing to look for Nathaniel again, though there was no use in lying. I definitely wondered if he was still here. Jamie's words had really struck me. Never in a million years would I ever have considered he was attracted to me. He wasn't. The last time we'd crossed paths, he'd called me an overprivileged brat, and his opinion probably hasn't wavered since then.

I set down my second drink and decided to not have another. Between the Jell-O shots and these drinks, I'd definitely met my quota for the night. I wasn't normally a lightweight, and even if I was, that was something I'd never admit aloud. My father owned a beer company, for goodness' sake. I couldn't be a lightweight, and yet I knew my limits.

"Let's dance," Jamie shouted over the music.

Danika stopped talking, mid-sentence. I shot her an apologetic look. "You can keep talking later. I definitely want to hear more about the church seating arrangement though."

She smiled. Jamie tugged my hand and pulled me out to the dance floor. "Oh my God, that girl doesn't shut up."

"Jamie." My mouth fell open. "We're supposed to be showing them the ropes. She's your Little, isn't she?"

"She is but that doesn't change the fact that she won't stop talking." She moved, swinging her hips side to side. We'd taken it upon ourselves to be Big Sisters in our sorority this year and that was the price we paid. "We can switch. You can have her and I'll take Morgan."

"No way. I love Morgan." I laughed. "Where's Mark anyway?"

"Getting me another drink."

"Where's—" I looked around. Jamie grabbed my arm.

"Stop worrying and start moving."

I did as I was told, letting the music drown out my thoughts and worries. I'd think about my unfinished macroeconomics paper tomorrow. Mark came back with Jamie's drink, which she offered me and I turned down. As they started dancing together, I backed away a little and danced with the guy behind me, then another. Somehow, moving around had led me to right beside Nathaniel. We looked at each other at the same time, and he stopped talking to his friend, mid-sentence. His eyes ran down my body and back up slowly, and he smiled when he caught my gaze again.

"*Grease?*" he asked. I nodded, blushing, grateful it was dark in here. "It looks good on you."

My brows shot up. "You're saying something nice to me?"

"Oh, come on." He chuckled. "I'm not that bad."

"You are, actually."

He reached out and pulled me toward him. I felt every single nerve ending explode inside me. What was he doing?

"Have you spoken to your father lately?"

I rolled my eyes. "Seriously? That's what you want to talk about?"

"He's worried about you," he said. "I told him I'd check up on you, but I didn't want to be . . . creepy about it."

"Creepy meaning what?"

"Showing up at your apartment at midnight."

"Is that why you're here? Because you knew I would be?"

"No." He frowned. "Ryan dragged me here."

"Right, you don't do the party scene."

"I have too much to prove," he said. "I don't have time for the party scene."

"Some would say you're wasting the best years of your life working. Do you even date?"

"You're worried about my love life, princess?"

"Just asking a question." I groaned. This was why we didn't get along.

"Well, don't you worry about me. I definitely date."

"Hey, we're going to head to Erica's party. Do you still want to skip that one and go home? We can drop you off on the way if you—" Danika stopped talking when she saw that I was standing with a guy, or maybe it was the guy I was standing with that made her words catch. Either way, her bright green eyes looked about ready to bulge out of their sockets.

"I'm good. I'll take a cab home from here." I smiled.

Danika nodded, still looking at Nathaniel. I rolled my eyes and moved to block her from continuing to make a fool out of herself. Nathaniel looked perplexed and amused by this.

"You don't like your friends looking at me?"

"I don't like my friends making a fool out of themselves," I said. "And there's not much to look at."

His mouth twitched. "Is that why you were staring at me when I got here?"

He hadn't even looked at me when he got here, because he was right, I had been staring, so how he knew that was a mystery to me. I wasn't going to admit that though, so I shrugged it off.

"I was just trying to figure out the easiest way to get out of here without having to talk to you."

"Yet here you are." His barely-there smile turned into a full-on smile that made him look stupid handsome.

I wanted to slap myself for thinking that. It was the alcohol, I told myself, not that I was drunk, but it had to be the effects of alcohol in my brain. That was it.

"Do you like me?" I blurted out. Definitely the alcohol.

His expression turned serious. "What?"

"Do you like me, like do you think I'm attractive and like me, like me?"

"I've never thought about that before."

"Ever?" There was a hint of disbelief in my voice because I truly couldn't believe that he'd never thought about whether or not he found me attractive. I was attractive.

"Not once."

My eyes narrowed. "I don't believe you."

"You think real highly of yourself, princess." He laughed.

"Don't call me that."

"Then stop acting like a brat who needs to get her way even in this."

"I'm not, I'm just asking a question."

"Which I answered. Twice." He raised his glass to his lips and took a sip, his eyes never leaving mine. He brought it back down slowly, still watching me. "It's not my fault that you don't believe that someone in this world wouldn't find you attractive."

"Whatever." I turned away from him and started walking toward the door.

I wasn't going to continue to make a fool of myself in front of him. If he didn't like me, he didn't like me. It stung, but what could I do? I sighed, taking my phone out to text Jamie. Maybe I should go to that party, after all. *How could he not find me attractive at all?* God, I was starting to sound like a narcissistic idiot, which was probably why he didn't like me in the first place. How could I be stupid enough to believe that there was a chance he did? The guy called me a princess and a brat every chance he got.

"Need a ride?"

His voice startled me. I glanced at him briefly. "Nope, I'm good."

"I'm heading out anyway. You might as well let me take you."

I looked at him again. "Did my dad let you keep one of his cars? Is that what you're driving?" Now I was really being a brat, but I really didn't care.

"No, actually, I turned him down on the car note."

Of course. I rolled my eyes. It didn't surprise me in the least that my dad would offer to buy Nathaniel a car. Even with Mom's ridiculous alimony payment, Dad had money he didn't know what to do with. He wasn't flashy or anything, but he definitely liked to make sure his people were living comfortably, and no one was more his person than Nathaniel.

"Come on. Let me take you home, princess."

The way he said those words made my face burn. *Let me take you home, princess.* He made it sound like an explicit promise. I shivered, because of the wind, not the words. I brought a hand up again to hail the next cab, but not fast enough. He drove by with no means to slow down.

"You'll be here all night," Nathaniel said. "They're not allowed to stop here anymore. You'll have to walk to the corner and try from there."

I started walking in that direction.

"I'm right around the corner, you know."

"Don't care."

"Presley, stop being so stubborn for one second and accept the ride."

When we rounded the corner, I was stumped to see a large mass of people dressed in costumes congregating in the area. I knew I'd be there for at least another hour if I didn't accept the ride from him.

"Fine. Can you please take me home?"

He smiled. "Gladly."

"I don't even know why you drive in the city. It's completely unaffordable to park a car, if you can even find decent parking establishments." I walked alongside him toward his car. "A friend of mine got his Maserati keyed pretty bad in one of these lots."

"I can't even afford to look at a Maserati, Presley, let alone be stupid enough to park one here." He glanced down at me.

A part of me felt bad for talking about money to him, but another part of me didn't care. That was the way the world was, and who cared that we were from different social backgrounds? The guy outsmarted me and would probably be worth much more than me someday soon. I looked forward and kept walking, wondering what he drove. I could picture him in any car, but I tried to think about older models. My very first car had been a used Honda Accord. Dad thought it would be best not to spoil me more than I already had been. I drove it most of the time, but every so often I would borrow one of his cars from the garage and drive that instead. The lesson hadn't been lost though. I knew I was much more fortunate than my cousins and I generally didn't take it for granted. I did, however, take my parents for granted. I knew I did, and even knowing it didn't stop me from continuing to do so. I was so messed up. It was probably another reason Nathaniel didn't find me attractive. He saw the real me. The ugly me. He saw past my porcelain, albeit freckled skin, and my *luscious* red hair. He saw past seductive curves and hip-hugging designer clothes. I couldn't tell you what it was he saw when he got past those things, because I didn't know who I was beneath those layers and the thought of asking scared me like hell.

"What do you drive?" I asked after a moment. He stopped walking in front of a motorcycle and handed me a helmet. I could only mouth, "Oh. *Oh*." I plucked the helmet from his hands and put it over my head. It was a little big for me, but it would do. "What do you think my dad would do if he knew you were taking me home on your bike?"

"I don't know, princess. Maybe lock me up in the dungeon? Do you really want to find out?" His eyes twinkled in amusement and it was hard to fight a smile.

"No, I don't."

"Okay then." He turned and swung a leg over the bike, then looked at me over his shoulder. "You coming?"

"Don't you need a helmet?" I was shouting so that he could hear me over the rev of the bike and one I had over my own head.

"You're wearing it, princess."

"Can you stop calling me that for one night?" I walked over, held on to his shoulders, and swung my leg over like he had. "Where am I supposed to put my feet?"

"Right behind mine." He brought his hands to my calves and positioned my feet, and then to my thighs and squeezed them on either side of the bike. "Get as close to me as humanly possible."

My pulse quickened as I followed his instructions wrapping my arms around him. I shouldn't have been surprised at how muscular he was beneath his clothes, but I was. I held on for dear life as he rode through the streets. He wasn't going as fast as I imagined we would, but it was fast enough that I yelped a few times, and each time I did he laughed. I couldn't hear it, but I could feel the vibrations on his stomach. He slowed when we got to my building and pulled into an empty spot across from it. I pulled my helmet off as I got off the bike and wobbled unsteadily for a moment. Nathaniel reached out and grabbed my arm.

"You okay?"

I blinked up at him, startled at how close his face was to mine. Even more startled at how much I wanted him to kiss me in this moment. I blamed Jamie and her stupid words for making me feel this way around him. His jaw clenched as he sat there, helmet in one hand, my arm in the other. My heart pounded harder and harder as I leaned forward.

"Presley." His voice was low and gravelly as his hand tightened around my arm, stopping me from completely closing the gap between us. Instead of kissing me, he placed his forehead against mine. "You have to know that this is not something you want."

"How would you know what I want or don't want?" I pulled back.

"Because I know you. You may think I don't, you can stomp around and yell and scream that I don't know you, but I do, and you don't want to do this."

"Because you're not attracted to me and you'd leave and pretend it never happened?" I whispered.

His eyes flashed and he swallowed. I thought he would say something to refute my statement, but instead, he nodded. "That's right."

"Okay." My chest felt like it was caving in as I stepped back, jerking my arm out of his grasp. "Thanks for the ride."

"Take care of yourself, princess."

I turned around and walked into my building without looking back. Why the hell had I thrown myself at him again? Learn from this, Presley. *Nathaniel Bradley did not want you, and never would.*

FOUR

THREE YEARS LATER

IT WAS SUPPOSED to be the happiest day of my life, so why did I have this gaping hole in my chest as if something was missing? I'd given myself a million excuses leading up to this moment—I was afraid of change and marrying Adam meant my life would be flipped upside down. I'd already put my own aspirations on the back burner in order to work on his campaign, and deep down I knew this was only the beginning. This was what it meant to be married to someone in public office though. It was putting your own dreams on hold for the sake of the bigger picture, and in this picture, Adam was running for mayor of the city of New York, which was unprecedented given his age.

It also meant I wouldn't be taking either of the jobs my father offered me as the accounts manager of White Oak. My heart still hurt a little when I thought about the last conversation I had with him about it, which had gone from a job offer to a screaming match. Dad was less than thrilled I was putting my career on hold for Adam. He said it was unlike me and frankly, disappointing. The door opened behind me, and I did a little jolt as I turned around to see my best friend Jamie walking in with a huge smile on her face.

"You look stunning," she said.

"I don't feel stunning."

"Is it because your mom's flight is running late?" She frowned as she walked toward me.

"No." I shook my head. "I'm surprised she's even coming at all."

"You know she wouldn't miss this."

That wasn't exactly true. Neither of us knew she wouldn't miss it, which further annoyed me. It wasn't like her only daughter was getting married or anything. God forbid she'd pick a flight that would've had her here a few days ago and not the day of. She'd been on a month-long vacation with her boyfriend in Greece, but surely she could have ended the trip a little sooner. I took a long, deep breath and exhaled it slowly. It didn't matter. It was my wedding day. Today was about Adam and me. I smiled as I thought of him and found it a little easier to breathe. At least my father was here to walk me down the aisle.

My relationship with my parents had gone from bad to worse. Because of the job thing with Dad and because I didn't approve of my mother's dating life. I liked to think it was in the mending stage now, especially with my mom. She'd found a respectable man her age, one she hadn't cheated on my father with, and I had Adam, a successful politician who'd take care of me. Of course, there was a lot more to him than only that, but that was what my mother appreciated about him because it meant she no longer had to worry about me.

Standing up, I adjusted my dress and let Jamie fix the veil on my head. I looked in the mirror and took another deep breath. I loved Adam. Adam was good for me. He was hardworking, loved me, and had offered me the world. He'd said as much more than enough times in the two years we'd been dating.

"I think I need a moment to regroup." I slid my gaze to Jamie.

"I'll make sure the rest of the girls are ready. Morgan is already here. I don't think any of the guys are running late, but I'll check." She put both hands on my shoulders, looking me straight in the eyes. "It's completely normal to freak out right now. If you need more than a few minutes, we'll stall. I'll go up there and sing and make half the attendees disappear if I have to."

I laughed. "I'll be ready in five minutes. No awful singing required."

"Okay, but if you need me to take one for the team . . ." She winked at me. "I'll be back in a bit."

I kept my smile intact until I heard the door click. Then, I sagged down on the chair in front of the mirror again. I looked perfect. My red hair was made in a perfect knot updo. My makeup was flawless, not a freckle in sight. My brown eyes were perfectly done, with minimal liner and fake lashes in place. I reached for the champagne on the little table beside me and sipped it. Liquid courage wasn't something I relied on, but the warmth that spread through me was welcome. I didn't know why we'd decided on a winter wedding at a grand estate. It was a little girl's fairy tale, I supposed. Not mine, but some little girl out there somewhere. Adam thought I would love it, and I went along with it because I loved him and public perception was important to him. The click of the door opening caught my attention. I steadied my glass, gripping the stem as I antici-pated my mother's arrival. When it opened fully and I saw Nathaniel, I was shocked. *Why the hell is he here? Now?*

I'd invited him as part of Dad's guest list. This wedding was partly for my parents and their social obligations and partly for Adam's. I'd invited two tables of friends and that was it. Nathaniel Bradley was one of the people I'd sent an invite to expecting it to be rejected. Not only was I not expecting him to attend my wedding, but I definitely hadn't expected him to come to my private room to see me. I stood up, setting the flute down on the table. He walked in, shutting the door behind him. He looked devastatingly handsome in his tuxedo. It was a phrase I never thought I'd hear myself think, but it was the only one that came to mind as he walked toward me, his dark blue eyes taking me in slowly. My heart pounded. I wanted to scream at him for making me feel this way. I wanted to scream at him for being here at all and catching me off guard like this.

"What are you doing here?"

He swallowed. "He's not right for you."

It took me a moment to register his words. I blinked. "What?"

"He's not the one."

"Seriously?" My mouth fell open for a beat. "You say that about every guy."

And I knew for a fact it wasn't because he was pining after me. He wasn't. I'd thrown myself at him a few times in college before Adam and I became serious, and the guy had practically laughed in my face. So no, Nathaniel Bradley didn't like me; he just didn't want to see me happy. He didn't like the idea of another man in my life and therefore my father's life. He wanted to be the favorite for all eternity. The thought alone made me angry.

"You have some nerve showing up here like this and expecting me to . . . I just . . ." I was breathing hard suddenly, my blood rumbling in my veins. I realized it was the first thing I'd actually *felt* all day. "Is this what you came here to tell me?"

"No." He frowned, shoving his hands in his pockets. "Your mother is five minutes away. Your father wanted me to let you know that he thinks we should wait for her to get here before you start the ceremony."

My eyes narrowed. "So you just threw the part about my

very-soon-to-be husband not being good for me in there for kicks?"

"I said it because I always tell you how I feel," he said. "You haven't exactly made yourself available to me. In the last six months, I've invited you to my housewarming party, to lunch, to grab a drink to catch up on things, and you turned me down every time."

"You've never wanted to hang out with me in the past." I shot him a look. "Besides, I've been busy."

"I've heard."

"Yeah, well, I've heard all about your whereabouts, too. Dad keeps me informed on his favorite pet."

"Glad to hear it." He smirked. "And what do you think of my accomplishments, if I may ask?"

I sighed. He wasn't going to leave, so I might as well answer truthfully. "On one hand, I think it's amazing that you've accomplished so much. On the other, I think the invention is completely disgusting and you're just contributing to one more thing society will get addicted to."

"You don't think it's innovative and smart?" He raised an eyebrow. "I mean, we're singlehandedly taking on the tobacco industry."

"Right, by replacing it with something else people will become addicted to."

"The company's already worth five million and it hasn't even fully launched yet."

"I'm not impressed with numbers unless you're finding a cure for the cancer that tobacco is already causing."

"Right, because the little perfect princess has never smoked." His rolled his eyes.

"My father smokes enough for the both of us."

"Well, my invention will make it safer."

"I doubt it."

"It's proven. We didn't just invent this and send it out into the world. These things need to be FDA approved, you know, tested and tested again."

""Do you want me to fall at your feet and tell you you're a genius and then smile at every word that comes out of your mouth?" I clenched my fists on either side of me. "I'm glad something you worked at for so long finally got picked up and is making you money, but I'm not going to agree with every word you say. I'm not one of your investors and I'm not one of your little model girlfriends."

"My girlfriend is a scientist," he shot back.

"Well, whoop-dee-doo. Good for her. Good for you for expanding your horizons past bimbos who drool over your rugged exterior and only see you as a plaything. You deserve that much." My jaw felt so tight that I had to fight to speak each word. "You can go now. Thanks for letting me know about my mom and thanks for coming to the wedding."

"Thanks for inviting me, even though we both know it wasn't your idea," he said, his jaw tightening.

For what felt like an eternity, we simply stared at each other, waiting to see who would win this tug of war between us. From experience, I knew the answer was simple: neither of us would. We'd get worked up and go our separate ways as we always did, and yet I realized I liked it. He always found a way to take me completely out of whatever was happening in my life and make me focus on something else, even if that something else was anger toward him.

"It's good to have you here," I said after a moment. "Only a jerk like you could make me see how lucky I am to be marrying such a kind man."

"Such a little brat." His eyes flashed as he shook his head slowly.

"I think that's your cue." I planted a hand on my hip and raised an eyebrow. "I need to finish up here before my mother arrives. Goodbye, Nathaniel."

Instead of leaving, he walked forward, closing the distance between us, standing almost flush against me, making me tilt my head to meet his dark hard gaze, a look I wasn't sure I'd ever seen before. My pulse kicked. What the hell was he doing? Why was he so close to me? Why did he smell so good? What would his chest feel like if I put my hands on it?

"What are you doing?" My voice was shaky. He brought his hand to my cheek, his eyes intent on mine. I was going to die. He was going to kill me before I even got to the altar. "Nathaniel. What are—"

He brought his face down slowly. I knew he was going to kiss me. I knew I could stop it at any moment if I wanted to, but the truth was . . . I didn't want to. God help me, I wanted this kiss. And when his lips met mine and his tongue slid into my mouth, I felt consumed by him. I forgot where I was and what I was wearing. I forgot that people were waiting for me and I had somewhere to be. I forgot I had a fiancé and that his name wasn't Nathaniel Bradley, and that he definitely didn't push my buttons like this. Even now, as he kissed me, Nathaniel was trying to take over my life. With the stroke of his tongue and the gentle pressure from his hand on the back of my neck, he made me feel like I was tumbling and out of breath.

When he broke the kiss, I was panting and left wanting more. He was breathing heavily, and his eyes looked glossy and out of focus as they searched mine.

For what? Did he expect me to tell him I loved it? My father had spent a small fortune on this wedding, and even though kissing this man had me feeling like I'd been kissed wrong all along, there was nothing I could do. *Why do that to me today? Of all days?* That he'd waited until this moment angered me even more.

"What the fuck were you thinking?" I pushed his chest.

"I had to do it and I'm not going to apologize." He ran his fingers through his hair, exhaling. "A few years ago, you begged me to kiss you and I didn't, and I didn't want the opportunity to pass me by forever."

I pushed his chest again. "So you decide to kiss me on my wedding day?"

"If not now, when? After you're married? I've been trying to link up with you and you kept brushing me off."

"You said that already." I closed my eyes, willing my heart to steady itself, my lips to stop yearning for his. I looked at him again. "Link up for what? To kiss me? To brag about how put together your life is and laugh at me when I tell you all the ways mine isn't?"

"I wouldn't do that."

"No, you just feel the need to tell me how every single person in my life is wrong for me and then proceed to kiss me on my damn wedding day."

"You're upset because you know this kiss is the best thing that's happened to you these last two years, and you don't know how to process that being that you're marrying the wrong guy today."

My mouth fell open momentarily before I reached up and slapped him. "Get out."

"Presley—"

"Get the hell out, Nathaniel."

"I'm not going to apologize for kissing you." He closed his eyes, took a breath, and looked at me again. "But I am sorry it was today, like this. More than anything, I'm sorry it was as good as it was."

With that, he turned and left. I was too shell-shocked to move or say anything else. When the door opened again a second later, I jumped, thinking it would be him again. Instead, it was my mother wearing a rouge dress that matched the wedding party.

"Oh, honey, you look beautiful," she cooed.

I'd been so angry at her for so long, blaming her for cheating on Dad and being the reason they divorced and broke our family apart, blaming her for basically everything that went wrong in my life, but in this moment as she looked at me with pride and love in her eyes, I wanted to crumble. Maybe it was the adrenaline rushing through me from my encounter with Nathaniel, but I rushed over and threw my arms around her.

"I'm so glad you made it."

"Are you kidding? I wouldn't miss this for the world. I had to take four different flights to get here in time, but I made it and that's the only thing that matters."

I hugged her tighter. I'd had so many differences with her over the years that it never even occurred to me that she'd genuinely be happy to be here. She pulled back and looked at my face.

"We need to fix your lipstick."

My hand flew to my mouth as thoughts of the kiss Nathaniel and I shared slammed into me. She started to tug me toward the mirror and I hesitated at first, but gave in quickly. When I caught a glimpse of myself, I was relieved to see I didn't look disheveled. There was no visible sign of the kiss, but inside, my veins roared with the memory.

"Mom," I whispered as she fumbled with the makeup bag. "What if Adam isn't the one?"

"Oh, honey." She walked over and tilted my chin up slightly. "You love him, don't you?"

I nodded. "Of course."

"It's completely normal to get cold feet right before you do something life-changing. You have to have faith that it'll all work out." She stopped talking and tilted her face when she realized her little speech was doing nothing to calm my nerves.

I didn't understand. I'd been fine before . . . I'd spent the entire year planning this wedding. I'd been looking forward to it, to creating a life with Adam. So what changed? *Nothing.* The only disruption had been the kiss Nathaniel attacked me with.

That's all it was—an attack on an innocent bride. Except I didn't feel innocent. I would've had it not made me feel like I'd been missing out on something major all along. I hated him for putting those doubts into my head. Hated him for making me feel things I shouldn't be feeling from someone other than Adam. *"I didn't want the opportunity to pass me by forever."* Forever. *There would never be another time . . .*

"Presley." My mom reached out and fixed my hair. I blinked a few times. I'd been staring at her without saying a word. She frowned slightly. "Are you not sure?"

Was I not sure? My heart pounded. I knew from the look in her eyes that if I said I wanted to hightail it out of here, she'd actually help me. Would I do that though? No, I wasn't sure. I wasn't sure at all, but I was already here. Would I risk marriage to a man I loved to explore something potentially hazardous with someone like Nathaniel because of a stupid kiss? I shook my head, then nodded, remembering what she'd asked.

"I'm ready. I'm ready. I'm doing this." I inhaled and exhaled and the minute I said the words aloud and my mom smiled, I knew I'd made my choice. Nathaniel Bradley was wrong. Adam and I were a team that would be strong. Unified. *Forever.* And it was time to get that journey started, nerves be damned.

FIVE

FIVE YEARS LATER

"THAT WAS A STRIKE. COME ON, UMP," Dad shouted beside me.

I glanced up from my phone and looked at the field in time to see the manager run up to the umpire, get in his face, and start a screaming match. I couldn't even understand what they were saying, but sitting in the third row, I was treated to a series of fuck you's.

"Finally. Something to spice the game up." I set my phone down and picked up my beer.

Dad scoffed but didn't take his eyes off the commotion on the field. He'd been talking about chasing ballparks for years and after his latest health scare, decided that he needed to scratch items off his bucket list. I was shocked he'd asked me to do this with him, partly because I didn't know a thing about baseball and also because I could name at least four people off the top of my head that he'd have more fun with while traveling from park to park. I was glad he'd asked me though. Traveling with him meant spending more time with him, which was something I was looking forward to. If I were trying to be the bigger person, I would say it was my fault we'd grown apart, but we'd both shared the burden of it. After years of barely acknowledging each other, I'd shown up on his doorstep, crying because of my failed marriage, and Dad had taken me in without hesitation.

"Why'd they throw him out?" I watched the manager as he walked off the field, still yelling.

"You're not allowed to get in the umpire's face like that," Dad explained.

"He called a strike on that guy even though it wasn't one."

"I'm surprised you caught that." He raised an eyebrow, shooting a pointed look at my phone. "They should make a no cell phone rule for the first fifteen rows in stadiums."

I laughed. "No one would come to games."

"Of course you would think that." He smiled, shaking his head. "You want another beer?"

I picked up my can and shook it confirming it was empty. "I can do one more."

"Two White Oaks, please. Keep the change," he said, exchanging his money for two cans of beer and handing me one. I took a sip.

"Ezra said we could do guava," I said, bracing myself as I glanced at him. He took a long sip of his beer, staring into the ballpark with a thoughtful expression on his face. I held my breath. Finally, after a moment of silence, he met my gaze.

"I know I was against adding different flavors, but I think we can make it a seasonal thing."

"Oh, thank God. I thought you were going to be mad I went and spoke to him."

"On the contrary, I think it's great you're taking such an interest." He took another sip, looked at the field for another long, silent moment. "I want you to focus your attention on the brew bar though. I know it doesn't seem like much right now, but I think this can be a big thing later on."

I nodded in agreement even though I didn't really agree, but I wasn't going to open up that can of worms again. Dad had invested in a boutique hotel last year and he wanted me to open a bar on the property. I loved the idea. I'd come up with it, for crying out loud, but in the last couple of weeks I realized I wanted to be more involved with the actual company.

"You studied hospitality," he said, taking my silence for what it was—disagreement.

"And business."

"This way, you can use both."

"I guess."

"I have things in the works right now and need your full attention on that."

"What else do you have in the works?"

He shook his head. "I'll tell you when I know it's going to happen."

"Okay," I said, even though I hated being in the dark about things.

"How's the divorce coming along?"

"Ask me this time next week." I sighed. "I'm going to an event with Adam on Monday and I plan on talking to him about it then."

"These things take time. I'm glad you're finally getting out of there though."

"Yeah, me too."

It had been a long time coming and now I was ready to start the process, I wished I could speed it up. I no longer wanted to be attached to Adam's last name. I no longer wanted to be attached to anything he did, but I knew that regardless of his cooperation, it wouldn't be that easy. We were considered high-profile people, at least he was. I was a socialite he'd bagged, his literal trophy wife. I'd been groomed for a man like Adam. I'd been taught to sit up, agree, and smile.

I was tired of smiling.

I was done pretending.
It was my turn to live the life I wanted to live.

SIX

I'D GOTTEN USED to being the subject of whispers at parties, but tonight it felt like they were shouts. I blamed Adam's camp for letting this get out of hand. We'd all agreed we wouldn't give attention to our separation and impending divorce for a few months. He'd been elected mayor for a second term and everything had spun out of control, including our marriage, which had already been rocky. The newfound attention he got right after we said our vows made the strain unbearable. It was more than just that, though. I felt like I'd been in forgiveness mode when it came to Adam for a long time now and I no longer had it in me. I'd agreed to stay on as an exec for the not-for-profit we started up only because I'd already done most of the legwork and helping underprivileged kids was something I was passionate about. What I didn't like was how that meant I'd be associated with him. Not that he was a bad guy, but he was a terrible husband, and I was still healing from indiscretions that took place with his assistant and his campaign manager and his supposed best friend—who according to him was nothing more than a friend . . . Basically, he hadn't kept his dick in his pants.

WAS it because we got married straight out of college? At first I thought, maybe it was me. Maybe I wasn't fun anymore, maybe I should have spiced things up, but nothing had worked. I gave it my all until I had nothing left but anger, because that's what infidelity did to the innocent party. It made us feel guilty. It made us feel like we weren't enough. It took me a long time to understand that I wasn't the problem. The one good thing that had come out of all of this was that it brought my father and me together in a way that nothing before had, maybe because we found common ground, as unfortunate as the stakes were. It reminded me of what Nathaniel said on that rainy, horrible day many years ago. *"You may want to ease up on him. He's going through a hard time right now."* Now I had an inkling of the hard time Dad had gone through. And it fucking sucked.

I smiled at a woman in a red dress as I stood by the bar, wondering if she too had fucked my husband, when I felt Adam walk up and stand beside me. I didn't acknowledge him, but I didn't have to. I knew his movements and the scent of his cologne. His presence was a colossal source of discomfort during times like these, when I knew what *they* knew and had to pretend I didn't understand their sympathetic smiles.

"We have a leak in our office," he said.

"No shit." I looked up at him, glad to see the clear look of discomfort on his face. "It's funny though, everyone keeps staring at me as if I was the one who had an issue keeping my dick in my pants."

"Presley." He cringed, exhaling heavily.

"The truth hurts. Trust me, I know." I shrugged a shoulder and reached for the drink he had in his hands, taking a big gulp of the whiskey. I handed it back and turned to face him. "I think you should put out a statement. You can call it a joint statement and say we're amicably separating, but that we respect each other or some bullshit like that."

"That's not bullshit." He took a sip of his drink. "I do respect you."

"Not enough to be faithful, apparently."

"That was—"

"A mistake? Please. Once may be a mistake but beyond that?" I shook my head, surprised when the anger didn't crash into me as it had before. "Stop bullshitting me, Adam. I already voted for you."

"I deserve that." He swallowed, nodding slowly. "And I don't expect you to understand what it's like to be pursued by all of these women constantly." *Fucking what?*

"You think men don't pursue me? I made vows to be your wife, so the only man I allowed into my bed was you. And it's rather ironic, don't you think, that your role is to be faithful to the vows you made to the people who voted for you? I know my boundaries, Adam, so don't make this about other women pursuing you."

He opened his mouth to respond, but evidentially thought better of it and shut it once more. I almost wished he would say something. Something that would make me angry and cause a scene, except we both knew I wouldn't. I knew my role, and I'd never openly flip my shit. We stared at each other for a long time, until I could no longer look at him without wanting to cry. He hadn't even bothered to tell me he'd try harder when I slapped him with the divorce papers. He'd just acknowledged them and agreed it was for the best because he knew he couldn't make me happy.

"I have to go." I grabbed my purse and put the strap on my shoulder. "Let me know when you're ready to put out that statement."

"I can try." He grabbed my arm before I could fully start walking away.

I glanced at him over my shoulder. "Try what?"

"Try to be better. To do better."

"That's nice, but I can't." I pulled away enough so he had to let go of my arm. "I can't stand by you anymore."

"Even if we both sign divorce papers tomorrow, it's going to take time to split our assets."

"Honestly? I don't need to fight you for money and even if I did, I wouldn't want any of it. Keep whatever you want."

"So you're really going to go work for your dad?"

I shrugged. "I guess I am."

"And you're really going to open up a brewery?" He frowned. "You don't even like beer."

I blinked. "Drug dealers don't necessarily like cocaine either, and yet they sell it anyway. What's your point?"

"I just think it's weird, that's all." He shot me a look. "You're spreading yourself thin with that and the foundation."

"The foundation is taken care of. I did my part to get it up and running. We have a full-time staff overseeing everything. They don't need me."

"You've never been interested in White Oak before. Winston must have offered you a lot of money."

"It's my family business, Adam." I didn't even bother to hide the warning in my tone. "I'll see you soon. Send me the statement by tomorrow afternoon. I'd rather get this over with as soon as possible."

This time, I walked away with finality. I had done my time, and enough was enough. I wouldn't let him make me feel guilty for taking the job with my dad, or anything else for that matter.

SEVEN

I WAS ALMOST at the door to my father's office building when I spotted a handful of reporters outside. My feet suddenly felt heavy. Why were they there? Did something happen to my dad? Panic rose in my throat as the thought hit me and I started to walk faster. Dad had been sick for a year now, but no one knew about it. He'd had a stroke. It had been covered up and reported as sleep deprivation that required medical attention. The reporters flocked to me when they saw me near.

"Mrs. Delaney, any comment on your father's recent sale?"

I blinked. Through Adam, I'd learned not to answer reporters and instead kept my head down and avoided interacting until I had something rehearsed to say, but the question caught me off guard. *Another sale?* Jesus, Dad. At this rate, I should've been scared he was going to sell me on the black market.

"I have no comment," I said quickly.

Dad had been on a mission this last year. After his stroke and diagnosis, he'd started selling everything in sight. He'd sold his house in Westchester on a whim and got a new apartment in Brooklyn, of all places. He'd sold his car collection and was down to his Porsche Panamera. I had no idea what his latest sale was, but it must have been a big one if people were people reporting it. Probably his esteemed painting collection, the one the museum had been dying to acquire for years. I pushed the doors and headed toward the elevator, waving at the front desk as I passed.

"Hold the door," a familiar voice shouted. I held it and waited until Victor Reuben, our family lawyer, walked into the elevator. He seemed startled to see me. Yeah, the feeling was mutual.

"I didn't know you were in town," I said.

"Jensen has a book launch," he said by way of explanation.

"Another one?" My eyes widened. His best friend was an award-winning author who seemed to release books pretty frequently. It seemed like every time Victor was in town he had a new one out. "I need to speak to you by the way."

"About this sale?" He signaled for me to exit the elevator when it opened. I glanced over at him as I walked out and he followed.

"Well, no, but now that you mention it, what the hell did he sell now?"

Victor stopped walking. "You don't know?"

"No." I stopped walking and turned toward him. "No one tells me anything until after it happens. What am I supposed to know?"

He eyed me curiously. "So what did you want to speak to me about?"

"My divorce."

His brows shot up. "You're getting a divorce?"

"Yes, long overdue and since you're the expert—"

"I don't work divorces anymore."

"I know, I know. You're all about estate law now." I rolled my eyes, annoyed that he couldn't handle it himself. He was the best divorce lawyer in LA. The divorce lawyer of the stars, they'd called him. He'd passed the bar exam in New York as well, so he was able to practice both. "I need you to tell me what to do in order to get it over with ASAP. How long will it take?"

"It depends. Is he contesting?"

I paused outside of Dad's office. "Like does he want to stay married?"

"Right."

"His dick obviously doesn't, so I don't really care whether or not he does."

"I'm sorry. I know this isn't funny." Victor chuckled before getting serious again. "If he doesn't fight you on this, it can take as little as six weeks. If he does, it'll take longer. It also depends on how many things tie you together."

"Six weeks?" My mouth fell open. "That's it?"

"You don't sound happy about that." He eyed me curiously. "You sure you can't work things out?"

"Positive." I shook my head and the reluctant thoughts away.

Did he not understand what I meant about Adam's dick? I'd given it one year longer than I should have and nothing changed. He didn't change and you couldn't change people who didn't want to change. It didn't mean I had to be jumping for joy about the whole thing. It didn't mean I didn't have the right to feel sad or angry about the whole thing. I took a deep breath and let it out as Victor knocked on the door to my father's office. When he called for us to come in, we did. He glanced up from his desk and smiled wide when he saw me.

"Look at you. My little exec is ready to work." He stood up and came around his desk to give me a hug and kiss before addressing Victor. "Victor, thank you for coming on such short notice. The papers are all here." He turned back around and handed Victor some papers.

We both sat in the chairs across from him and he went back around the desk and took his seat.

"What'd you sell now?" I asked. "There are a ton of reporters outside, so I'm assuming it's something expensive."

He glanced at Victor briefly. "Maybe you should go over that in the conference room. We'll meet you there."

Victor stood up and walked out without another word, leaving my father and me alone. A sinking feeling settled in the pit of my stomach.

"Dad, what did you do?"

"I'm selling the majority of the company."

My mouth fell open, and I tried to form words. People had been hounding him to sell the company for years and he'd never budged, always maintaining that it was a family business and would always be run by family, and now he'd sold the majority of it? Now, when I was freeing myself of all other ties to come and do what he'd always assumed I'd do and actually work here? I couldn't wrap my head around what he said. I also couldn't hide that I was blindsided and hurt. We'd just watched a baseball game together last weekend. These things took months to process. He should've told me then. But to wait until I came into the office ready to work on a job he'd offered me? I felt like I was being fired and I hadn't even started.

"But you . . . I just . . . " My voice was a bare whisper. "You told me to come work for you."

"Relax. You'll still have a place here and I still fully expect you to be in charge of opening our brewery," he said, sighing when my mouth remained open. "It's been stagnant for a while now and I want it to grow and flourish. It's a good move."

Maybe it was a good move. I didn't know. It wasn't my place to tell him what to do with his company, especially given I'd just agreed to start working here, but to sell the majority of the company was crazy. Unless he'd sold to a bigger beer company, in which case my role, big or small, would be eliminated the minute they brought their own people in and did a haul of this place. I wiped my palms over my navy-blue skirt.

"Who'd you sell to?"

"Bradley Investments—"

"Bradley?" I blinked. ""Nathaniel's company?"

"Yes."

"What the hell, Dad?"

He could've sold it to Satan and gotten better feedback from me. He was the one person in the entire universe I would've argued against. The one person. We butted heads on everything under the sun. My eyes fell to Dad's desk and instantly landed on the Forbes magazine. I scoffed at the sight of Nathaniel's picture on this month's edition. It was at the edge of Dad's desk, away from the rest of his things, as if it were some kind of award or something. It was even signed. My eyes rolled of their own accord. Of course he'd treat perfect Nathaniel's achievements like that.

At thirty-one, Nathaniel Bradley was the poster child for a rags-to-riches story and the media loved him for it. He'd invested in two successful companies and invented a device he'd sold for one billion dollars. One billion. With a B. He'd split that money with the five people he started it up with, so he himself wasn't a billionaire with a B, but still. Like the title of the article suggested, it was said he had the Midas touch when it came to money, which was saying a lot for a man who'd grown up with nothing. Not to knock my achievements, but at twenty-eight the only thing my parents seemed to dwell on for the last year was my unhealthy marriage and now impending divorce. Neither one of them was upset at me. My marriage had been great for all of two years before the beautiful surroundings I thought we'd built for our relationship had started crumbling down on top of me. They'd seen my struggle; they'd seen how it affected my mental and physical state. There had been no hiding it.

But alas, here I was, once again, sitting across from my father listening to him go on and on about the amazing Nathaniel Bradley and how perfect he was for this company. *My* company. Well, the company I'd inherit someday. This was not the welcoming I'd been expecting. I'd kept tabs on Nathaniel through Dad all these years and occasionally seen him at social events. The only thing we'd managed to do was bicker. We'd bickered about something as simple as the taste of water—that's how bad it was between us—prompting his date to walk away and leave the establishment before either of us even noticed her departure.

"Presley." My dad's voice snapped me back into the present. I blinked up at him.

"Yeah. Sorry." I cleared my throat. "I just really don't think it's your best move, but it's your company and I respect your decision."

"I didn't exactly call you in here to get your permission."

"Right." I bit down on my tongue but somehow opened my mouth again regardless. "I'm not crazy enough to think you'd ever ask my opinion or permission on anything."

"I value your opinion, but he knows what he's doing." He shot me a stern look but continued on regardless. "He's worked for me longer than you have."

"He worked for you when he was a child." I rolled my eyes. "Driving for you, mind you, not handling business accounts."

"I had no idea you knew so much about my business with Nathaniel."

"I don't." I ground my teeth. I hated when he was being sarcastic with me. It served me right, though. I knew it. "He's all you talk about. It's as if he's your favorite child or something. Kind of hard to miss."

"Oh, Presley." Dad shook his head. "You don't know what that kid has been through. I think you'd appreciate his hustle if you cared enough to find out."

"I do appreciate his hustle. I know he made a lot of out nothing. I know he got into the pocket of one of the richest men in the East Coast and somehow won him over, so much so that he's now taking over most of the company and soon enough the entire thing will probably be his. Is that in your will? You might as well tell me now, Dad. I'm going to find out sooner or later."

It was the wrong thing to say. I knew it the moment the words left my mouth and his eyes lit with the kind of fire he only held when he found out he was being screwed over.

"Get out." He pointed toward the door. "Get out, take a walk, and come back when you shed your teenage attitude behind." I closed my eyes momentarily, ready to apologize, but he continued. "I'm serious. We also have an office party tomorrow night to announce the new direction of the company and I expect you to be there. For now, take a break and come back when you're ready to act civilized."

I opened my mouth to speak again, but decided against it. Dad looked pissed. The tips of his ears were burning bright red and that was never a good sign. I didn't come here to antagonize him. Instead of arguing, I stood up slowly and swallowed down the words that threatened to tumble out.

"I'll be back in an hour."

EIGHT

I SHOOK the entire ride to the lobby. I planned my next steps before they happened. Sometimes that helped calm me down and get into the right frame of mind. I'd walk toward the lobby door with my head held high and go to the coffee shop down the block, get an espresso, and head back here. By then, I'd calm down. By then, I could apologize to my father for acting in a way I could only act around him. Well, him and his prodigal pretend son. I couldn't understand why it had to be Nathaniel, of all people. Why not some older man with a kind smile and encouraging words? Why did it have to be Mr. Know-it-all? I wanted to blame my outrage on him being an asshole, but the truth was, I knew it was me. My feelings were anchored by the fact that I'd always felt less than him in my father's eyes. I was pushing thirty, I didn't need anyone's approval, but for some reason I'd always craved for father's. I took a deep breath and with it, tried to let out my feelings of inferiority. I was his daughter, damn it. I'd do right by this company. I took my phone out and started to text my friend Jamie, hoping to meet for drinks later.

Me: *Up for drinks?*

Jamie: When am I ever not?

I laughed as I stepped out of the elevator and gasped as I crashed into someone stepping in. "Shit, I'm—"

"Might want to watch where you're going, princess."

My pulse throbbed in my ears as my gaze clashed with his. For a minuscule of a second I felt like what I could only imagine a fish out of water felt like. I couldn't breathe, couldn't think, couldn't process the conflicting and tormenting emotions jarring through me. *What the fuck, Presley?* I blinked.

"Sorry," I said finally.

Nathaniel looked surprised that I was capable of apologizing, and for some reason that pissed me off again. I was capable of a lot of things, including apologizing. I couldn't bring myself to say anything though, so I brushed past him and walked away, the sound of my heels tapping more rapidly as I reached the door. He grabbed my arm before I could fully exit the building. What was up with men grabbing my arm to try to stop me from leaving? I yanked it out of his grasp as I turned to face him.

"What? Do you want to gloat about the way you're effectively taking over my company?"

"*Your* company?" He didn't laugh, but his blue eyes filled with amusement. "Last I checked, in order for one to have stakes in a company you actually have to invest in it."

"It's my family's company. You know what I mean."

"I don't think I do. Why don't you elaborate?"

"Maybe you haven't heard, but I'm working here as of yesterday," I said.

"Is that supposed to deter my investment?"

"Yes, actually. I have plans for the company and I don't need you meddling in it."

"You have plans." He scoffed. "You took interest in this two seconds ago and suddenly you have plans?"

"Laugh all you want but I do, and I'm prepared to throw all

of my attention into learning the ropes and opening up this brewery, so you may want to re-think your next move."

"The move's already been made, sweetheart. This merger is going through whether you like it or not and if you want to be a part of this company, I suggest you get on board." He turned around and walked back to the elevator, leaving me standing by the door, gaping at his broad shoulders. He walked with command, as if he already owned the damn place and it did nothing to simmer my boiling blood. I turned and stomped out of the building, eyeing the bar across the street. I wasn't sure coffee would be enough for me to go back in there today.

TWO GLASSES of red wine and one hour later, I headed to my father's office.

"They're in the conference room," Rosa said when she saw me lift my hand to knock on Dad's office. Rosa had been Dad's personal assistant for as long as I could remember. "Your cheeks are a little red, baby, is it cold outside?"

"No." I was warm, actually. The wine helped with that and I felt much more at ease with everything. "Must have been something I ate," I lied, though I didn't know why. Rosa knew me better than that. She stood up and walked over to me.

"Let me walk with you," she said, smiling as she hooked our arms together. "I spoke to your mother yesterday. She seems to be doing well."

"She is." I smiled. "She's totally smitten with her husband and he loves to dote on her, so I'm sure that helps."

"He seems like a nice guy."

"Very nice guy." And not even super rich, which was shocking when it came to my mom. I didn't want to think of her as a gold digger, but I couldn't help but put her in that category when I thought of her boyfriends between my father and her new husband, Constantine.

Rosa opened the conference room door for me and walked in. My attention was still fully on her, but I felt Nathaniel's presence in the room. I couldn't ignore it if I tried, with the way my chest tightened.

"I found this one in the halls," Rosa said, smiling at me.

"I hope you're in a better mood," Dad said.

I hated that he said it in front of Nathaniel, but then, I'd already unloaded my anger on him as well, so it didn't really matter. I turned to face the three of them: Dad at the head of the table, and Nathaniel and Victor across from each other. Instead of answering, I smiled at my dad—the apologetic smile I used so often around him. He shook his head, smiling back. Rosa let go of my arm and started walking away.

"Oh." She turned around. "I didn't ask you how your husband is doing. I saw him on the news the other day looking all dapper."

"He's doing well." My smile faltered. Oh, what the heck, people were going to find out soon enough anyway and I didn't want Rosa to find out through the press. "He's also my soon-to-be ex-husband."

She gasped, bringing a hand to her mouth. "Oh, sweetie."

"I'm fine." I let out a shaky laugh as she moved to wrap her arms around me. Maybe it was the wine I'd consumed that had me feeling emotional, but my eyes teared up as she held me. *God, when was the last time I was hugged? Held? Comforted?* Come on, Presley. Get it together. Now was not the time to lose my shit. "I'm fine seriously."

"It's okay not to be fine," she said, pulling away and looking me in the eyes. "You call me if you need anything at all, you hear?"

"I will." I smiled again. "I'm really fine though."

She let go of my arms, shot a warning look in my father's

direction, and walked out of the room. I jumped when someone clapped their hands together and turned to see it was my father.

"I can hold on to these papers and swing by your place later if you want," Victor suggested. He smiled. "Or we can meet over drinks and discuss the other thing."

"I think it's best if she signs them now," Nathaniel said.

I eyed them both as I walked to them, feeling like I was picking between two teams on the PE field. Obviously, I took a seat next to Victor. I couldn't even look at Nathaniel right now, but I definitely felt him looking at me. Victor slid some papers over to me and leaned in to point at where to sign.

"Your cologne is distracting," I said.

He chuckled. "It's officially my new favorite."

I laughed as I signed.

"Did Adam make it official?" Dad asked.

"I told him he had to by this afternoon." I glanced at him as I turned the page. When I looked back down, I saw Nathaniel's name and was reminded why I was here. I started clicking the pen nervously.

"Let me take you to dinner," Victor said. "Help you get your mind off things."

I knew it would be fun. He was most likely here with his wife and kids and I always had such a great time with them, but I felt off and I hated being Negative Nancy especially when I was around kids. I'd always felt that your energy affected those around you and my energy was dark right now. I shook my head.

"Another time."

"Come on, it'll be fun."

I signed the page. I wondered if he was doing this so I'd stop overthinking it and just sign. If he was, he was a damn genius because it was obviously working. My hand seemed to move of its own accord, quickly signing every page he pointed out. Dad and Nathaniel started talking about something, but I tuned them out, only paying attention to Victor. When I was finished, I clicked the pen and set it down, daring to look at Nathaniel who I knew was staring at me. Sure enough, his blue eyes found mine and stayed there. My heart flip-flopped. How someone could annoy me as much as he did and still manage to make me feel whatever it was I felt around him was absolutely mind-blowing. I didn't even feel this way around Adam. That thought made me frown. Surely I'd felt that way around Adam at one point, hadn't I? I tore my gaze from Nathaniel's and glanced at my father.

"We still on for Saturday night, kid?" Dad asked.

"Of course." I smiled. "I got the tickets."

"Will you be here this weekend, Victor?" Dad asked.

"We leave Sunday."

"Interested in going to the Yankees game?" Dad looked at me. "Can we get more tickets in our row?"

"Um . . . I don't see why not." I licked my lips hesitantly.

It's not that I didn't want Victor and his family to join us, but this was supposed to be father-daughter time. Then again, there were thirty baseball stadiums to visit this year, so I was going to be spending plenty of time with him. The ballpark chasing was a way for him to take it easy and pull back from the company a little. In retrospect, I should've definitely seen this sale coming.

I never would have guessed the buyer being Nathaniel. *Had I missed the signs there as well? After all, I hadn't known the full extent of Adam's transgressions. Dad hadn't been subtle in his acknowledgment of Nathaniel's successes. Had he been grooming him all this time, especially given I'd shown no signs of interest?*

"Would you like to join us, Nate?" Dad asked.

My eyes widened. I'd never heard Dad call him that. But, what the hell was he doing? Inviting everyone to father-daughter time? He may or may not have seen my hesitation at this idea, but in true Nathaniel fashion, he grinned and said, "I'd love to go."

I groaned. Out loud. I didn't even care.

"Presley." Dad cut me a look.

"I didn't say a word," I said, smiling as sweetly as I could muster. "I'll work on getting the tickets."

"Leave them on my desk. Top—"

"I know. Top right corner." I pushed away from the table. "If that's all you need from me, I'll be on my way. I want to make sure I get the same row and my ticket girl leaves in"—I glanced at my watch—"twenty minutes."

The three of them stood. I gave my dad a kiss on the cheek first. I was unsure how to say goodbye to Nathaniel, so I gave Victor a kiss on the cheek next. Yes, he was our lawyer, but he was also a good friend of mine. But Nathaniel? I wasn't sure what I should do. I'd been sort-of friends with him once upon a time . . . if you could call two people bickering about everything friends. His lips had been on mine once though, and *that* hadn't felt like friendship. My cheeks burned at the thought of that kiss and I swear to God he knew it, with the way his gaze darkened on mine.

"What?" he asked. "No kiss for me?"

My eyes felt like they'd bulge out of their sockets. Dad and Victor were already halfway out the door as Nathaniel grabbed his briefcase, so I know they hadn't heard, but even if they had, so what? It wasn't out of the ordinary. He was just being his usual self. He had the reputation of being a cheeky, charming, gorgeous guy . . . and he was. There was no denying it. I hated that he knew I wasn't immune to him. I looked toward the door and back at him, and decided what the hell. As I reached up to kiss his cheek, he held my elbow. Maybe it was to steady me, maybe it was to control my movement, but I felt the warmth of his touch spread through me as my lips touched his cheek. His gaze seared into me as I pulled back.

"I guess I'll see you Saturday," I said.

"You'll definitely see me Saturday."

"Should I get you an extra ticket?" Was I seriously fishing for information on his personal life? Is that what he would think? I mean, it was definitely what I was doing, but would he know that? I wanted to slap myself. Of course he'd know.

"I'm good with just the one." He cocked his head slightly, amusement clear in his eyes.

"Okay." I nodded, heart pounding, and walked away.

This was too weird for my liking. Once again, I blamed Adam. It was his fault I was reacting this way to Nathaniel. I hadn't been with a man in a long time. It had to be that. *Please let it be that.*

NINE

"IT WAS SO WEIRD." I put a hand over my face. "First he gets the company and then that awkward experience."

Morgan laughed. "Oh, honey."

"What?"

"Nothing." She bit her lip. "Have you told Jamie?"

Morgan and Jamie were my go-to people for everything. If the world were ending tomorrow, I'd probably make sure of it in our group text. Otherwise, I wouldn't believe it. This thing with Nathaniel was not something I wanted to be discussed in the group text though. Not yet. Not ever.

"Hell no, I haven't told Jamie. She's on the other side of the world. The last thing she needs is to hear about this and ridicule me. Besides, what's there to tell?"

"You've always been attracted to each other." She raised a hand to stop my impending complaint. "I know, you hate his guts, but you also think he's hot. I mean, he is. There's no denying that."

"I'm not saying he's not, but that doesn't mean I'm attracted to him."

"Okay. When he walks into the room, how do you feel?"

"Like I want to take a stapler to his lips and seal them together."

Morgan laughed. "Sure."

"I'm serious though. I don't like him like that."

"Remember in college when you practically begged him to kiss you?" She raised an eyebrow.

"I should have never told you that." I lifted my vodka soda and sipped. "Besides, I slapped him when he actually did kiss me."

"That was because it was poor timing." She shook her head. "But now here you both are, single."

"I don't know if he's single. I never asked." I frowned. "And I don't care. I'm not even divorced."

"Oh, please. You've been separated for well over a year and you've been acting like a nun in a convent for just as long, too. You need to get over this hump."

"I'm not in a hump, I'm just taking time to heal."

"Does that mean you're not over Adam?"

I shot her a look. "Don't be daft. You know I'm over him. It doesn't mean I have to jump into bed with Nathaniel, of all people." I shivered at the mere thought. "I hate him."

"So you say. Can you imagine how happy your dad would be if you guys actually dated?"

I scoffed. "He'd probably be scared I'd totally mess up his prized possession."

"You say that like he's innocent or something. I remember him in college, with his motorcycle and his girlfriends."

"He's not the settling-down type."

"That's not true. He dated that one girl for a couple of years . . . what was her name? She was pre-med."

"Larissa."

"Right. Larissa." Morgan smiled. "You didn't need to reach very deep into your memory for that one, huh?"

"Oh my God, will you stop?" I laughed. "You're impossible."

"I'm just here for the entertainment." She winked, taking a sip of her drink. "Tell me more about this baseball game situation. Are you guys planning on going to every single park? So like, one a weekend? Won't that leave you with no time to date?"

I laughed. "Have you not been paying attention? I don't want to date."

"Sure. That's what you say now. Let's see what a few weeks working with Nathaniel does to you."

I rolled my eyes, because that would not make a difference. I had too many reasons not to like him to like him. "Why don't you tell me more about this new venture you have going on?"

"Oh my God. The dating app." She clapped her hands, shimmying in her seat. "So, it's like a regular dating app—"

"Like the one your boss came up with?" I supply.

"No. He came up with a friendship app. This is a legit dating app, but it's a group date. So like, you know how it's super awkward to go on a date one-on-one?"

"Yeah."

"Here, you get a group together on the app, like four or six, and then you go on a group date. Something that interests all of you. Cool, right?"

"Very cool."

"I'm going to launch the speed dating aspect first to get my name out there, which is why I would love to rent out a few tables at the brewery when it opens at the end of the month."

"Totally. Count me in." I smiled at the light in her eyes. "Will your boss care? That you're going all out with this dating app project? Is there a conflict of interest?"

"Nope. The company only focuses on e-games and stuff like that. The app I'm making for them is so people can sign up for e-game events."

Morgan was only two years my junior. She had been my Little in our sorority, and while two years didn't seem like a big difference in age, it was, at least in our case. Despite wanting to explore love apps, she wasn't looking to settle down any time soon. From where I was sitting, she looked like a damn genius. I seriously needed to learn a thing or two from her, starting with not letting Nathaniel get to me.

TEN

I'D JUST PLACED the envelope on Dad's desk with the tickets
and walked out of his office when I spotted Nathaniel on the
other side of the hall. As usual, my body reacted—blood racing,
adrenaline pumping, mouth going dry. I hated it. He wasn't
even doing anything that warranted this reaction from me. He
was on a phone call, pacing the hall, looking broody as fuck and
God help me, all I could do was picture him turning that potent
energy my way as he pressed me against the wall and kissed me .
. . or maybe more. I gasped as I stood there gaping. What the
heck was wrong with me? Maybe Morgan was right. Maybe I
did need to get laid. *Or maybe you need to get laid by him.* No.
Absolutely not. No. Jesus. I shook the thought away and started
walking again. I had to go that way in order to get to my cubicle. Yes, cubicle. Nathaniel Bradley had a damn corner office
with a view, and I had a freaking cubicle with the peasants. And
they said life was fair. In Dad's defense, they were working on
the offices and I wasn't really going to be in here often. I mostly
expected to be working at the brewhouse.

I remind myself for the millionth time that I brought no
money into this company—he did. It didn't make me feel any

better, but at least by the time I reached him, my attraction—or whatever—was replaced by annoyance. He glanced at me and my pulse kicked again. It was the way he looked at people that held them captive. I wasn't a stranger to the look, as Adam had the same effect on people, but Nathaniel's was raw, like he didn't give a fuck whether or not you liked him, he'd take you prisoner anyway.

"Princess," he said by way of greeting. "I wasn't aware you functioned this early in the morning."

"I wasn't aware successful businessmen took calls in the hall."

"Yet here I am."

"Yeah, it seems you're also effectively blocking the path to my desk." I shot him an impatient smile.

"Your father's in?" He stepped out of the way, closer to his office so he was no longer in my way. The move brought him closer to where I was standing, close enough that I could smell the scent of his cologne.

"Not yet. Doctor's appointment."

"I thought I saw you come from that direction." His nodded toward my dad's office.

"Well, the elevators are in that direction." I tilted my head. "But if you must know, I dropped off the tickets to tomorrow's baseball game on his desk like a good employee."

His mouth twitched. "Trying to get your own parking spot next month?"

"I don't know. Is it in the budget? You would know such things, right?"

"We can work something out. Do you also want to wear a crown and a sash for the marvelous effort it must have taken for you to do this task all on your own?"

I felt a muscle tick in my jaw as I crossed my arms. There was definitely no attraction. I could never be attracted to a man who made my face do things that would surely cause premature wrinkles. I glared at him and he stared right back, unblinking. His eyes were like an endless dark hole, a place people got lost in, and I would not be one of those people. Yet, the longer he looked at me, the more I felt the air between us shift. This was the problem with staring contests—no one got out unscathed, and I swear the longer we stood there, the more stifling the air got. They must have turned up the heater. I needed to say something to break this spell. I licked my lips to do just that, but then his eyes shot to my mouth and I felt myself breathe a little faster. Oh my God, what was happening?

"I really hate you," I whispered. He raised an eyebrow, a challenge, a question. I continued. "I hate how rude and arrogant you are. I hate that you . . ." My chest was getting heavier with each word I spoke, so I stopped. *Why bother? He always had an argument ready*.

"Go on, princess. It seems like you have a lot to get off your chest today," he said, his voice was a soft purr. Something I could envision in my ear, in bed, and that made the whole thing worse. It made me want to keep going like he asked. And after a beat, I did because I couldn't hold it in any longer.

"You make me feel like I can't breathe."

My mouth clamped shut the minute the words left my mouth, as if I could shove them back in and hold them there. Nathaniel's lips parted slightly. He looked completely caught off guard by my words. Shit, *I* was completely caught off guard by them. Where did they come from and more importantly why had I said them? I felt hot suddenly, my face burning. Instead of getting completely out of the conversation, completely out of the building, I continued . . . because I was an idiot.

"In conclusion, I hate you," I said.

His eyes crinkled. I was sure if I stood there longer I'd finally see the charming smile I'd only seen in pictures, because he never smiled at me, but I couldn't. I didn't. I walked to my cubicle, sat down, and pretended to busy myself with things—

sorting papers (all blank, for the printer I needed to refill), counting the pens in the jar, powering up the computer. I really did have things to do, but I couldn't even think of one right now. I needed to look at my calendar. I closed my eyes as my computer came to life. Why had I said those things? Had I hurt his feelings? Not that I should care. He'd said some pretty mean things to me without caring if he hurt mine, but I didn't want to hurt his feelings. I just didn't want to feel this way. I was seriously going out of my mind. Thankfully, I got to my calendar and read through the tasks of the day: meet with the contractors at three, settle on the floors for the inside portion of the brewery, decide on the five beers we'd showcase the first month of opening.

I took a deep breath. I could do this. I was dying to look over my shoulder. I knew Nathaniel wouldn't be standing there, but I could see into his office from here unless he shut the blinds. My phone vibrated in my purse, and when I brought it out, I saw Adam's name on the screen. I answered.

"This better be about the statement."

He breathed into the phone. "It'll be on the eleven o'clock news."

"So like, fifteen minutes?" I looked at the time on my computer. "You didn't even send it to me."

"Jill wrote it."

"Okay." Jill was the only person in his camp I trusted to get anything done right, especially when it came to our personal lives. "Send it to me anyway."

"I did."

I clicked my email and sure enough, he'd sent it fifteen minutes ago. "I'm nervous."

"I'm outside your building. I'll be up there in five. We can read it together."

"You haven't read it?" My voice came out a shrill.

"I was waiting to do it with you."

"It'll be on the news in a few minutes."

"I'll be right there."

I looked around. I was sitting in a fucking cubicle. I needed more privacy than this. Dad said the reason he didn't give me the other corner office was because they were working on it, and there were two guys painting it right now. I didn't exactly want to go to my father's office. I could use the conference room. I grabbed my phone and walked over to Nathaniel's door, knocking lightly.

"Come in."

I turned the knob and poked my head in. "Hey, are you using the conference room in the next hour?"

"I have a meeting scheduled at eleven." He glanced at his watch. "Do you need it?"

"Um." I bit my lip and looked around his office. It was completely plain. He hadn't decorated yet, but he had a television, a desk, and a computer and that was all I needed, really. "Can I borrow your office?"

"Sure," he said, slowly.

He clicked something on his computer, gathered some papers and stood, buttoning his suit as he walked around his desk. He did everything effortlessly and it made me a little jealous, because despite what he may think about my upbringing, nothing came effortlessly to me. I opened the door wider as he walked toward me, his gaze set on mine. I licked my lips.

"About earlier . . ."

He shook his head. "Don't sweat it, princess."

"Okay." I breathed in and out, losing my balance as I fully inhaled him.

"You okay?"

"Yeah. Of course."

He looked over my head and his expression hardened. I turned around and caught Adam heading toward us. He looked handsome in a form-fitting navy suit, crisp white shirt, and blue tie.

"This is what you need my office for? To impress your husband?"

My temper flashed as I turned back to him. "Think what you want, Nathaniel. I don't give a shit. I need a private place to have a conversation, and it's either your office or my supposed office." I pointed across the hall, where the painters had stopped working and looked over. They both threw a wave in our direction. I waved back. Nathaniel didn't. Jerk. I met his gaze again. "Or the conference room. I would meet in my dad's, but he's due to get here any minute and I don't want another fight."

Adam reached us by the time I was finished talking. He glanced at Nathaniel and down at me, placing his hand on my elbow. "You okay?"

"I'm fine."

"You're bright red. You look like—"

"I said I'm fine." I clenched my fists and glared at Nathaniel, who thankfully, walked out of the office and signaled for us to go inside.

I stomped in, leaving them behind me to make small talk. They still looked like old buddies when I'd finished setting the television to the news network and logged into my email from Nathaniel's computer. It was his laugh that did me in. That was what made my temper come back full force. My face snapped in their direction.

"Are you coming inside, Adam, or are you going to blow him out in the hall?"

Both of them blinked at me. It would've been comical, but I was too anxious to laugh.

"Presley," Adam said, frowning. Nathaniel glanced away, but not before I saw his smile. "We'll catch up later, Nathaniel.

Good seeing you again." He turned to me as he walked inside. "You're in such a bad mood today."

"I'm *always* in a bad mood." *Around Nathaniel,* was what I should've added, but I didn't though. I didn't like the fact that they were so buddy-buddy. How long had they been cordial like that? I shook my head and looked at the statement on the screen in front of me. It was good.

"I told you, Jill wrote it. She knows us."

I took a breath and stood up, raising the volume when I saw Adam's face on the screen. It was stupid to feel nervous about this. I'd read the statement while he was talking to Nathaniel, I'd pushed for it to happen, and now it was. So why did I feel this tightening in my chest? Adam's hand found mine as the news anchor read the script that told the world my marriage was over. We were officially done. My throat clogged up. I couldn't remember when we'd last held hands without being in front of a crowd, but I knew this would be the last time. I squeezed his hand when they finished reading it and turned it off, yanking my hand from his when they started talking about speculation of Adam cheating.

"I hate that they said that," he said.

"It's the truth." I met his gaze. "Why wouldn't they report the truth?"

"It's my personal life."

"You're a public servant. Nothing you do is considered off-limits now. You're a public persona now."

"That's bullshit," he scoffed. "There has to be a line."

"Well, there isn't. You should've thought about that either before you signed up for the job or before you started fucking other women." I shrugged. "Either way, it's done."

"You realize this means that our divorce is open to discussion," he pointed out. "You're okay with that?"

"Obviously not, Adam, but it's not my place to tell reporters what they can and can't talk about. Freedom of speech and all that."

"It's messed up." He glanced back at the television's black screen as if it would be enough to shut them up.

"For me, maybe. You deserve everything they could possibly conjure up about your personal life."

"I deserve to get shit from you." He looked at me, pointing at the television. "Not from them."

"You are getting shit from me. It's called divorce papers that I expect you to sign and cooperate with."

His eyes searched mine. "I just want to do this amicably."

"I'm glad we agree on something."

"I'm really sorry," he said, moving closer. "You didn't deserve any of that."

"I know." I swallowed, licking my lips.

He was going to kiss me, and I would let him because it would be our last. We hadn't kissed in nearly a year. It was the only reason I could see him and not claw his eyes out. It was the only reason I leaned into him. When our lips met, I expected to feel something more. What I felt was familiarity. It was warm and safe and spread sadness through me. I'd once imagined being kissed by him for the rest of my life. I'd imagined children and grandchildren and trips to Europe. When I pulled away, his eyes were still closed.

"Call me if you need anything."

"I won't, but thanks for the offer." I smiled as he walked toward the door.

"Let me know when I can visit the brewery." He walked out.

"That I will do." I followed, walking beside him toward the elevator.

"And I'll see you at the auction for the foundation," he said.

"Right." I sighed heavily. Public appearances were part of our agreement. He wanted the public to see that even though things hadn't worked out between us, we were cordial and in turn, he was still worthy of their trust.

"Bradley wants to donate a chunk of change." He pushed the elevator button and put his hands in his pockets as he looked over at me.

"To the foundation?" I frowned. "It's not even tax season."

Adam chuckled. "Not everyone donates based on their tax deductions. It's a cause he feels close to his heart. The man was one of those kids once upon a time, you know."

No, I didn't know. I mean, I knew, but not to the extent that apparently Adam did. I eyed him suspiciously, walking forward and raising an arm when the elevator doors opened and he stepped in. "How do you know so much about him?"

"He went to our wedding, Presley. I've spoken to him a few times." He pushed the button inside the elevator. "Besides, the man has been on every magazine I subscribe to the last two years. He's a wise addition to your father's company."

I dropped my hand and stared at him as the doors closed. Was this what it felt like when Julius Caesar realized what was happening during the Ides of March?

ELEVEN

NATHANIEL

THE THING about working in close quarters with someone like Presley Rose was that everything was a power struggle. It may have been a long time since I'd seen her, but I knew how she handled things, which was why I didn't take offense to her poor attitude or the way she was glaring at me across the table. I'd worked with people in a lot of industries and dealt with a lot of levels of arrogance and hers was the only one I'd willingly put up with. Maybe it was because I'd met her and got used to her irreverence at a young age. Maybe it was because the fire in her eyes made me feel things I rarely felt around others. Truth be told, I probably wouldn't have had much of an appreciation for her if it weren't for my friendship with her father. I'd probably still think she was a spoiled brat who was thrust upon me to annoy me, but I knew better. I'd heard of the way she'd left meetings that could have taken her career to another level in order to be by her father's side. I'd heard the way people in her husband's circle spoke about her, with the utmost respect, as if she were the one with his career in her hands and not the other way around. There was a mystery to her that I hadn't yet uncovered that, if I was being completely honest with myself, I'd been yearning to uncover since we were in college.

That time had come and gone though. Not only because she was married, but because she was the kind of person who would never jeopardize herself or her relationship, especially for a guy like myself. I was an outsider in her eyes. She may not say it, but we both knew it. She'd always treated me as such, with good reason. Had she let me in before, I would've probably crushed her in my attempt to attain more, more, more like I had been since her father took me under his wing. I'd achieved a lot in a short amount of time, but for some reason, it didn't feel like enough. *For her.* My mother was still asking me when I was going to settle down with a woman and Winston was always telling me to slow down, to not let life pass me by like it had his. The way he said that unsettled me. I continued to stare at Presley. She was talking to Rosa now, but the moment she felt my eyes on her, she met my gaze in a flash, a challenge. I felt myself smile because there was nothing I loved more than that fucking challenge.

TWELVE

PRESLEY

I BIT the inside of my cheek as my father told the employees about the future of the company. He was cheerful, boastful, as only he could accomplish in a time of crisis. I, on the other hand, felt numb. It was like my entire world was crumbling and I was struggling to stand on the one solid piece of concrete left. How did all of this happen without me even realizing? Had my marriage blinded me? By trying to do right by Adam and helping him with all of his endeavors? I'd been so caught up in Adam I'd obviously forgotten to see to my own, not that it mattered. I'd made my newest endeavor this brewery and I'd see it through. It made my dad happier than I'd ever seen him when I told him my idea and started working on the space. It gave us something to talk about, to bond over. Me coming on board with the company had changed our relationship in a way I wasn't sure much else could, and for that reason alone I was willing to give this Nathaniel thing a shot. Not that I had been left much of a choice. I looked up from where he was staring at me.

"I hope you're ready to take all of this on," I said. "I know you like to have a million projects going at once, but you can't be the reason this company fails."

"You think I would've invested if that were the case?"

I shrugged in response.

"I just hope you can carry your weight with the brewery. I know you're not the most equipped to work under pressure."

My eyes narrowed. Fuck him. I wanted to say that, but wouldn't just in case any of these people heard me. "I hope you can keep up. As it is, I'm having a hard time thinking about having to lug you around. If I wanted to babysit, I'd have kids."

"With who?" he scoffed. "Is that what your ex-husband was here to discuss earlier?" He spat the words out in such disgust, that I felt myself cower slightly, even the smile that followed was mean-looking. "Your dad says you don't make any time to meet new people. Who the hell would you have kids with?"

"My dad said that?" I felt something like betrayal spread through me, coating my cheeks with warmth. I didn't owe Nathaniel an explanation about my personal life, but the fact that he'd discussed it with my father made me feel low, small, and despite my effort to push the feeling away, it stuck. I grasped for my confidence. "For your information, I have a date in a few days. Would you like to call a conference meeting. with my father and discuss it?"

He didn't smile. Not with his mouth anyway, but I could see the gleam in his eyes as he lifted his glass of water to his lips. It didn't really matter that I didn't really have a date.

It's not like I couldn't get one, but with the divorce, the brewery, my father's health, the very last thing I needed was to add a stupid, annoying, needy man to the mix.

THIRTEEN

I WALKED into my dad's place and called out for him as I looked around. Apparently the cleaning ladies had just left. It smelled like clean linen and looked immaculate—the marble floor so glossy, I almost felt bad for stepping on it with my dirty Converse.

"I'll just be a minute, Pres," Dad called out.

"Totally fine. I'm early."

I walked over to the floor-to-ceiling window that covered the entire living room and looked out. Dad had sold his place on Fifth Ave last year and traded it for a Brooklyn apartment. Of course, apartment was a bad choice of word for it. It was more like a penthouse. He owned the entire upper floor, which normally consisted of four apartments, but after tearing down the doors between them, he'd built his own mini-mansion. After Adam and I separated, I started staying in one of the guest rooms but moved out a few months ago to one of the downstairs apartments. Much less lavish, much less room, but it gave us both our privacy and I still had a doorman and an elevator, which was more than I could say about a lot of apartments in Brooklyn.

"It doesn't look like it's going to rain," I called out unnecessarily.

He was probably in the shower and couldn't hear me anyway. Sure enough, he didn't answer. I turned and walked to the kitchen, but before I made it there, the doorbell rang. Another difference between our apartments. Mine wasn't big enough to require a doorbell. I looked through the peephole and saw Victor standing on the other side, wearing a polo and jeans. I looked around as I opened the door.

"Where's Nic?"

"She's on her way. She had to help Mia with something last minute." He gave me a hug as he walked inside. "How are you feeling today? Did you review the papers I sent?"

"I did until it started to look like it was written in a different language."

"I'll help you." He chuckled, pulling away and walking toward the kitchen. "I'll have some Macallan while I'm at it."

"Of course you will." I laughed as I walked over to the bar and looked through Dad's stash of liquor, finding the right bottle. "Is 1926 okay?"

"Is that a trick question?"

"Guess it's fine." I served him a glass, served myself some red wine from the bottle Dad and I were sharing the other night and walked back to the kitchen.

"So, what part did you get up to?"

"I got through most of it. I just don't know if I like the whole thing about splitting our assets fifty-fifty."

"Shocker. That's the part everyone has an issue with." He took a sip of his drink.

Dad walked out of his room wearing jeans, a Jeter jersey, and a blue Yankees cap. Basically, everything I was wearing. He gave me a once-over and grinned. "That's my girl."

"You took forever." I gave him a kiss on the cheek.

"The water took an hour to warm up," he said. "Do you have hot water downstairs?"

"Yeah."

He frowned, then shook his head. "Hey, Victor. I see you went for the pricey stash."

Victor smiled, raising his glass. "She served it."

"That's because she doesn't know what the hell she's serving," Dad said, but he was smiling. The doorbell rang again.

"That's probably Nicole. I'll get it." I hopped off the stool and walked toward the door as Dad and Victor talked about my divorce papers.

When I pulled the door open, it was Nathaniel standing on the other side. My heart bounced into my throat. "Oh. Hey. I wasn't expecting you."

"You don't look through the peephole before opening the door for people?"

"I assumed you were someone else."

"That's your problem, princess." He brought his hand down, brushing up against my neck, and tugged my ponytail. "You assume too much."

"Stop calling me princess." I closed the door and followed behind him, taking in the lingering scent his cologne left behind. He looked damn good in his blue Yankees T-shirt and jeans.

He greeted Dad with a hug, and Victor a little stiffly, with a shake of his hand and a serious look on his face. I wondered what his deal was? Had he had a bad experience with him in the past or was he just acting like an asshole because that's what he did for kicks? He walked toward the bar like if he'd been here a million times. I wondered when. I'd never seen him.

"Apparently Presley thinks the Macallan is a good idea before a game."

Nathaniel chuckled. "The twenty-six?"

Dad shrugged, lifting his glass. "The one and only."

"Guess you were due. If not now, when?" Nathaniel said, a twinkle in his eyes.

Dad grinned. I felt like I was missing an inside joke and I didn't like it. Why did they have inside jokes?

"So, I think her best bet is to settle or buy him out now," Victor said to Dad when he turned his attention toward him again. "Rather than waiting."

Nathaniel walked back and stood beside me, on the other side of the kitchen counter.

"Buy out the brewery?" I reached for my glass of wine and took a sip. "I don't know if he'd go for that. I wouldn't even know how much to offer. Do I just tell him I'll pay back the money he spent?"

"You can, or offer a little more as an incentive so he won't come back and argue," Victor suggested.

"Or you can just dissolve your responsibilities with the foundation," Dad said.

I set my glass down with a clink. "No way. I built that. I'm not just going to give it to him."

"He'll fight you on it if you try to take it," Victor said. "He's a politician. The foundation makes him look good. Softens his persona."

I closed my eyes, tossing my head back. "I can't with this right now."

"You know I'm with you every step of the way," Victor said. "Penn's a good lawyer though. You'll be comfortable with him."

"Thank you. I seriously don't know what I'd do without you."

Victor winked. "Aren't you glad you never have to find out?" The doorbell rang again. This time, Victor stood up. "I'll get it."

Dad patted his pockets. "Let me get my wallet."

Nathaniel was still standing beside me, quietly sipping his drink. "So, this is your date?"

I blinked up. "What?"

"The lawyer." He set down his tumbler. "He seems your type."

"Wealthy and selfish?" I fought a smile.

"Right."

My eyes fell to the tattoos on his left arm. "Why don't you have tattoos on your other arm?"

"You're avoiding my question." He met my gaze, suddenly seeming to be much closer than he was before.

Footsteps approached. I pushed off the counter in time to see Victor walk back into view with Nicole following closely behind. She smiled wide and picked up her steps when she saw me, throwing her arms around me.

"I've missed you so much," she said against me. "I'm so sorry you're going through all of this."

"Thank you, and I've missed you too." I squeezed her harder. "How's the baby?"

"Not so baby anymore. Mia and Jensen are watching him tonight." She pulled back. "Tell me about you. How are you?"

"Good. I mean, really. It's been a long time coming." I squeezed her hands in assurance, knowing she'd completely understand me. Nicole had gone through a high-profile divorce while Victor was still practicing divorce law. It definitely got messy but, in the end, they ended up together, and now I couldn't imagine them without each other. *God, I was thankful to have her in my corner. Especially here today.*

"Well, if you need anything you know I'm here in a heartbeat." She smiled.

"I know."

"I'm sorry, I'm being rude. I'm Nicole." She turned around, still smiling.

"My wife," Victor added completely unnecessarily.

"I'm going to need to add that title to my résumé." She laughed, looking over at Victor briefly before shaking

Nathaniel's hand. "My husband gets a little possessive when he's had some drinks."

"I haven't even finished my first." Victor rolled his eyes.

Nathaniel chuckled. "It's a pleasure to meet you, Nicole."

"Got my wallet, got the tickets, finished the call I was on, so I'm ready to go. Is everyone here?" Dad came back into the kitchen, smiling when he saw Nicole. "Nic, so great to see you."

"Likewise. I love your place. It suits you."

"Thank you."

"Speaking of, where are you living, Pres?" She looked at me.

"Downstairs." I laughed at the confusion on her face. "Like seriously, the floor beneath this one."

"Fancy," Nathaniel said.

"I would love to see your place, Mr. Hot Shot."

His expression darkened. "You're always invited."

My heart did a little flip. I looked away, because what the hell? We were in front of people. He shouldn't have said that. I walked toward the door and mentally slapped myself as a reminder that I hated him. He shouldn't be making my heart flip like this.

WE WERE SITTING in the second row, behind home plate, which wasn't my dad's preference, but it was the only thing I could pull together for this many people on such short notice. It wasn't the ideal situation for me either, with Nathaniel on one side of me and my father on the other. Victor and Nicole, unfortunately, were sitting on the other side of Dad, so I couldn't really avoid conversation with Nathaniel.

"So, Dad mentioned you have plans for the company," I said, hoping he'd take over the conversation.

"I do, but I need to run some things by you."

"You're going to run things by me?" I placed a hand on my chest. "Well, damn. Color me surprised."

"You're impossible, princess," he said under his breath, shaking his head. He looked at the game again.

"When are you going to stop calling me that?"

"When you stop acting like the world owes you something."

I glared at him. He gave me a passive stare, but I swear I felt that look all the way to my bones.

"Oh, come on, ump!"

I jumped at Dad's shout and focused on the game again.

"So how has this ballpark chasing adventure you've been going on been?" Nathaniel asked taking a sip of his beer. I picked mine up from the cupholder and took a sip.

"Well, we've only been to a couple of games so far and you're sitting in one of them, so I'm not sure."

"I would apologize for coming along, but I'm not sorry." His eyes twinkled when he said those words. I forced myself to look away. "So, you scouting parks we can sell our beer to?"

Our beer. I took a deep breath and let it go. "Do you think I should? I think White Oak is in most parks now."

"Not most." He tilted his head. "It's in fifteen of the baseball stadiums. We need to get the other half."

It was hard to believe it wasn't everywhere already. I reminded myself that even though my grandfather started the company, it was practically brand new in comparison to others out there. As far as beers go, White Oak was a baby, and up until recently, there was a monopoly with the larger beer breweries that made it difficult for Dad to get his foot in, even though he did it anyway.

"Okay, so how do we do it?" I asked, genuinely curious.

"We speak to the person in charge of sponsorships and try to get in through them," he said, shooting me a sly smile. "Don't worry, I have someone on it. You can just sit back and enjoy the game."

"But . . ." That made me frown. I turned my attention toward my dad. "If it's that easy wouldn't you have tried, Dad?"

He shrugged. "I didn't think I needed to give them money for them to sell my beer. I'm already giving them a cut of my product, so why should I have to pay?"

"Because we have to play their game," Nathaniel said.

"You weren't playing the tobacco industries' game when you came up with your vape thing," Dad countered.

"Those were different circumstances. We had a product that people wanted and got bought-out fairly early into the game." He shrugged. "I know people are quick to give me all the credit for it, but the truth is, I got lucky."

"You call making a billion-dollar product getting lucky?" I laughed. "You worked like hell all through college to get it right. I hardly call that luck."

"Surprised you noticed," he said.

The way he was looking at me when he said it made me think that he was noticing whether or not I noticed what he was doing. I licked my lips. His eyes clocked that. We were sitting too close for this conversation, for the way he made me feel, like I was missing air, when he looked at me. I cleared my throat, lifting my beer to my lips, needing something to quench the sudden dryness in my mouth.

"I guess I was good at pretending not to notice."

He smiled with his eyes, the way he often did, the lines around them pleating into smiles of their own. I told myself the beer was the reason for the warmth I felt spread through me, but I knew I was lying. I knew it was him.

FOURTEEN

WE'D INVESTED in a space that wouldn't need too much work. Dad sent eight containers of beer to brew here and the process had started long before anything else was in place, so in essence, I was trying to turn a brewery into a family-friendly bar. It really wasn't that difficult, or it wouldn't have been that difficult if the contractors working on it wouldn't have been so unreliable. My phone vibrated on the table and I swiped to take the call from my dad.

"Hey."

"Uh-oh. That doesn't sound like a good hey."

"It's not." I sighed, feeling like I was on the verge of tears. "Nothing is going right. The wood they installed isn't the right one, the lanterns were supposed to cross throughout the yard are colorful instead of white, the beer taps haven't been installed, the heater won't turn on, and I just . . . I'm overwhelmed, and I can't seem to do anything right."

I'd tried to stay calm throughout my recount, but the tears streamed down my face nonetheless. Maybe I was due for a good cry anyway. Everything in my life was falling apart. Everything. I'd tried to meticulously hide it for so long—my failed marriage, my father's ailing health, my inability to run a business the way it was supposed to run because I had zero experience in this setting, yet here I was, faking it until I made it work. The issue with real life was that you could fake it until money was involved. Once you were playing Monopoly with actual currency, all bets were off. I needed to get this right and I needed to do it fast.

"Presley," Dad said, his voice fighting with the static of the phone line. "Take a deep breath . . . Every . . ."

"Dad, you're cutting off."

"I called because . . ."

I slapped the table and stood up, wiping my face as I walked toward the door. The reception in this place was shit. That was another thing we needed to work on. I unlocked the door and opened it, gasping when I saw Nathaniel standing on the other side. He glanced up from the phone in his hand, took one look at my face, and frowned. My heart thumped loudly in my ears, and then I remembered I'd been crying and probably looked like a mess.

"Dad, I have to go." I hung up and slid it into my back pocket, keeping my eyes on Nathaniel. "What are you doing here?"

"What's wrong?" He was still frowning.

"Nothing is wrong. Why would anything be wrong?"

"Is it Adam?" His jaw ticked as he asked the question.

"What?" I crossed my arms. It was a defensive stance, but in this moment it felt more like comfort. I stepped back, allowing him to come inside. "No."

He was quiet as I turned around and faced the mess in front of me. "I came by to see the progress," he said. "Will we still be ready to open in a few weeks?"

I felt the mixture of panic and defeat rise inside me once more, and again I couldn't stop the tears from falling. I never once cried in front of Adam, not when he'd shouted at me in frustration of a poor reception after one of his fundraising events, not when I'd found an exchange of dirty text messages between him and his assistant, or got proof from the private investigator I'd hired to confirm his affair with his campaign manager. I hadn't cried when I'd made the motion to file for divorce, or when I'd moved my things out of our shared apartment in SoHo. I refused to let him see my tears, refused to let him see any weakness from me. Nathaniel had seen me on my worst days though, so I allowed my weakness to be visible, ignoring that he might use it against me because I knew he wouldn't.

"Everything is wrong," I managed to whisper.

I still hadn't faced him. I'd allowed him to know I was crying and I was okay with that, but actually looking at him was another story altogether. I heard his heavy exhale behind me, and his footsteps as he came around to stand in front of me. He brought both his hands up and cupped my face, pressing his thumbs to wipe my cheeks as he brought my gaze to his. He was blurry through my tears, but somehow I saw his empathy. He should hate me as much as I hated him. He should laugh at my tears and at my obvious failure. Instead, he held my head high before dropping his hands.

"You're not going to make fun of me?" I blinked, trying to stop fresh tears from coming, and failing at that as well.

"Why would I?"

"Because it's what you do." I swallowed, pushing past the painful knot in my throat. "It's what you always do."

"I don't poke fun at you out of spite, sweetheart."

"Don't call me sweetheart."

His lip twitched. "Why don't you wash your face and then we can talk about what's going on?"

I nodded, swallowing as I pulled away from him. He was standing too close and I was feeling too vulnerable and as much as I wanted to push myself onto him, I didn't want to make past mistakes and be pushed away . . . again. Something flickered in his eyes, something that made me think maybe he wouldn't push me away this time, but then I remembered this was Nathaniel. He didn't like me. Not like that. I took a deep breath and walked past him. I went into the bathroom and did as I was told, washing my face and drying it. When I looked in the mirror, I could barely recognize myself, but I walked out of there and headed toward the mini fridge I'd installed, and pulled out two bottles of water. He was sitting in one of the long picnic-style tables when I got to the main room. I handed him a water as I took the seat across from him.

"I can get you a beer if you want," I offered.

"I'm fine with this." He opened the bottle and took a sip. "Now, tell me what's going on here."

For the next ten minutes, I went through everything I'd told my father over the phone. The entire time, as I ticked off points, Nathaniel looked around the brewery, mentally clocking each thing. When I finished, he stared at me for a long, silent moment. I didn't dare speak up. He wasn't staring at me because he was waiting for me to talk, but because he was thinking. He did that often—focused on one thing in front of him as his mind ran off into his thoughts.

"The lights outside is an easy fix," he said, finally. "I can do it myself."

"Why would you do that?"

"Because I can." He shrugged. "Because it'll help you and we wouldn't have to waste time hiring people who may get it wrong again."

"What about the floors?"

He glanced at the hardwoods they'd installed. "It looks fine to me."

"It was supposed to be rustic."

"Give it time. When people start coming in here and dropping their keys on it and denting it, it'll look rustic enough." He chuckled at my expression. "Personally, I would've chosen different flooring, but it'll do."

"The beer taps are a mess right now." I looked over my shoulder to where they were on the bar.

"I can install those."

My head whipped around again. "You can't be in here fixing everything. Don't you have things do to?"

"I do actually." He looked around again. "But this is important. I need this to open on time and you're in over your head."

"I can get it done."

He shot me a look. "You were crying when I got here. You're obviously overwhelmed."

"I'm not . . . that's not . . ." I stopped talking and tore my attention from him to look around the brewery. I couldn't exactly lie to him after he'd seen the state I was in when he got here. I took a deep breath and tried again. "I have a lot on my mind."

"So let me help. I have to be in here anyway."

My gaze shot to his. "What do you mean?"

"I want to try to fuse liquor with one of our beers, but in order to do that, I have to be here during fermentation."

I felt my brows pull together. "Why don't you just let the head brewer handle that?"

"I will, eventually," he continued, not fazed by my weighted stare. "If you want something done right, you have to do it yourself."

"You can't possibly do everything yourself," I scoffed. He continued to look at me wordlessly and I knew my statement was wrong. "How do you find the time?"

"I make time." He watched me closely. "When you want something bad enough, you make time for it."

The words pierced my chest. It was a foreign concept to me. When I was young, my parents were too focused on their own dreams to make time to teach me to cultivate mine. When I was married, my husband was too caught up in his political career to glance my way for too long. I'd never even really noticed it until this moment, with Nathaniel sitting across from me, watching me like he was waiting for my reaction to what he'd said. I wasn't even sure what reaction to give him. Which one did he want? Did he want me to agree with him or tell him I understood? I didn't and couldn't. It was something I still needed to learn. *But how? For so long, I've only made time for what everyone else wanted.* Or so I'd thought. But Nathaniel thinks I'm selfish and conceited, that I never look past my own issues.

The silence between us seemed to stretch longer than I normally allowed, because *normally* I would've thought of a snappy comment to say to him, but not anymore. I was tired of snapping and if I was being completely honest with myself, I was sad, and when I felt like this, the only thing I wanted to do was crawl under a blanket and sleep. Let the time pass me by and ignore my worries. Of course, I didn't have that luxury anymore. I'd promised my dad and myself that I'd have this space ready by the end of the month, and I'd make good on that promise even if it meant accepting Nathaniel's help. I put my elbows on the table and rested my chin on my hand. I was also tired of fighting.

"I'd really appreciate your help."

"Damn, princess." He raised an eyebrow. "Who knew you had it in you to be nice?"

I rolled my eyes. "You always fucking ruin it."

His chuckle echoed in the empty space, and inside of me somehow. A reminder that I wasn't as hollow as I sometimes felt.

FIFTEEN

"I HEARD Nathaniel's helping out in the brewery."

I coughed around the kernels of popcorn I'd just shoved in my mouth. It wasn't an accusation, but a matter-of-fact statement, and I think that bothered me more than if it had been an accusation. It meant he'd expected I'd need help. It meant he didn't trust I'd do it alone to begin with, and he was glad a man had stepped up to take on the challenge. I grabbed the water bottle and took a large gulp of it, hoping to get rid of the poor taste left in my mouth. It didn't work. I glanced at Dad, who was watching the baseball game intently. We were in Safeco Field today, and the Mariners were taking on the Marlins.

"I don't know what he told you, but he's not helping because I can't get it done. He simply wanted to be a part of it."

"He didn't tell me much." He met my gaze. "I'm glad he's helping you out."

I took a deep breath and tried to let it go, but I couldn't. I was tired of feeling inept, and worse, letting people make me feel that way. I turned my attention to the game in hopes that if nothing else, butt watching would keep me entertained, but all I could do was replay his words and focus on the tone he'd said them in. I did this until the words felt more like shouts than I was sure he'd intended. Until the only thing I wanted to do was scream just as loud. That was the thing about my relationship with my father though. Any response felt like backtalking, and that was something I was raised not to do. Growing up, I never wanted to be rude or seem ungrateful, but sometimes it was inevitable. One thing I did learn throughout my life was that the weight of unspoken words always felt heavier than the burden of the consequences they carried. And so, I spoke.

"You've never had faith in me." I glanced at him. He met my gaze. "You've always thought little of me because I'm a woman. You'd rather sell your company to Nathaniel Bradley than leave it for me to be in charge of it."

"You don't know what you're talking about."

"Enlighten me then."

He shook his head. "This isn't the time or the place."

"It never is. It never will be." I shook my head and looked forward. "It doesn't matter. At the end of the day, you're always going to choose him or any other man over me." *It stings. It's yet another punch adding to the doubt-sized bruises on my heart.*

He was quiet for so long, I thought he wasn't going to acknowledge what I'd said. He did that often, ignoring me or shrugging my emotions away. When I was young, I hated it. Now that I was older, I took it for what it was—he was a man who had grown up in a time where parents ignored their children, where children were expected to know how to solve their own issues, the way they had as kids themselves. My grandparents were loving toward me, but even they admitted they'd been bad parents by today's standards. We were a needy generation; we wanted to be seen, heard, and acknowledged. Dad's generation wasn't like that. They let their actions speak for them. It occurred to me, as I sat there making excuses for his aloofness toward me, that maybe he liked Nathaniel because he reminded him of himself. *But I wasn't sure what to do with that yet.*

"I'M NOT DOING WELL," Dad said finally. My gaze flew toward his. "Health-wise. I'm not doing well. Between the stroke, the diabetes, and my inability to quit smoking . . ." He shrugged.

"You told me you quit." I blinked rapidly, trying to clear the unexpected tears I felt forming. "You told me you felt fine."

"I feel fine enough." He smiled sadly. "But according to my neurologist, things aren't looking so good for my brain."

"What does that mean?" My voice was barely a whisper.

"My brain isn't recovering as well as we'd hoped." He turned his attention back to the field. "Therapy isn't helping like it used to in the beginning. My face feels different. I feel different."

"That's why you sold so much of the company."

"That's part of it, yes." He met my eyes again. "After the divorce, I had a hard time getting back on my feet."

I let that sink in. My parents divorced when I was in high school, still in that ritzy private school, doing ritzy private school-girl things. Mom's lifestyle didn't change much. We'd stayed in the house I'd grown up in, a mansion by most accounts, in a high-end neighborhood, attending fashion shows and galas. My life hadn't changed at all. Dad's had, but he'd made excuses for everything he sold and the changes he made in his life. He was living by himself, so he didn't need such a big house, and he definitely hadn't needed more than one. He'd said he didn't need a driver or more than one car. He'd said he didn't need the excess of things we'd been afforded our entire lives.

It was reasonable and easy to believe because nobody needed any of that. Those were luxuries few people were afforded. The possibility that my mom had taken him to the cleaners was not something that would have ever occurred to me or crossed my mind. Of course it wouldn't. I was a selfish brat. I could practically hear Nathaniel saying that about me right now. If he was here, he'd probably give me the *I told you so* look. And hadn't he? Hadn't he tried to tell me that my father was having a hard time? Hadn't he tried to get me to open my eyes? I closed them now and wished I'd been a little kinder to the man sitting beside me. God, I was so stupid. And now I was running out of time. Now, all the years of bickering and ignored phone calls on my end seemed so petty and insignificant. I wanted to say something, to tell him I was sorry, to express so many things, but the words wouldn't come. The blockage in my throat was too heavy, too big and painful. So instead of speaking, I laid my hand on his and squeezed. When he squeezed back, I knew words hadn't been necessary. *He knew.*

SIXTEEN

THE BUILDING FELT DESOLATE when I got there, only a few people had their office lights on. The entire marketing area was still empty and neat, a sign that none of them had been here yet to disrupt the space. I walked over to see if they'd left anything out by any chance and had started working on ideas for the brewery. I'd ended up naming it Hops BrewHaus, not because I loved it, but because Dad had formed an LLC and bought the domain years ago and it was the easiest name to use in such short notice.

"What are you doing?"

"Fuck." I jumped at the sound of Nathaniel's voice and dropped the stapler I'd picked up to move off the table. "Damn it, Nathaniel. What is your problem?"

"What is yours?" He switched on the lights. My eyes widened. What was he doing? He crossed his arms and leaned against the doorframe. "Are you snooping?"

"I'm not . . . I'm . . ." I blinked a few times. Damn it, I was snooping. "I was just trying to see if they'd started working on stuff for Hops."

He chuckled, pushing off the frame and walking toward me. "So, you are snooping."

"Sort of." I bit my lip, no use in denying it.

"Did you find anything?"

"No. Not yet anyway. You came in before I had a chance to look at whatever is underneath this cover."

"You don't think you should wait until they show you?"

"I guess."

"The plumbing inspector called me," he said. "Said he'd been trying to get hold of you but couldn't."

I frowned. "I don't have any missed calls or messages from him."

"Must have been Friday. That's when he called me."

"Oh. How'd he get your number?"

He searched my face for a beat before saying, "They have their ways."

"Hm. What'd he want?"

"He said one of the sinks wasn't working properly."

"Oh fuck." I took a deep breath. "I'll get it fixed ASAP."

"You better," he said, the amusement vanishing from his tone. "A lot depends on this opening. It's not only about you looking good, you know?"

"I never said it was."

"I'm reminding you in case you forgot. I know you have a difficult time thinking about others sometimes."

My mouth dropped. "What the hell are you talking about?"

"I'm talking about you opening up this business in time," he said. "You hired all these people but haven't given them an exact start date. You keep going out of town with your dad, which I respect, but you have a job to do and you can't expect me to pick up the ball every time you drop it. I'm an investor in this company. I'm helping sort shit out here, I told you I'd help out with a few things over there, but I don't want you to take that as me doing all of your work for you."

"I don't want you to do everything for me. I'll call the plumber and have him—"

"I already did that. The sink is fixed. You need to call the inspector to go back and re-inspect."

"When did you fix it?"

"When you were gone. I didn't want to have one more thing pending."

I swallowed back my pride. "Thank you."

He nodded sharply. "I have a few things to take care of before I go back to my office, but I should be in the brewery later on with the drop for the boiler."

I wanted to ask him about that. I wanted to know how he planned to change the game when it came to adding flavors to the beers, but I bit my tongue. I didn't want him to think I was interested in anything he was doing. Not after his outburst. And maybe that was petty and stupid and small, but around him, I felt immature. *I don't want you to take that as me doing all of your work for you.* Why bother fighting? I wanted to understand the process involved and what Nathaniel thought it would add to the bottom line in the future, but I didn't. I'd simply never measure up, so it wasn't worth pushing against another testosterone-infused wall.

SEVENTEEN

NATHANIEL

I WAS PISSED. I'd spent my weekend at the brewery fixing shit and making sure everything was running well enough for the inspectors to sign off on it while she'd been traveling across the country with her father. I'd done it because it was in my best interest as well as Winston's. I'd done it because I knew what it was like to depend on a paycheck, and the people we were hiring needed theirs, especially right before the holidays. None of this seemed to cross Presley's mind though. She was always so caught up in what was happening in her own life, that she didn't stop to think about it. I'd gone off on her because of that —because all I'd wanted was a simple acknowledgment that I was doing things she should have been doing—but the moment she thanked me and I saw the look in her eyes, I regretted being so harsh.

Despite her poor attitude toward me, I knew she wasn't selfish. I knew she was kindhearted and wanted to prove to her father that she was a worthy employee. She was in over her head—especially when it came to starting a business from scratch—but I wanted to fortify her not vilify her. She needed to know that I wanted her to succeed because she deserved to.

96

Especially after what her husband put her through. *I'd been right about him not being the man for her but had no idea that union would scar her so deeply.* Fuck, how many times had I wondered if I should have done more than kiss her on her wedding day? I'd never forgotten it. *I'd* wanted her then, and I knew I wanted her more than anything now, even after all of these years. As if she'd know that after my brutal attack just now. *Idiot.*

I needed to simmer down on the insults if I wanted her to even entertain the idea of dating me.

EIGHTEEN

"I seriously just want to be done with all of this."

I was in a high-rise office, sitting across from Adam and his lawyer. Beside me, was the lawyer Victor had put me in touch with, the one who'd been trying to get me to take something, anything from Adam even though I steadily refused.

"I'm with her on this," Adam said, looking between my attorney and me. "I want this to be as painless as possible. I've already put her through enough."

"You called the meeting." That was my attorney.

"Because we need to discuss the future of the foundation. Realistically, neither one of us has the time to deal with it right now."

"We have staff, Adam. Cut the bullshit. You want to keep it solely under your name." I raised an eyebrow, waiting for him to deny that.

"I do."

I took a deep breath. Fuck. I knew it would come to this. We'd discussed it before and agreed I'd stay on the board, but I hadn't really thought about completely handing it over. It was

what I worked on the most during our marriage, building relationships with different after-school programs for underprivileged kids. It was a not-for-profit and right now there was
absolutely no profit being made by either of us. The foundation
hadn't recovered any of the money we'd invested in it and it
probably wouldn't for a couple of years even though we both
knew once it did, it would blossom fully and beautifully.
Someday soon, it would be worth a lot of money. My attorney
cleared his throat beside me. I knew what he was thinking. *How
much is this worth to you? Let's take it.* I thought about my father
and the way he'd lost so much—his marriage, living under the
same roof with his family. Everything flipped for him in the
blink of an eye in such similar circumstances. We'd both been
cheated on, taken advantage of, and yet we held no ill will
toward the person responsible. Under different circumstances,
maybe I would've fought for the foundation, but I already had
so many things I needed to right in my life. I needed time with
my dad. I needed to build this brewery and make it the best I
could, for him. For me. For our family name. I looked up
at Adam.

"You can have it."

"Mrs. Delaney—" my attorney started.

"Miss Rose." I cut him off with a glare. "Like I've said a
million times, I want to be done with this."

We finished the meeting and signed the last of the agreement. Apparently, that was all politicians needed to do in order
to get a divorce because our attorneys congratulated us on
getting it done and announced us divorced. I didn't thank them.
It felt weird to go that far. I walked out of the room and left the
three men behind me. Normally, I called Jamie in a time like
this, but she was out of town. Most of our other friends were
married with babies, so I couldn't exactly ask them to meet me
at a bar. I had too much work to do to stop for a drink anyway,

so I headed to the brewery instead. Hopefully within those walls there would be solace and peace. Besides, at least there I'm needed.

NINETEEN

I WAS on the phone with my mother when I got to the brewery and saw Nathaniel's sports car in the parking lot.

"Mom, I have to let you go. I just got here."

"Okay, sweetie. Call me when you get a chance. Even better, come visit me. I know you promised your dad this year, but I want to spend time with you too."

"You're like a twelve-hour plane ride, Mom. Not exactly a hop, skip, and a jump."

"Well, it'll be worth it. There are a lot of cute boys here who are dying to meet you. Constantine's nephew has been staying with us the last few weeks. He's so handsome and I just know you'd hit it off."

"That sounds a little incestual, Mom." I laughed as I pulled the door to the brewery open.

"Oh, nonsense. I'm going to send you a photo."

"Mom."

"Check your phone in five minutes. I love you, sweetie. Talk to you soon."

"Love you too." I hung up the phone and sighed heavily.

"Long day?"

I jumped and turned to face Nathaniel, who was dressed in jeans and a T-shirt that looked like it could've been white once upon a time, but was now as filthy as his large hands.

"What in the world have you been doing?"

"Working." He raised an eyebrow. "What have you been doing? Obviously *not* working."

"I was in a meeting. Last I checked, I can totally work in this outfit though." I looked down at the lacy black dress I was wearing. Okay, so it was too short and flowy for work, but my entire chest was covered. I met his eyes again. "It was hot today and I hadn't been able to wear this since I got it off the summer clearance rack."

"You buy things off the clearance racks?"

"You don't have to look so shocked." I rolled my eyes. He didn't need to know that it was off the clearance rack of a high-end boutique. "I am in the middle of a divorce, you know?"

"I took you as the petty type," he said, with a twinkle in his eyes that made it difficult to measure whether or not he was totally kidding. "You know, the type to max out your husband's credit cards right before you leave him."

"Well, I'm not, but it's nice to know you still think so highly of me." I turned around and walked toward the back of the brewhouse.

It seemed like there was still so much to do. As I reached the large wooden door that led to the coppers, I focused on the questions I had for Ezra, the head brewer. The main one was, when will the first four beers be ready to drink and how many glasses of it would we be able to fill? I was hoping the answer was now and a lot. Pulling open the door, I instantly smelled the malty aroma that the brewing process provided.

Even after all these years, if you made me take a test to name all the steps in brewing, I'd probably fail. I recognized the large kettles and the mash tuns nearby, and knew that the lauter tun was used to separate the wort from the solids of the mash like a giant sieve. Where most breweries had large stainless-steel vessels, we had the classic copper. Dad was willing to compromise on a lot—cheaper floors than he would've liked, more affordable alternatives for the taps and bar area—but the coppers were where he drew the line. I finally spotted Ezra with a tiny clear cup in his hand near one of the coppers.

"Drinking on the job?" I joked.

"I have to walk the walk." He laughed. "Can't be selling beers we don't appreciate ourselves."

"Definitely not." I smiled, giving him a hug when I finally reached him.

I'd known Ezra since I was a little girl. He was probably a little younger than me when he started working for Dad in the main brewery. In the past few years, he'd scaled back on his hours, but when he heard I was opening this place up right by his house, he asked if he could work here. We would've been stupid to turn him down. He knew every recipe for every beer to the point that if you blindfolded him and let him compare two different brands, I'd bet he'd name them correctly.

"How's this one?" I asked, pulling away from him.

"I'll let you decide." He turned around, picked up a cup and poured me some. I took a sip and felt my face light up.

"This is the guava?"

"This is the guava." He smiled wide. "Your creation is going to be a hit."

"Oh my God, I hope so." I laughed and drank the remainder of my cup in one large gulp. "I can't believe it tastes so good."

"It still needs to brew another week, but I think it's safe to say it'll be great."

"Thank you for trying it."

"Of course, my girl." He took the empty glass from my hand and tossed it into the recycling. "What can I do for you?"

"I just wanted an update on the beers. We're supposed to open by the end of the month, but nothing is ready and I hadn't even considered how much it would suck if the actual beers weren't ready either."

"They'll be ready." He looked around, bringing his hand up to stroke his long, red beard. "The only one that may not be ready is the Deutsche brew, but the October will be, the guava, the lager, White Oak. You'll be fine."

I closed my eyes and relished the relief that came with those words: *You'll be fine.* I sampled another beer and waved him goodbye as he closed up and left through the back of the building. I'd completely forgotten about Nathaniel until I started making my way back to the dining hall. He'd probably left and I hadn't even gotten a chance to ask him what he'd done today. I walked behind the bar and reached down for a glass and the bottle of whiskey I'd stashed there. Once I poured myself a good amount, I walked around the bar and sipped as I headed outside to examine the light situation. It was a gorgeous day, conflicting with the rest of the days this week.

With no sign of Nathaniel, I plopped down on the two-seater cocoon swing outside and closed my eyes. I was no longer Mrs. Delaney. I was officially Miss Rose again. The thought hurt a little, but not as much as I thought it would. Maybe it was because we'd been living such separate lives for so long, sleeping on polar ends of our California king, not touching in any way that mattered, not discussing anything other than his politics.

"You look like a picture, princess."

I jolted, spilling some of my drink on my exposed knee. "Damn you, Nathaniel. Look what you made me do."

He chuckled, his eyes clocking the liquid I was currently brushing off my leg. "I would apologize, but that was the best thing I've seen all week."

"You must not get out much."

"You would be correct." He went inside.

I closed my eyes again, glad to be left in peace, and exhaled heavily when I heard his footsteps approach once more. I opened my eyes just as he sank down in the open seat beside me, rocking the swing back with the force of his weight.

"What the hell are you doing?"

"You think you're the only one having a bad day, princess?"

I scowled. "What's so bad about your day?"

"Hm. Let's see." He took a sip of the whiskey in his glass. "My girlfriend broke up with me last night because I wasn't willing to take things to the next level."

"You have a girlfriend?"

"Had." He shot me a sideways glance. "Are you not listening?"

"What's the next level according to her?"

"Probably give her a key to my place." He shrugged a shoulder. "Move in together. Get engaged. Who the hell knows?"

"You didn't ask what she considered the next step to be?"

"In order to ask, you have to care, and I simply don't."

"How long were you together?"

He tilted his head. "How long ago was your wedding?"

"That long?"

"On and off."

"And you wouldn't give her a key to your place?" For some reason, I found that funny.

"Well, that would mean I didn't anticipate ever being off. I would've had to go through the trouble of asking for my key back, changing the locks . . ." He shrugged. "I don't have time for that shit."

"Wow." I felt my brows rise as I took a long sip of my whiskey. This was the man who just a few days ago had told me you make time for the things you care about.

"What?"

"Nothing." I shrugged. "I guess it feels good to know you're an all-around asshole and it's not just something you reserve for me."

He winked and shot me a smile that made something in my stomach flutter. I pulled back slightly, suddenly needing to put some distance between us, because my reaction wasn't something I could handle right now. He sipped on his drink, but kept his eyes on mine, as if he knew what I was feeling and thinking. As if he was okay with that, but that was bullshit. I knew Nathaniel and hearing his admission of his breakup because he wouldn't commit to something more was all the more reason I needed to chill out. I tore my gaze away from his and looked up at the tealights, which were off.

"They're solar powered," he said, as if reading my mind. "And they're white."

"Oh. Wow." I smiled. "You installed them."

"I told you I would."

I met his gaze again. "People say a lot of things and don't make good on them."

"Only liars do that and I'm not a liar."

"Well, thank you. I do appreciate you doing this." I took another sip, leaning back in my pillow and closing my eyes as his foot kicked the swing into a steady, slow motion.

"I like this swing," he said.

"Me too." I didn't open my eyes. "It's so soothing. I could seriously sleep in here."

"So could I. It's bigger than the bed I had growing up."

"Really?"

"Really."

"What was it like? Your life growing up?" I turned my face toward him and opened my eyes again. He was looking straight ahead.

"Pretty normal. My dad died when I was eighteen, so my mom put up with a lot of shit from me. Mom's a nurse and worked day shifts, so she was gone a lot and we were very frugal, but a lot better off than the kids I went to school with." He glanced back at me. "Your dad gave me a job, offered me guidance. Sometimes, I think of how different my life would've turned out without Winston giving me something to do all those afternoons." He looked away again, taking another sip of his drink. "I sure as hell wouldn't be sitting here. That's for sure."

"That's why you want to donate to the foundation," I whispered. "Because you could've easily been one of those kids growing up in the streets."

He looked at me briefly and nodded sharply.

I swallowed. "I gave it to Adam."

"What?" His attention whipped toward me.

"The foundation. I let Adam have it."

"I thought you built it." His frown looked more like disappointment than disbelief. I didn't like the way my chest squeezed at the sight of it. *When had I started caring what Nathaniel thought of me?*

"I did." I finished off my drink and set the glass on the floor beside me. "But I wasn't ready to fight as dirty as his lawyer was for it. The foundation was never about who did what. It was about doing something with our money that went further than first-class seats and our images that had nothing to do with politics, though, let's be honest." I shot Nathaniel a look that I hoped would help him read between the lines.

He stared at me for a long moment. He didn't say anything, but he didn't have to. His expression said it all—he was disappointed in me, and that pissed me off. I sat up straight and turned toward him.

"You know, this entire year has fucking sucked for me, so I would appreciate it if you wouldn't get all judgy with me right now. Yes, I gave him an organization I built from the ground up. Yes, it hurt, but you know what? I have my freedom, and there's no price for that."

"You know what your problem is, princess?" He set his glass on the floor and leaned closer to me. "Everything has been

107

placed on your lap. You don't know what it is to fight for something. That's why you let things go so easily."

To hell with him. He has no clue what means what to me. I hadn't realized I was gripping the front of the swing until I pushed myself up. It takes me a second to gather my bearings, the alcohol I just drank swishing in my head making my feet sway slightly. He looked perfectly content sitting there, his long leg still rocking the swing lightly, as if he hadn't just insulted me. His expression was expectant, like he couldn't figure out why I hadn't said anything the minute I stood. I continued to glare at him.

"I let him keep it because I wanted to move on. I don't expect you to understand. You can't even give a woman the key to your damn apartment, so I don't expect you to know or comprehend what it's like to be in a marriage. A loveless marriage, at that. I don't expect you to know what it's like to be unwanted or . . . or . . ."

I paused to swallow back the inevitable tears, but it was no use. I felt them right there. I knew if I spoke another word I'd crack, and I couldn't crack. Not now. Not like this. I ended my marriage today. Five years of my life gone with nothing to show for it. I felt utterly alone. *Desperately lonely. Unlovable.* I turned to walk away, when he grabbed my hand. *No. Just let me leave.*

"Stay."

"I'm done with this conversation." I shook my head, blinking rapidly. "I'm tired of men trying to make me feel small."

"I'm sorry." He tugged my hand, still in his. This time, I turned around and faced him.

"I hate you," I whispered.

"No, you don't." His lips twitched ever so slightly before he got serious again. "You should never feel unwanted."

"That's rich coming from you." I scoffed, taking my hand from his.

"What does that mean, coming from me?"

"Surely I don't have to say the words aloud." I glanced away, wondering when it started getting dark out.

The tealights flickered on and off once, twice, three times before they stayed on. At least that was functioning, unlike everything else in my life. It was the self-deprecating part of me that smiled at the thought. The swing creaked as Nathaniel stood up. I didn't look back, but I felt his presence loom behind me. He walked around and stood before me.

"Say the words."

"Where should I start?" I looked up at him. "Back in college when I asked you to kiss me on like three different occasions and you turned me away, or when you showed up at my wedding and finally did it knowing nothing could come of it? Why'd you do it anyway? Why'd you show up there and do that? I never made sense of it. Or was that your point? To make me think about it for years to come?"

"Did you?" He inched closer and licked his lips. I fought to keep my attention on his eyes. "Did you think about my lips on yours all those years?"

"No."

"Liar." He moved closer, bringing his hand up to cup my neck, his thumb grazing my chin. My pulse jumped. "Tell me again, with more confidence this time."

"Why are you doing this?" I whispered. "Just kiss me if you're going to kiss me or leave me alone if you're not. I'm so done with this."

The folds that cased his eyes crinkled as he leaned closer yet, the tip of his nose brushing mine, his soft lips rubbing against mine. Mine parted on their own accord, expectant, but he pulled away again, his eyes on mine. My heart was pounding so hard I thought if he didn't kiss me right this second I might pass out, but I didn't care, I wouldn't be the one to do it. Not this time.

"Do you think about my lips on yours, princess?" he asked, his voice a low gravel that intensified the yearning inside me. I shook my head, fighting it. He brushed his nose against mine and pulled back again. "Do you wish I'd stop talking and kiss you now?"

"I wish you'd stop calling me princess." I tried to narrow my eyes, but it was no use with my breath coming in short spurts and my heart beating like a rapid staccato

"Do you really?" His lips pulled up to a lazy smile, his thumb caressing my jaw. "I think you like when I call you that."

"You think wrong."

"Hm." He moved his hand, his thumb brushing against my neck. "I think you're lying about that too."

"You're so annoying, Nathaniel. Either kiss me or don't." I tilted my face a little more, begging without words. "I'm not going to beg for you to do it. I'm not that girl anymore."

His eyes flashed with an array of emotions—alarm, regret, lust—as he brought his other hand to cradle the other side of my face. The possessive motion matched the look in his eyes as he finally brought his mouth down to mine. His lips were warm and soft, a complete contradiction to who he was. He took his time exploring my mouth, his thumbs caressing my jaw ever so slightly as if to ask for it to part farther, to move with him. I felt myself sway with him, my lips parting to allow the intrusion of his tongue.

When it met mine, I felt the air whoosh out of me. My heart took a leap, and I felt myself leap with it, pushing my body flush against his, bringing my hands up to tug the back of his hair, pulling his face to mine, unwilling to part from his lips. My life seemed to balance on that kiss. He groaned into my mouth, his teeth nipping mine, sucking, his fingers burying in my hair and pulling to the point of pain, my eyes watering with the bite. I pushed on, wrapping a leg around his waist, and then another as he lifted me up, his hands gripping the backs of my thighs and pushing their way to my ass, bare in the thong I wore. He tore his lips from mine, pulling back, his expression cloudy.

"Are you trying to fucking kill me?"

"You act like I planned for this to happen."

He let out a little growl as he took my mouth again, his fingers gripping me tighter. My back arched. I rocked against his stomach, wishing I was a little lower. As if reading my mind, he lowered me slightly, pressing me to his hard erection. Even through his jeans, it felt thick, hard, and long. The thought alone made me grind again. He hissed out a breath, letting go of my mouth, dragging his lips down my jaw, my neck.

"You have no idea how long I've wanted you," he said, a murmur against my neck.

"Now who's the liar?"

"I'm not lying."

I wanted to roll my eyes and call him out on it. Instead, I pulled his hair hard enough that his face aligned with mine and when it did, I kissed him harder. I'd heard stories, watched movies, read books about people being consumed by a kiss. I thought I'd experienced it before, but this teeth-clinking, tongues-clashing, hair-tugging kiss that left me gasping for air was incomparable. He broke the kiss first. His grip loosened on my ass, just a touch, but he still had a wild look in his eyes.

"Come home with me."

"Yes."

It was a split-second decision. One I'd probably regret tomorrow, but right now? I wanted to be consumed.

TWENTY

WE STUMBLED into his apartment like two drunkards, even though by the time we made it there we were completely sober. This would be a rebound hookup, but not one I'd blame on the alcohol. I told myself that I had to keep kissing him because if I stopped, he'd say something to piss me off and ruin the moment, but in reality, his mouth felt so good on mine I couldn't bear to come up for air. When he dragged his mouth from mine it was to push me back on his bed. I fell upon it with a whoosh and took in the scent of him on the comforter beneath me. As I inhaled, he was all I smelled.

"Take that dress off for me, sweetheart." The way he said that, all low and gravelly, made my stomach flip. I sat up in the bed and obeyed his wish, pulling it over my head, revealing my bare chest and thin thong. He closed his eyes, breathing out through his mouth as if I was testing his patience.

"Are you going to undress or stand there fantasizing about fucking me?"

His eyes snapped open. The heat in them was palpable. I felt every inch of me burn with it, yearn for it. He started undressing, his eyes on mine the entire time, as if he was afraid

I'd go anywhere. I was sure my legs wouldn't abide by my wishes even if I wanted to get away, which I didn't. When I saw the first sliver of his toned torso, I licked my lips, savoring what was to come. My heart pounded as he drew near, placing his hands on either side of my head and dropping his head to kiss me slowly, deeply, with a gentleness I hadn't imagined could ever come from him. He broke the kiss, dragging his lips down, kissing and sucking as made his way down my neck, my chest, stopping to explore my breasts. My hand went to his hair, tugging, begging for more as I moved against his mouth.

"I've dreamed about this moment more times than I can remember." He kissed his way down my stomach, biting the top of my thong and tugging it down my thighs and calves with his teeth. He brushed his nose against my leg until he reached my inner thighs. He blew out a breath over me. "I have to say, the reality beats out every single one of my fantasies."

"You fantasized about me?" I arched and threw my head back when he ran his tongue through my slit.

"All the time."

The grip I had on his hair tightened. "Liar."

"Hm." It was a sound he made as he sucked me into his mouth.

"Holy shit, you're actually really good at this," I gasped. His rumbled laugh vibrated through me. I gasped again. He seemed to want to consume me completely yet still keep me on the edge. I'd lost track of the number of times he'd brought me to the brink and then toned it down once more.

"I need to come," I said, fisting his hair tighter in my hand. "You need to make me come."

"Hm."

That was all he'd give me. *Hm* as his tongue slid across my sensitive flesh once more, swirling right where I ached. I felt like I was on fire, the blaze lit from inside of me seeping into each of my pores. I couldn't do this. I wouldn't survive this kind of pleasure. Adam never did this—took his time with me. I'd never been with anyone who had before him either. Everyone had always chased their own pleasure. They hadn't made time to let the other person enjoy it. I arched my hips, rocking against him. It felt like a bold move, daring, something I'd managed to control up until this point. He groaned loudly, as if the move pleased him, as if one of his fantasies was coming to fruition, though I couldn't imagine this being one—me grinding against his mouth, charging after the orgasm I felt building inside me. When I came, it felt like fireworks had gone off inside me, blinding me, deafening me, completely exploding all my senses. I thrashed and yelled embarrassing things. I must have said every single name in the bible as that orgasm hit me—Jesus, Mary, Joseph, Holy Moses . . .

Nathaniel had managed to position himself between my legs, teasing my entrance with his cock, which was huge and thick and standing at attention in a scary way. I bit my lip, arching my hips as I reached between us to stroke him. His nose flared with each touch. After a couple of beats, he pulled away so he was out of reach. I pouted, but soon after, he reached for a condom and started unwrapping it slowly onto his shaft, and every single one of my complaints left me.

"I want to memorize this moment forever." He shook his head, lids heavy, as he moved forward again, his cock teasing my entrance. "I want to replay it every morning and every night."

He continued to glide along me, but not inside, and I rocked against him, pleading for more. It wasn't long before I said, "Please. Just please."

"Tell me." He rocked against me again. "Say it, princess."

"I need you. I want you." I rocked. "Please."

He closed his eyes as if savoring the words, and opened them once more as he slid inside me, achingly slowly, little by little, inch by inch, stretching me until I felt almost painfully full. I bit down on my lip hard. It'd been a while, and even so, he was bigger than I was used to.

"God damn, sweetheart."

I bit down harder as he growled out the words, and harder as he grabbed my hips and started to move, rocking against me just so. His gaze met mine, wide, echoing the same surprise I felt. It was terrifying. Rebounds were supposed to help you forget – they weren't supposed to make you feel. As he held my gaze, I felt beholden to him. This no longer felt like comfort, it felt big and whole and all-consuming. He continued to move inside of me as he brought his face down to mine, his lips capturing mine in a deep, thorough kiss, his tongue as deep in my mouth as he was inside me.

I felt him everywhere, I couldn't escape him, and when he brought his hand between our chests and tweaked my nipple, making me moan loudly into his mouth, I knew I didn't want to. I wanted to live this moment forever, and whether or not he was lying about memorizing it, I knew I'd never forget it. I felt myself clench around him, felt my orgasm build so tightly until it exploded inside me, making stars rain down in its wake. I gasped, eyes wide, as I watched his own orgasm climb and felt him spasm against me. He bit down on his lip and closed his eyes as if he was savoring the moment, and I finally closed mine and let out a breath, emotionally and physically sated.

TWENTY-ONE

I LAY in my bed for hours, unable to sleep, thinking about his hands on me, his fingers in my hair, his mouth on my skin as he moved inside of me. His words came back to me. *You have no idea how long I've wanted you.* I didn't question them in the moment, too caught up in the lustful haze to pause and break it, but now I was alone, those words rang louder than everything else I learned about him last night. I'd slept with Nathaniel Bradley, my nemesis of over eleven years. *And he'd wanted me.* For a long time, if what he said was to believed. But how? We'd only ever bickered. He had thrown more criticism my way over the years than I'd eaten hot dinners, so how was that akin to wanting me? I shook my head. It was too early to work that one out. I looked up as the sun was coming out. It was moments like these where I cherished taking my dad's offer to move into this apartment. I let my head thump onto my pillow and closed my eyes once more. I'd really hoped I could avoid today, that maybe by some miracle I could stay in bed and let my life sort itself out. With that thought, I stood up and got ready for the day then headed to my dad's apartment. I let myself in quietly, careful not to wake him. It was our morning ritual since I moved downstairs: I let myself in, prepared us breakfast, and after we ate, we both went about our day. He played music in the mornings, old songs that reminded him of his youth, of a time when he stood on top of the world. Not that he wasn't still on top. I looked outside as a reminder. He was still on top, despite what he'd given up. The scenery had changed though, from pretentious yuppies to creative hipsters. No shame in that.

I was setting the coffee to brew when the doorbell rang. My attention flew to the time on the microwave.

"Presley, will you get the door? I'll be right out," Dad called out from his room.

"Sure." I eyed the eggs, the stove, and the toaster before making sure it was safe for me to walk out of the kitchen.

Wiping my hands on the kitchen rag, I walked toward the door and looked through the peephole. I dropped the rag. Nathaniel was standing on the other side of the door wearing a dark navy suit and white button-down, no tie, first button undone as if he'd left his house before he got around to considering wearing one. I bit my lip as I thought about what I'd find if I unbuttoned the rest of that shirt, then righted myself by slapping a palm on my forehead. I can't think about that right now. I bent to pick up the rag I'd dropped and looked through the peephole one last time before steadying myself to open the door. So what if he's crazy handsome and insanely good in bed? He was still Nathaniel Bradley, and it was only a matter of time before he said something to piss me off. With that thought, I lifted my chin and pulled the door open. His eyes seemed to burn into me when he saw me on the other side. My heart was pounding so quickly, I felt it everywhere except where it was supposed to be—in my ears, in my throat, roaring through my body. I gripped the door handle and pulled it open wider, so he had room to come inside. He did, stopping when he stood in front of me.

"You left," he said. "And you changed your number."

"What?"

"I tried to call you and your old number belongs to Dustin Castro."

That made me laugh. "You called the wrong number and asked for his name?"

"I got worried you'd either had your phone stolen or that you'd been stolen."

"So you called because you were worried I'd been kidnapped?"

"No."

"So then, why would you want to get hold of me?" I licked my lips.

"Give me your number and you'll find out." He took his phone out of his pocket and handed it to me.

I'd managed to avoid giving it to him so far, but I knew I'd cave sooner or later, if not for the brewery, for myself. I knew regardless of how hard I tried to fight that urge, he'd win that battle. Anyway, it was just a phone number. I plucked it from his hand and typed in my number, saving it under the first thing that came to mind. I smiled at the thought of his face when he searched for my name in his contacts as I handed it back to him.

"There. Now you have it."

"You're in a good mood today," he said. "Wonder if I had anything to do with that."

"You think too highly of yourself." I turned around and walked ahead of him. He grabbed the end of the rag swinging from my hand and tugged it, effectively stopping me. My pulse spiked as I pivoted around to face him and found his blue eyes on mine, his expression serious. He tugged the rag harder. My feet moved taking one step, then two, closing the gap between us. I tipped my head back and looked at him.

"What are you doing?"

"Last night wasn't a one-time thing."

"Yes, it was."

"Let me take you out."

"Like on a date?" I whispered, looking around in case my dad sneaked out of his room. The last thing I needed was for him to think there was something going on between Nathaniel and me.

His mouth curved. "Yes."

"I can't go on a date with you." I tugged the rag from his grasp. "Your girlfriend just broke up with you like yesterday and we . . . oh my God. We seriously shouldn't have done what we did."

"We fucked, princess. You can say the words." He raised an eyebrow.

"This isn't a good time for me to date."

"Because of your divorce?" His expression was no longer amused.

"Yes. Exactly." I backed away a step and then another, hoping he didn't realize I was full of shit.

"We don't have to call it anything. We don't need labels." He stepped forward, bringing a hand to my face. The tenderness in his eyes made it impossible for me to breathe. "It's time to call a truce, don't you think? One date."

"Fine. I'll agree to one date." My voice was a whisper, but I wanted to scream it, the way I'd screamed his name last night countless times. "But we're not telling my dad about this."

"That's fine." His lips twitched.

I took another step back, away from his grasp, and walked away. My father would never let me live it down if he found out about this, not after all the crap I'd talked about Nathaniel over the years. Jamie would probably say *I told you so.*

"Do you want coffee? Eggs? I'm making breakfast." I looked over my shoulder just as Nathaniel was undoing the button of his suit and taking it off.

Flashes of the previous night came back in quick snaps: him taking off his clothes, slowly, then taking mine off, his fingers caressing between my thighs as he slowly dragged my panties down my legs. *Oh God.*

"Breakfast would be great," he said, his voice low and husky. My eyes flashed up to meet his and I could see the fire in them. I turned around and focused on beating the eggs. "I didn't know you cooked, princess."

"There's a lot you don't know about me."

My phone rang, interrupting whatever he was about to say. I knew that ring. It was my mother calling me on WhatsApp video. I glanced at the time. It seemed about right that she would call me at this time. She was probably out shopping or having dinner. I turned around, swiped the screen as I picked up the phone and went back to what I was doing. It took a few seconds for her face to clear on the screen.

"Are you making your father breakfast again?" she asked, smiling. "He's so spoiled."

"Go back to your picturesque scenery and stop telling our daughter what to do, Wendy," Dad joked as he walked into the kitchen.

Mom and I laughed. Dad focused his attention on Nathaniel and started talking to him as I poured the eggs in the pan and poured three mugs of coffee.

"I want you to meet someone I'm having lunch with." She moved the camera to a man sitting beside her. I kept smiling because I had to, but I swore I'd kill my mother for this. "This is Constantine's nephew, Alexander."

"Hi, Alexander." I smiled wide, picking up one of the mugs and turning to place it in front of my father who was sitting beside Nathaniel on the other side of the kitchen island. "My mom speaks very highly of you."

"Of you as well. She kept telling me how beautiful you are, but nothing could have prepared me for your smile."

I felt my cheeks flame. It was such a cheesy line, but in this particular circumstance, I couldn't fight my blush. I was in front of my father, for Christ's sake, and a man I'd fucked just hours ago. I picked up the second mug and placed it in front of Nathaniel, taking a chance to glance at his face. He didn't look amused. *At all.*

"Careful not to burn the eggs, princess."

I rolled my eyes and turned back around. I'd set the stove on the lowest of lows. I wouldn't burn the damn eggs. I picked up the spatula and started jabbing at the eggs, alternating my attention from the pan to the phone.

"So, are you coming to visit?" Alexander asked.

"I hope to. I'm just not sure when. It's on my to-do list though."

"Maybe I'll come to the States and see you one day."

"That would be nice." I really wanted this conversation to end like right now.

"I'll turn you over to your mother. Is it okay if I ask for your phone number? We can keep in touch."

"Um . . . I guess?"

Behind me, I heard Nathaniel exhale heavily. His *annoyed* sigh. I shot him a glare over my shoulder. My father was sitting right next to him, on his phone, but right next to him none-theless. You couldn't really hide reactions like that.

"Okay sweetie, I see you have your hands full. I'll call you later." Mom winked at me. "Love you. Talk to you soon."

"I will. Bye, Mom." I set the phone down and started plating our food. Instead of taking the seat on the other side of Nathaniel, I stood across from them.

"Who was that on the phone?" Dad asked. "A new suitor?"

"Hardly." I scoffed. "You know how Mom is."

"Well, now that you're officially divorced you can date whomever you want," Dad said. "Not that I think dating a man who lives halfway across the world is a smart move."

"I'm not *officially* divorced." I glanced up. I wasn't. I was almost divorced, but it wasn't completely over and done with yet. "And I'm not dating anyone."

Nathaniel scoffed. I glared at him again. Seriously, what was wrong with him?

"Did you read the paper today?"

"Nobody reads the paper anymore, Dad. It's all online."

"Well, they took your side," he said, ignoring my annoyed tone. "They called Adam a cheater and said you were a victim."

"Doesn't matter." My cheeks flamed. I hated being called a victim. I wish the media would save that word for people who actually deserved it. I'd been cheated on and chose to stay in the marriage. I'd hardly call myself a victim.

"They've been outside the office this week again," Dad said.

"Then it's a good thing I've been at the brewery." I saw Nathaniel's grin from the corner of my eye and felt my entire face heat up. I turned around, walking to the fridge to hide it, but I was sure he'd noticed.

"Are we still on schedule to open in two weeks?"

"I think so." I pulled out a bottle of water and walked back. "Ezra is happy with where the beers are at."

"And the staff?"

"Ready when we are." Thankfully I'd spoken to Jennifer, our staff manager, yesterday. She'd already begun training with the waitstaff, all of whom had prior experience. We had three baristas fully appraised in White Oak beers, especially the new guava blend, and each one capable of creating any cocktail off the menu. They were meeting with the chefs on Thursday to sample the meals provided and to be better versed in what wines and beers would match which dish.

"So, only final touches?"

"Yup. Nathaniel's been helping out a lot."

"I bet he has. He gets a little obsessive when it comes to

these things." Dad smiled, glancing at Nathaniel, who was scowling.

"I don't get obsessed."

Dad shrugged, still laughing. "Why don't you two stay at The Boutique until it's all done? It'll speed up the process, and it's right down the street from the office."

"I don't think they'll have space. There's a convention across the street next week and the hotel is booked to the max."

"You can stay at my place," Nathaniel suggested, his gaze intent on mine. "I have a guest room."

"That's not a bad idea." Dad winked at me. "I have meetings here all week and hired a chef to stay, so you won't have to worry about making me breakfast."

"I"—I looked between the two of them—"I guess I can stay there a couple of days to save time."

"Nate's going to join us on our trip next week. We have too much to catch up on and every time I think we're going to knock it all out, I go out of town." He stood up slowly. He looked uncomfortable today.

"Okay." I agreed even though I did not like the idea of him going anywhere with us. I was supposed to stay at his place and spend the entire weekend with him? Next week's game was in Boston and we'd opted for a train ride instead of plane to make things more exciting. I'd been excited about it until now. "I'll see if I can add an extra train ticket."

"Traveling by train?" Nathaniel raised an eyebrow at my dad. "I thought you said you'd rather jump out of a plane than ride a train."

"I can't believe you remember that." Dad's shoulders shook with his laugh. "Presley has never ridden a train. I thought I'd take her."

Before I die. He didn't say the words, but I knew he thought them. I could see it in the way his eyes lost the light that was there a second ago. The loss of light threatened to choke me.

"Get the extra tickets and leave them on my desk," he said as he walked away. He took a pack of cigarettes out of his pocket and tapped on the top of the box before opening it. "I'll be back in five, Nate."

"I'll be in your office," he said.

"You shouldn't be smoking." I took off after him, chasing him to the door that led to the rooftop. "Dad. Please."

"I know, but it makes me happy." He shrugged, smiling sadly as he pushed the door open. "Can you just let your old man be?"

He closed the door between us before I could respond. I crossed my arms and pressed into it, the weight of my body on my forehead against the cold metal. I closed my eyes, willing myself not to cry. The urge to open the door and run up those steps to argue with him felt like a noose around my neck. *Could I just let him be?* Did he want me to let him kill himself? Finish the job before whatever was going on in his brain did it for him? My shoulders shook with that thought, a low sob escaping me without permission. I took a deep breath and wiped my face, standing tall. If he was a child, I could handle him. Punish him and send him to his room until he changed his attitude or abided by my demands, but he was my father. I couldn't make him do anything.

Nathaniel was still in the kitchen, his back pressed against the counter, legs crossed at his ankles. He'd rolled up his sleeves, revealing his muscled, tattooed, forearms. I avoided his eyes as I looked at the sink, intending to wash the dishes before I left, but they were all neatly stacked on the drying rack.

"I washed them," he said, pushing off and walking toward the living room. "I didn't know where to put them."

"Oh. Thank you."

"I've been trying to get him to quit too you know."

I sighed, pressing my hands on the edge of the sink. "He's too stubborn for his own good."

"He's gotten better."

I bit my tongue. No use in going there. If Dad hadn't told his favorite person that he was dying, I wasn't going to do it either. It wasn't my place. I heard him approach, but stayed in the same position, facing the sink, unwilling to turn around. I'd already met the amount of emotions I was able to handle in one morning. He was standing directly behind me. He wasn't touching me, but he might as well have been squeezing me in his arms for how much I felt his presence. I saw his arm from my peripheral vision as he set something on the counter beside me. A key. I blinked, looking at him over my shoulder.

"To my place," he said. I felt the weight of it press onto my chest. He must have noticed my panic, because he added, "Since you're going to stay there a few days. Don't make this more than what it is."

"Oh. Um. Thanks?" I exhaled with a nod, picking the key up and sliding it into my back pocket. "I'll probably stay there Wednesday night if that's okay. That dating thing is exactly two weeks from today. I'm starting to worry everything won't be perfect by then."

"What dating thing?"

"A speed dating company booked the brewery." I pressed my lips together, trying not to laugh at his bewildered expression.

"They want the entire space?"

"Not the entire space. Just a few benches."

"That is just weird. Did you offer them a special or something?"

"Well, yeah. The owner of the speed dating company is a friend of mine."

"Do I know this friend?"

I rolled my eyes. "You don't know all of my friends."

"I know. I'm just asking. I'm always curious about what happened to the group of vultures you used to hang out with in college."

"Vultures?" That made me laugh. "Why would you call them that?"

"Oh, you know, they'd survey the perimeter, squawk around when they saw prey, and go in for the kill in a pack, hoping to secure the prey before the other. You have to admit, it was weird."

"You watch way too much Animal Planet."

"National Geographic."

"Right." I walked over to him and pressed my hip against the island. "Did any of them ever catch you?"

I didn't even know why I asked. I really didn't want to know. How upsetting would it be if one of my friends had managed to land him back then when I couldn't and I'd known him longer? What if it was someone I kept in touch with?

"The one I wanted never tried."

"Oh." Something squeezed inside my chest. I'd tried many times, so he obviously was not talking about me. I pushed off the counter and started walking away. "I'm going to go book the extra ticket. It'd be nice if you give me a heads-up for the rest of the cities you're thinking about joining us, by the way. This whole getting extra tickets thing so last minute is a bit annoying."

"If you can't handle such simple things, how the hell are you going to run a business, princess?"

I bit my tongue, hoping to remain in control of the situation. It was something I often did with Adam. He'd say something that made me want to murder him, and I'd smile and bite my tongue, picturing myself doing it but not actually going through with it. There was power in holding back emotion. Of course, I hadn't achieved Morgan's level in this, but I was perfectly content with what I did now. Giving him one last glance, I walked away. I'd half expected him to follow me, but I was glad he didn't. Why did I even care that he hadn't wanted me back then? In the grand scheme of things, what did it matter? *You have no idea how long I've wanted you.* He was such a liar. I reached into my back pocket and touched the key he'd given me. He hadn't even given his ex-girlfriend a key. *It doesn't mean anything, because Nathaniel Bradley had offered this option to my father, not me.* His actions reflected his respect for my father. Nothing more. Never nothing more.

TWENTY-TWO

I TOOK a deep breath as I approached a mob of journalists that had gathered in front of my father's building. There were only four of them, but their camera crew made them eight, and in turn, felt like a mob. They all walked over to me in a wave.

"Mrs. Delaney—"

"Miss Rose," I corrected.

"Miss Rose, what do you have to say about Mr. Delaney's cheating scandal?"

"I have no idea what you're talking about."

"Is his infidelity the reason you are divorcing?" another asked, bringing her microphone up to my face. I put a hand up to lower it. They were so fucking rude.

"Why don't you address these questions to Mr. Delaney himself? I'm sure he'll be of better assistance to you," I said. "I'm not the one who's sitting in office."

"There are reports circulating that he had an affair with the senator's wife. Can you confirm this?"

My eyes widened slightly. Jesus, Adam. I shook my head, trying to keep my breath under control. "I don't know anything about that. Adam and I haven't been together for quite a while. What he does with his private time is none of my concern."

"The senator is the biggest donor the foundation has," another one chimed in. "There are rumors that Adam is funneling some questionable money into his campaign from the foundation."

"This may be your only opportunity to speak on the matter and clear him," another said.

At that, I scoffed, shaking my head. I powered through them, demanding them to part way for me to get into the building. As I pulled the door open, I looked back one last time. "I have nothing but respect for Adam Delaney. Our marriage may not have worked out, but our friendship remains the same. I would appreciate it if you'd stop following me around."

I wasn't sure how I managed to keep my head held high as I walked through the lobby and into the elevator. I couldn't tell you who was riding up with me or what they said as I nodded. My ears were ringing loud, a mix of the reporter's words and my regret filling them. It was a miracle I heard the elevator ding when I got to my floor. I waved at the receptionist sitting in front of the big White Oak Beers sign and walked past Rosa, who was on the phone and to my dad's office, knowing it would be empty. I pushed it open and placed the envelope on the corner of his desk, the way I always did the Monday before our trip. I could've easily taken it to his apartment, but this way he had a reason to come down to the office. It was another way I felt connected to him throughout this mess. When you feel like your grasp on your life is slipping, you cling on to things you can still control.

After setting it down, I stood in the middle of the office and looked around. What would I do once he was gone? Would I really fight to keep the remainder of the company or would I sell it all to Nathaniel? The thought made my heart hurt, but these were things I really needed to think about. Dad was meeting with lawyers and doctors and all sorts of people and unfortunately, he wasn't a man who liked to let his family in on those meetings. It was as if he thought not having me be a part of the process would shield me from the pain. As if the pain itself didn't come from the thought of losing him and having to live the rest of my life without him. He'd never see me happily married, never see my children, never see whatever it was I accomplished career-wise, whether it be effectively running the brewery or the company, or something else altogether.

With a deep breath, I walked out of the office and closed the door. I made my way to my office, which was now complete, and sat behind the desk. It was a similar desk to the one Nathaniel had in his office. I wondered what his other office looked like, the one in Queens I knew he worked out of a couple days per week. I'd heard about it from Dad, and in all honesty, was dying to go see it, but I couldn't just show up there. I reached for the key he'd given me. The one I'd attached to a separate keyring, careful not to mix it with my others, as if the key would get too comfortable there blurring my emotions about where we stood. He didn't even give a key to his ex-girl-friend, I reminded myself of that once more. What the hell did I care? My phone buzzed. I let go of the key as if I'd been caught doing something illicit and answered Adam's call.

"I saw you on the news," he said.

"Okay?" I leaned back in my chair. "Did you call me to criti-cize my wardrobe or to tell me what I should have said?"

"Presley, don't be like that."

"Like what, Adam? Honest?"

He was quiet for a beat. "Thank you for defending me."

"You're welcome." I closed my eyes. "Why were they saying the thing about the foundation?"

"You know how reporters are. They spin whatever story they want."

"Yeah, but how would they even know what money is going in and out of the foundation and what it's being used for?"

"I don't know."

"You were the one who said you had a leak in your office." I opened my eyes and switched my computer on, typing in the first news outlet I could think of. Sure enough, there I was, smack in the middle of a headline: *Beer Heiress Denies Delaney Wrongdoing.* "Beer heiress? What the fuck does that even mean?"

"You know how they are."

"Adam, you need to get your shit together. I agreed to let you keep the foundation because I didn't in a million years consider the possibility of you using it for shady political shit. Are you really that low? Have you forgotten all of those values you like to unleash on everyone?"

"I haven't," he said, his voice rising, "But in case you forgot, I have a million fucking people breathing down my neck with their demands and I have to try to keep the peace somehow."

"In conclusion, the media isn't lying. You're using the foundation to benefit yourself."

"That's not what I said."

"You didn't have to." I clutched the phone tighter. *I have nothing but respect for Adam Delaney.* Why the hell had I lied so blatantly? I had nothing but loathing and disgust right now. "I want my name completely off any papers that have to do with the foundation. I have things to do. Goodbye, Adam."

"Wait. I need a favor."

"When do you not?" I rolled my eyes. "What is it now?"

"I need you to come to the auction with me this weekend. You know, clear the air a bit. Let people see we're capable of working together."

"But we're not," I said. "Working together. You made sure of that when you demanded to keep the foundation to yourself, which I'm grateful for now, and which is also why I need my name out of there."

"Please?"

"I can't. I won't even be in town this weekend."

"Because you'll be off traveling to a new ballpark with your dad? This is important, Presley."

"Fuck you, Adam. My father's more important than your stupid web of lies."

I hung up the phone and slammed it on my desk. It took me two counts to twenty to calm down. There was a knock on my door two seconds later, followed by Nathaniel peeking his head in before I could tell him to come in. I raised an eyebrow.

"Seriously? What if I was changing?"

"Why would you be changing?"

I blinked. "Because I'm going to the gym? Or something?"

"Or something?" He chuckled, a sound that didn't sound warm at all, and walked inside, closing the door behind him. He took a seat across from me. He looked pissed, those dark blue eyes narrowed on me. "The building inspector is scheduled to arrive at the brewery any minute. You should be down there, not giving interviews or sitting around here doodling."

"I am not doodling." I slammed my palm on the desk. "I came to drop some things off. I'm going over there now."

"Good." He stood up.

I followed. "Why are you being such a jerk to me?"

He blinked. "Am I?"

"Uh, yes," I sputtered. We were walking side by side toward the elevator.

"Because I'm telling you what you need to get done for the business you signed up for?"

I shot him a look. "You're not my boss."

"Technically, I am," he said. "And here's the thing, princess, I know you're not used to having actual responsibilities on your shoulders, but people are depending on this brewery opening.

People like Ezra who left the main brewery to help you out with this one and needs to sustain the job, people like the bartenders you hired and the waitstaff, and what about the night chef? All of these people are depending on this opening in two weeks. They're not going to understand that there's a delay in their paychecks because they see you giving interviews on the news."

This was the second time he'd pointed this out to me and he wasn't wrong. I knew he wasn't. A part of me was in full agreement with everything he said, but I was also pissed. Pissed that he sounded so condescending every time he wanted to drive a point home. He had no idea what it was like to be hounded by the press and constantly be asked questions about my divorce. He had no idea what it was like knowing that Adam was most likely using the foundation for ulterior motives and I'd let it go because I felt like I was in over my head all around. He had no idea what it was like to be in my shoes. I jabbed the button for the elevator and faced him.

"I don't expect you to understand everything going on in my life right now, but you seriously need to work on being nicer." I pulled the key he'd given me out of my back pocket and handed it to him. He took it, confused. "I don't need or want any favors from you."

I stepped into the elevator and glared at him as the doors closed between us. I'd had enough of men treating me like shit. Surprisingly, I was completely calm as I walked through the lobby. I felt light. Was that what standing up for yourself felt like? If so, I could definitely get used to it. I pushed through the circular door smiling and smiled wider when I realized there were no longer any journalists out there. I was halfway down the block when I heard my name being shouted and turned to see Nathaniel beelining toward me. He seemed out of breath when he got to me.

"What are you—"

"Here." He put his hand out. Instinctively, I opened mine, blinking up at him when I saw the key I'd given him back.

"No. I don't—"

"I don't care," he said. "I don't care that you don't want my help, I'm going to give it anyway. I don't care that you think I'm an asshole, I'm going to give you my opinion anyway. I expect the same from you because contrary to what you may think, I'm not doing any of this to hurt your feelings. I'm doing it because I believe in you and I know you can do better."

"Oh."

"I'll see you at my place later."

I swallowed. "I'll think about it."

"Please be at my place later." His brows furrowed as if he couldn't believe he wanted me there. "I know I'm a jerk sometimes but . . ." He exhaled heavily, running his fingers through his hair. When he zoned in on me again, he looked like he was still trying to find words. "I'm sorry. But please be at my place later."

I couldn't believe I was nodding. "Okay."

"Good luck with the inspection, princess." He winked and turned around, walking back to where he came from as if he hadn't just completely flipped my world on its axis. *He has no clue.* No clue that his words and attitude made him out to be a total asshole. *"I'm doing it because I believe in you and I know you can do better."* How was that possible? *And why had that softened my heart somewhat? Shit.*

TWENTY-THREE

I HELD my breath as I followed the inspector around the brewery. He kept looking at things and making notes on his electronic device. By our third go-around, I started chewing on my fingernail. What if we didn't pass the inspection? What if he made me get the electrician out here again? As it was, he'd taken a billion years to come add more outlets. I couldn't imagine having to wait for him again. I massaged my temple as I watched him walk outside. What if he said something about the way Nathaniel had installed the lights? Fuck. Why was it so damn difficult to open up a brewhouse? The inspector made his way back to where I was, standing in front of the main bar. He turned the clipboard around and tapped his pen on it.

"Sign here."

"Okay." I took the pen from him and looked at him. My chest hurt from not being able to breathe correctly. I couldn't bring myself to sign the paper. I scanned it to see what it said, but all I could see were check marks. "But . . . what does this mean?"

"It means, I fully expect to get a free beer as early as next week," he said, grinning. "Everything looks perfect."

"Oh my God." I let out a relieved breath, rushing my signature on the page. "Thank you so much."

"No problem" He took the clipboard, gave me a copy of the paper, and looked around. "It's a damn good brewery. Good luck with the opening."

"Thank you." I smiled wide as he left.

We'd passed all of the inspections and were ready for business. Take that, Nathaniel. I took out my phone and scrolled until I landed on his name. I'd had it saved from when I was younger, but I couldn't recall using it once. I guess I'd never wanted to, but right now the urge was unbearable. I texted.

Me: Hey, according to the inspectors, we're set to open.

I stared at my phone a while, waiting for his reply. When I didn't get one, I put it in my back pocket. He was probably busy, but I hoped he'd get the text before I headed to his place. As it was, I was having serious doubts about staying over, especially after we had sex. No. Because we had sex. Mind-blowing sex that I couldn't seem to stop thinking about. It felt wrong to feel this way about him. I'd spent so much of my life being angry at every word he said and now I was vying for it. I focused my energy on re-arranging the long picnic tables, which were nearly impossible to move, when my phone vibrated in my pocket. The only people who called me instead of texting were my mom, dad, and Adam, and I didn't want to speak to any of them at the moment, but I pulled it out anyway, surprised when I saw Nathaniel's name on the screen.

"Hey."

"Not Your Princess?" he asked, laughing. "That's what you saved your number under?"

"I forgot about that." I laughed.

"Well, you'll be thrilled to know that I'm going to drop the *Not* part and keep the rest."

"Oh my God, you better not," I groaned. "I should've just saved it under my name."

"I would've changed it anyway." I could hear a smile in his voice. For some reason, it made me keep smiling. "Are you at Hops now?"

"Yeah. We passed all of the inspections, so we're officially set to open." My voice was cheerful.

"You did it," he said, and I could definitely tell he was smiling now.

"We did it. I'm just re-arranging these ten-ton tables that I can barely move."

"What else do you have to do there?"

"Honestly?" I looked around. "Nothing crazy. I'll be cleaning all day tomorrow. The graffiti artists are coming in the morning. The beer guys come on Friday, but Ezra's handling that, and the kitchen staff and bartenders we hired are from Jamie's parents' restaurant, which means they're fully trained. They come Monday. I think everything is finally falling into place."

"I'm sending you an Uber," he said. "He'll drop you off at my office. By the time you get here, I'll be done and we can go celebrate."

"Um . . . okay. Yeah. That would be nice."

I didn't bother reminding him that I had a key to his place and would be there later, because I was dying to see his office and celebrating the brewery was definitely a good idea in my book. I locked up and rode the Uber in silence. Anticipation spread through me when the driver told me we were one minute away, the butterflies taking over my stomach when we finally stopped.

"This is the place?" he asked, pointing at the building beside us.

I looked out the window. "I guess so. I'll get off here either way. Thank you."

My high-heeled boots hadn't even touched the ground before the door directly in front of me opened and Nathaniel walked down the stoop of the building. He was still wearing the dress pants I saw him in this morning, but he'd ditched his jacket and tie and rolled his sleeves up to expose his tattooed forearms. He looked comfortable and hot and it took me a minute to stop checking him out before I could speak.

"I thought maybe we were in the wrong neighborhood."

"Cheap rent."

"As if you can't afford expensive rent." I raised an eyebrow as I reached him. His arm came around me, pulling me into his side. My heart galloped as his face lowered to mine.

"I'll tell you a secret, sweetheart," he said, his mouth tickling my ear. "I'm not a big spender."

"You invested a lot of money in White Oak." I turned to face him. Our faces were so ridiculously close right now that all I wanted to do was pull his face down to mine and kiss him.

"Invested being the key word. I don't consider that throwing away money." He searched my eyes for a beat, then another.

"Are you going to kiss me?"

"Do you want me to kiss you?"

"More than anything."

As he brought his lips to mine, I wrapped my arms around his neck, pushing myself into him. I kissed him unabashedly, with no reservations. I realized as our tongues moved and his hands roamed my body, that it was the only way I knew how to be with Nathaniel. I'd never generated a filter to keep my emotions hidden from him, so even as I tried to hold a part of me back, I found myself faltering. He broke the kiss, breathing heavily as he placed his forehead against mine.

"Thank you for coming."

"Are you kidding? I've been dying to come here for years." I dropped my arms and looked at my boots, biting my lip.

Had I really just admitted that? And had I really told him I wanted him to kiss me more than anything? A filter would be nice right now. Yes, he'd kissed me again, but I'd asked for it.

Yes, he'd told me he wanted to continue hooking up, but he was single and I was a rebound. I needed to keep these things in mind before I made this out to be something it would never be. He pulled away but grabbed my hand to usher me into the building.

"What do you mean for years?"

"I wanted to see where the CEO of Whiz came up with his ideas." I smiled. "This was where you guys came up with the vape thing, right?"

"Not exactly. We came up with the idea at a bar. We rented out this space shortly after realizing it was something we could achieve." He stopped in front of a set of stairs and shot me a lazy smile that I felt everywhere. "No fancy elevators here."

"I think I can handle it." I walked ahead, but stopped suddenly, looking down at my attire.

I was wearing a short tie skirt that was literally made of ties, a birthday gift from Morgan that Adam would've never let me leave the house in. I'd worn a white blouse and blue blazer, making the ensemble look chic, not skimpy at all, but the thong I wore beneath it was definitely questionable. If I walked ahead of him, he'd be able to see up my skirt. The thought made me bolder. I started making my way up, not daring to look back to see his reaction. His footsteps behind me were the only indication I had that he was behind me.

We made it to the first landing. From memory, and Dad telling me about the place, I knew there were three more since his office was all the way up on the fourth floor. The second floor was silent, maybe used for storage? I made my way to the third, where I heard a lot of buzzing and commotion. When we rounded the corner and stepped into the massive space, I was taken aback. It was nothing of what I'd pictured Nathaniel's workspace to be. This was vibrant and fun, and every single person in here seemed to be working on something and excitedly talking to his or her peers. There were about thirty people in the room. Some of them looked up and acknowledged us. The ones who did, smiled and waved at me, obviously having seen him earlier.

"Let's go up one more floor." He grabbed my elbow. "We'll come back down later for introductions."

Instead of walking toward the employees, I rounded the stairwell and continued walking up the stairs. This time, Nathaniel was really close behind me, like probably eye level to my ass.

"Why are you walking so close to me?" I asked without turning around.

"Trying to block these motherfuckers from the perfect view of your perfect ass."

For some reason, that made my stomach flip. When we reached the landing, I stopped and admired the space. It looked like a high-end bachelor pad with gray walls, beautiful wood floors, a huge television, gaming system, a ping-pong and foosball table. To the left, there was a door that I assumed led to his actual office. On the opposite end, there was another.

"Which one's yours?"

"This one." He started walking left. I followed.

"I can see why you had a hard time going home after a day here. Your poor girlfriend had to compete with all of this."

His office was simple. He had his degrees up and framed, a bookshelf, desk, computer, his chair, a chair across from it, and a futon in the corner that really didn't match the vibe.

"Do you sleep here often?" My chin jutted to the futon.

"Not as often as I used to when I first got this place."

"Before you sold the invention?"

"Before I made enough money to get my own place," he said. "I was still rooming with Ryan when we got this place and this futon was as good as it got. It gave him and Mirna space from having me around and gave me space from them."

"I'm sure there were plenty of women who'd have let you stay at their place."

"You think so?" He stepped closer, closing the distance between us.

"I know so."

"Would you have been one of them?"

I squinted at him. "Possibly."

"You were engaged." He brought his lips down to my neck. "Would you have welcomed me in your bed despite the ring on your finger?"

"Would you have wanted me to?"

"It's hard to tell. I don't condone cheating. I've seen how it rips people's lives apart, but I wanted you so badly, I probably would have."

"I wouldn't have," I breathed, holding his forearms to keep me steady because the way he was moving his lips all over my neck and now exposed shoulders was intoxicating and completely unsettling. "In hindsight though? Knowing what I know now? Hell yes."

He pulled away. "What do you know now, sweetheart?"

"That men like Adam don't deserve saints for wives."

"You're not a saint." His lip tugged. "And I'm not a cheater."

"You say that now, but who knows." I shrugged. "Maybe if you had me every day you'd tire of me."

"Doubtful." He let out a laugh, then raised his eyebrows when he realized I was serious. "Presley, I can barely think when you're around." He brought his large hands to my waist, running them on either side of me, pulling my skirt up slowly until his hands were covering my ass beneath it. "It took everything in me to lead you up those stairs and not into one of the broom closets so I could bend you over and fuck you in this skirt."

"Do it now then." I licked my lips, moving away from his grasp.

I walked to his desk and bent over it, reaching back to lift my skirt so my ass was exposed. His gaze roamed over me slowly, as if he was savoring the moment. I swear the heat in his eyes was palpable, burning me from the inside out. He turned his body slightly and closed the blinds, but kept his hooded eyes on me as he did so. He came to me slowly, his gaze on mine until he was standing behind me and I could no longer see him.

"This is a dream, princess," he started, his voice low. He crouched behind me, sucking my calf before dragging his lips up along the length of my leg. "I'm waiting to wake up from it, but I hope I never fucking do." He brought his lips to my other leg, doing the same. When he reached my ass, he bit me. Hard. I yelped.

"What's a dream?" I whispered, panted, it was one and the same.

"Having you bent over like this. Exposed to me in my office." His hand rubbed my ass before he tugged my panties down slowly. "God, you're too fucking much."

Before I had a chance to ask what he meant by that, his mouth was on me, his tongue moving along my folds, nipping, sucking. I gasped loudly.

"Nathaniel."

"Yes?" he murmured against me, licking again, sucking my clit into his mouth. "You want me to stop?"

"No." I pushed back closer to him, needing him to rid me of the pressure building inside me. "Please don't stop. Never stop."

"Never?"

"Never," I whispered, squeezing my eyes shut. I was so close.

He teased and licked and nipped and sucked, and brought a hand up to help tease even more. It was as if he wanted me to accumulate so much pressure, I'd explode. He was definitely achieving that. I was definitely going to any minute, all over his mouth and his face. I said as much and he groaned, bringing both hands to my thighs and squeezing.

"Do it," he said as he sucked. "Let go."

Ecstasy felt like a firework I never wanted to dim. I continued gripping the desk as I shook, fully expecting him to slam into me, but it never happened.

I came loudly, wondering if I'd ever come so forcefully, so exquisitely. Every part of me convulsed with sensation. Adam had never made me feel so satisfied . . . as if my orgasm was his goal. I felt languid and so turned on, even though I'd just come in Nathaniel's mouth. *God, his mouth.* I wanted him inside me. Hard. Fast. *Now.* I was so ready for him to slam into me, but that was when it clicked that he was silent. Still. I stood up slowly to find him watching me with a peculiar look on his face.

"What happened? You're not going to . . ."

He stepped forward, cupping my face. "We have plenty of time for that later. I want you to meet everyone." *He what?*

"But you're . . ." I looked at his very obvious erection.

He smiled. "I can deal with it."

I wasn't sure I wanted him to, but he helped me find my underwear and went to the bathroom before I could demand anything else. I really, really wanted to have sex with him again. I really, really wanted to do anything with him again. When was the last time I'd felt like that? I couldn't recall.

We walked downstairs and Nathaniel introduced me to all of his employees. I small talked with Ryan, whom I'd met in college a handful of times. He showed me pictures of his newborn daughter, and I marveled at how crazy it was that he was a father.

"Not that crazy." He grinned, his brown eyes twinkling. "Crazy is our friend Nathaniel still not having a long-term partner."

I laughed. "I wouldn't doubt it if he's a bachelor for life."

"That sounds like a nightmare," Nathaniel said. He looked

more pensive than usual as he looked up at me from where he was sitting, cross-legged on the beanbag chair beside me. "I'm working on a long-term commitment."

"Not with Lisa," Ryan said, clearly hoping it wasn't with Lisa.

"Definitely not. She's out of the picture."

I kept my eyes on him because the long-term comment had completely taken me by surprise. Was I the rebound before his long-term woman? *Still not the woman he actually wanted, but the stand-in until the woman he actually wants notices him.* The thought bothered me. Ryan changed the subject and kept talking about an innovative baby bottle he and Nathaniel were working on and how it was taking up so much of their time, but it would be worth it if they could find a way to create it and get it approved before he had another kid. I kind of tuned out, my mind staying on the whole long-term thing longer than it should've, but I couldn't help it.

"Presley and I are off to celebrate." Nathaniel stood up. "Her brewery is finally ready to open."

"Nice." Ryan smiled wide. "I'll be sure to stop by for a beer or two."

"That would be lovely. Send my regards to Mirna."

"I will. She'll be excited to hear from you."

We walked out of the building in silence. Outside, a mother was struggling with opening her stroller while carrying her baby, and Nathaniel stopped to help her, opening it with ease. Everything was like that for him—easy and seamless. Like he didn't have to try, though I knew the truth. I knew he'd tried like hell before he got to this comfortable space in his life. I was quiet as he spoke about getting an Uber, about where we were going to eat, about strollers and bottles and how behind the times we were in both and how he hoped to change that alongside Ryan. He talked so much and I let him, because for once, I enjoyed listening to him. I didn't feel the same jealousy about his relationship with my dad, nor want to roll my eyes at his arrogance. This Nathaniel deserved respect and a little awe. I wanted more of this man. Of his fire. His energy. That was why my skin felt itchy when I thought of the woman he didn't get. When I thought of his future, one where I'd have to watch from the sidelines as he found his forever woman. Yet for the moment, I had him to myself, so I enjoyed the light in his eyes and how animated his hands were when he incorporated them into a topic he was passionate about. I was trying so hard to follow along and be a good listener, but my eyes kept focusing more on his mouth than his words, more on his hands than his gestures. Finally, halfway through our Mediterranean dinner, he slapped his hand on the table so loudly I jumped.

"What are you doing?"

"What am I doing?" He raised an eyebrow. "What are you doing? You haven't said a word since we left the office."

"I'm listening."

"Bullshit, Presley. You think I don't know when you're listening and when you're not paying attention?"

"I'm sorry." I closed my eyes. "I'm trying to be present, but I keep thinking about other things."

"What are you thinking about?"

"Just . . . stuff."

He reached across the table and put his hand over mine. "What stuff?"

"You said you were working on a long-term relationship." I swallowed, hating that it was so difficult for me to bring this up. "Where would that leave whatever it is we're doing? Is this a rebound?"

He blinked. "That's what you're thinking about?"

"Don't make fun of me, Nathaniel." I pulled my hand from his.

"I'm not trying to make fun of you. I just . . . where did this come from? You were the one who said you wanted this to be a hookup."

"I know what I said." I went back to my food. "I'm allowed to change my mind."

He grinned. "You're allowed to want whatever you want."

"That doesn't mean you have to give it to me. I know." I rolled my eyes. Should've seen that one coming.

"Who said I won't give it to you?"

I exhaled. "Let's change the subject."

"I don't want to change the subject. I want to hear you say what you want from me."

"Why? So you can make fun of me?"

"Why do you think everything will turn into me making fun of you?"

"Because it's you and it's me and we don't know how to just be. We make each other mad and then we're okay and then we go back to making each other mad again. That's our normal."

"No, princess. That's your normal. Your way of coping with your emotions is to lash out. I'm just along for the ride."

My mouth dropped. "What does that mean?"

"It means I humor you. I'm not going to let you sit here attacking me without giving something back."

I shook my head. "Why are we even talking about this?"

"Because you haven't told me what you want from me."

God, that was the million-dollar question. But was I really willing to answer him, because it was putting my heart on the line again with a man almost as well-known as my ex-husband? I would be in business with this man, and it felt as though more was at stake. But then I thought of my dad and how we weren't guaranteed long happy lives. So, I was taking a giant leap and hoping with all I had that Nathaniel would break it to me more gently if I were once again asking for more than he'd ever wanted to give me.

"I want you."

His gaze heated. "You have me."

"I don't mean . . . I don't mean just sex," I whispered.

"So tell me. What do you mean?"

"I can't." My voice was as meek as I felt right now.

I'd never had to have this conversation with Adam or any other guy for that matter. They'd started something and I'd gone along for the ride, and sometimes that ride was fun and other times it ended awfully, but I was strapped in for it all along. I wasn't navigating the whole thing. I wouldn't know where to start or what gears to shift.

"Presley." His stern voice beckoned my attention. "The first rule in a negotiation is that you have to state your terms. If you get a seat at the table, you need to take advantage and make demands. Otherwise, how will you ever get what you want?"

"I don't know what I want." No. That wasn't true. I wasn't able to articulate what I wanted, and Nathaniel wouldn't allow me to get away with that.

"Mistake number one." *As I thought.* He raised an eyebrow. *Let the lecture begin.* "Besides, you think I'm going to that bullshit? You know damn well what you want. I'm not one of those clowns you've dated in the past. Or married. This is me and you. What do you want?" He brought his hand over mine again.

"I want you, but I don't know in what capacity."

"We'll work with that." He brought my hand up to his mouth and kissed it. *We'll work with that? What the hell did that mean?*

"We'll work with that? Do you want that? For me to want more with you?" *Oh good God, Presley. Shut up.*

He shook his head and smiled against my fingers. "Yes. I want that."

"I have to say, you have a lot of control."

"In what sense?" He kept eating the tabbouleh and kibbeh on his plate.

"In the sense of you bending me over in your office and then

147

going downstairs like nothing happened, and not trying to make a move on me since." I tilted my head. "I mean, it could be that you absolutely don't want to make a move and that's understandable."

"Understandable?" He raised an eyebrow and continued eating. "How's that?"

"I don't know." I shrugged. I kept putting my foot in my mouth tonight. I didn't want to seem needy, but here I was with another comment that practically begged for a compliment.

"You think I normally fuck women and then take them out to dinner?"

My eyes widened. "I don't know. Didn't you have a girlfriend the last four or so years?"

"On and off, sweetheart." He shot me a pointed look. "You think I didn't sleep with other women during that time?"

"I don't know. I guess it makes sense if you did." I glanced away briefly. "I mean, it's what I was planning on doing."

His chewing slowed down. He kept his gaze on mine as he lifted his water to his lips and set it down again. "What were you planning on doing?"

"Sleeping around." I shrugged. "That's what single people do, I guess."

"You guess?"

"I haven't been single in a while and I definitely haven't been single in the city. It seems so . . . fast." I felt my eyebrows tug as I said the words. "Meaningless."

"That's what you want? A meaningless hookup? That's what you want with me?"

I licked my lips. I could totally see how he'd concluded that after the reaction I had when he showed up at my dad's place the morning after, but how could I tell him it wasn't? For the first time since my separation, I felt like maybe being single again didn't have to mean meaningless hookups. Maybe it meant a second chance to be honest with myself and with the world about what I wanted, what I felt. I wasn't sure I'd ever been honest before. And so, I took a deep breath, looked into Nathaniel's deep blue eyes, and said something I never in a million years thought I'd say to him aloud.

"I don't think any kind of hookup with you could ever be meaningless, Nathaniel Bradley."

He seemed just as shocked as I felt. For a moment, he just sat there, across from me, staring at me. Then, he cleared his throat, set his napkin on the table, and said, "Let me get the check so we can get out of here."

TWENTY-FOUR

"A FRIEND of mine from high school had an marriage arranged." I glanced at Nathaniel in the back of the taxi we were sharing. "Like she knew the guy she was going to marry from an early age."

"Was she able to date other people?"

"I think she was, but she didn't. She was smitten with this guy. I always thought it was the weirdest thing because I couldn't picture myself marrying anyone I dated back then, even as I dated them."

He smiled. "Is there a reason you're telling me this?"

"Other than the fact that I'm a little tipsy?" I smiled. He smiled back. "I've been thinking that the reason those things work so well, especially amongst older people, or so I think, is because they tell each other every single thing right up front. They're brutally honest, so there are no secrets at all."

The taxi slowed and Nathaniel paid before we arrived in front of his building. Nathaniel held my hand to stop me from walking toward the front desk.

"I took it upstairs earlier."

"My bag?"

"White with pink polka dots?" he asked. I nodded. "It's upstairs."

He stood close to me in the elevator, his fingers brushing mine. "So, what you're saying is that you want to be up-front with me?"

"With anyone I date," I said.

"Is that what we're doing, princess?" He moved closer still. "Are we dating?"

"Not if you keep calling me princess."

"That's fair." He chuckled, pushing closer to me until our bodies molded together. He pressed his lips to mine and pushed me onto the back wall of the elevator. When he pulled away, he kept his gaze on mine. "I don't know if you're doing this runaround for my benefit or yours, but I want to date you. I want the label."

"I—"

"I'm telling you what I want. That's what I'm bringing to the table right now. You can come back to me with what you want whenever you're ready."

"Okay."

I was confused. That was not the way anyone I knew stated what he or she wanted. He wanted me to think about it? A part of me really wanted to explore this thing between us past just sex, but the smarter part of me was sure it wouldn't end well. How could it? He gave me a quick tour of his apartment, which I hadn't gotten the last time I was here. In addition to the nice-sized kitchen, there was a living room and a guest bedroom, both appointed with dark furniture and understated fittings, which truly matched Nathaniel's personality.

"Where's my bag?" I asked as we walked back toward the living room.

"My room."

"Your room, huh?" I raised an eyebrow. "You're highly sure of yourself."

"I don't think I have to keep telling you where you stand with me, but if you need me to continue to repeat it, I will." He walked into the kitchen. "Want something? Water, wine, whiskey, beer?"

"Wine please." I sat on the couch. "Red."

"Half a glass?" he asked, amusement lighting up his eyes. "You've always been a lightweight and you said yourself that you're already tipsy."

"I was tipsy in the car. I sobered up in the elevator." I stuck my tongue out. "I've gotten better."

"I know." He grinned. "Otherwise, I wouldn't have brought you back here the other night."

"I have a question."

"I hope I have an answer." He walked toward me with our glasses, handing me one as he took a seat beside me.

"You said my friends were vultures." I took a sip out of habit. "And that the one you wanted never tried. Which one did you want?"

"Was it not obvious?"

No, Captain Arrogant, it wasn't, otherwise, I wouldn't ask. Was he making fun of me again? We'd never spent this much time together without fighting, so I was on uncharted ground. He took a sip of his wine and set the glass down, then reached for mine and did the same.

"What?"

He chuckled, searching my eyes. "Oh, princess."

"Will you stop calling me that?"

"It's a hard habit to kick," he said, looking way too amused for my comfort. "I'll make you a deal. If I tell you who I was talking about, you have to go with me to my mom's house next Tuesday?"

"What happens next Tuesday?"

"It's my birthday, and she always bakes me a cake and does this whole thing that I hate because I hate acknowledging my birthday."

"Your birthday?" I smiled. "I never knew it was in October."

"You never asked."

"Does my dad go?"

"To my mom's house on my birthday? When he can. We normally take the boat out when he does, but it's on a Tuesday this year, so that's not going to happen."

"Okay, I'll go. Just tell me who you liked so much you didn't pay attention to any of the other girls."

His smile was slow. "You."

"Liar." I rolled my eyes. "Tell me the truth."

"That is the truth."

I pinched his arm. "Liar."

"I'm not lying." He laughed, moving away. I pinched him again, moving closer as he laughed. "I swear I'm not lying."

I pinched him again, this time when I moved closer, I straddled him, enjoying his laughter way too much. How many times had I dreamed of making him laugh like this? Who would've known the way to get it was to pinch the shit out of him.

"I'm going to keep pinching you until you tell me."

He grabbed my hands, still laughing. "I'm telling you the truth, dammit. I've wanted you since I was eighteen years old and had absolutely no business wanting a girl like you."

"What?" I felt the breath leave my lungs with his admission. I lay my hands flat on his chest and continued to stare at him. The only sound audible to my ears was that of my own pulse. "But you . . . I . . . I hit on you all the time."

"You wanted me the way you seem to want me now," he said, shifting so my legs spread wider, so my sex was on the bulge in his pants. "You want to have fun with me, have sex with me, and then move on to another man, one with political ambitions or a trust fund baby."

"That's not true," I whispered. How had this changed from me fearing I was simply the rebound to him believing that of himself? He'd never showed me this sort of attention before, so I was still stunned and struggled to believe it was true.

"It's okay, princess. I'm not good enough for you. I never was and never will be." He leaned into me, his lips on my jaw, kissing to my earlobe. "But I want you anyway. And I'll take you any way I can get you. I'm tired of denying this to myself. I couldn't handle it before, but I can now."

I'm not good enough for you. I never was and never will be. What the hell? Why would he think that? Before he could say more, I leaned in and kissed him, dragging my arms up and around his neck. My hips moved on their own accord as our tongues met. It wasn't a demanding or frantic kiss. It was slow and teasing, his teeth on my lower lip, my tongue sucking his, my fingers tugging his hair as his seemed to get lost in the sea of mine. With Nathaniel, I felt present. His lips brushed over mine gently, the stubble on his face scratching my skin as he licked his way to my collarbone, his hands working on taking off my jacket. My blouse was undone next, the buttons popping with his desperation. He unclasped my bra with a skill I didn't want to think about, his mouth coming down on my breast, teasing, tugging, his groan filling the air between us. I grabbed his hair and tugged it so he'd meet my eyes.

"Stop saying you're not good enough for me."

He stared at me for a long moment, his gaze hazed with a lust I felt deep in my core. He didn't say a word as he lifted my skirt up to my hips and brought his hand between us, his thumb finding my clit as he moved in a slow, circular motion. I gasped and writhed against him. Our gazes were still locked, neither one of us willing to break first. The intensity in his, the way his lids lowered and how he bit his bottom lip as he watched my face, was what made me come apart on his fingers. I grabbed his hair harder as I shook.

"You come so easily like this," he whispered.

I bit my lip. I didn't want to tell him that it was him. It was the things he did to me and the way he watched me as he did them. I didn't want to give in to the notion that there might be something real, something more here. He leaned in and kissed me, a long, hard kiss that made me forget my thoughts. His thumb continued to move.

"I can't come again," I groaned my protest.

"You're going to come again." He kissed me. "You're going to come when I bury my cock inside you." He bit my bottom lip and pulled it into his mouth. My hips rocked against him on their own accord, chasing another orgasm. "I'm going to fuck you so hard, you're going to see stars, princess."

"Stop talking." I was panting as I scrambled to undo the buttons of his dress shirt. "Just stop talking and fuck me already."

I lifted up onto my knees, and his lips worked on my neck as he undid his belt and pulled his pants down. He didn't even take time to undress me completely, instead pulling my thong to the side and lifting me so he was rubbing his hard length against me.

"Oh my God." It was all I could say as I threw my head back. "Why aren't we naked?"

"This is only the prequel, sweetheart." He thrust into me, filling me slowly and completely as he grabbed my hips and lowered me until our pelvises touched. My entire body shook with the intensity of him filling me, and when he started moving me over him, I completely forgot my next protest. Nathaniel owned my body in that moment, and nothing could have broken that hold he had on me. *And I wouldn't want it to be any different, which terrified me a little.*

TWENTY-FIVE

"I GOT TWO CABINS." I massaged my temples with both hands and closed my eyes.

I had two cabins and a killer headache. It was only a five-and-a-half-hour train ride, so I didn't need two full cabins equipped with beds. I needed one for the three of us, but when I booked, I didn't realize I was booking actual cabins. I thought they were just pricy because they were in the front of the train. I smelled Nathaniel as he stepped closer, but continued my head massage until he moved my hands out of the way and replaced my fingers on my temple.

"Oh, that feels so good."

"Good." He pressed his mouth to my forehead. My eyes flew open and I took a step back, looking around. "Relax, princess. Your dad is checking out the second cabin you booked unnecessarily."

"Ha ha." I rolled my eyes, then cringed. Even that hurt. I followed Nathaniel as he walked out and into the cabin across the hall. Dad was sitting there, setting up his laptop.

"These are nice." He looked up when we walked in. "I could live in one of these."

"I'm glad you think so because you paid double and they won't refund me."

He shrugged a shoulder. "I can room with Nate and you can get your own room. I'm sure you'll appreciate that."

I smiled wide and nodded my agreement, which was contrary to what I was feeling. I'd been staying at Nathaniel's place all week and even though I'd officially finished everything I needed to do at the brewery last night, I was contemplating whether or not to go back to his place once we returned from our trip. I hadn't brought it up to him yet though. How was I supposed to spring that on him? He hadn't even let the woman he dated on and off for years have a key to his place. Speaking of which, I hadn't given mine back to him.

I sat down across from Dad and Nathaniel sat beside me, keeping a little distance between us, which felt odd after a week with few personal boundaries. I'd worked hard, but at night behind his closed doors, we'd fucked even harder. I hadn't truly accepted that he'd wanted me for so long and never acted on it, especially given how cruel he'd been to me. His barbs had been hurtful, and if I was honest, had probably hurt me more than Adam's infidelity. Both had left me feeling scarred and inadequate. At least *now* I knew that Nathaniel hadn't always said things with the intent to hurt. He'd simply known I was capable of more than I'd attempted, and it had angered him. So, he'd lashed out verbally. *Strange man for thinking I had no idea he'd wanted me.*

"How many parks do you have left on this ballpark chasing journey of yours?" Nathaniel asked.

"A lot," Dad said at the same time as I said, "Too many."

Nathaniel chuckled, bumping my arm with his. "Which one was your favorite?"

"Yankee Stadium. Obviously."

"That-a-girl," Dad said, winking at me.

"Aside from that one," Nathaniel said.

"Hm. San Francisco Giants."

"Mine too," Dad agreed. "And the Braves. They have a great park."

"And Wrigley." I smiled. "That one is incredible."

"Sounds like I have a lot of catching up to do," Nathaniel said.

I bumped his arm with mine. "Maybe you should start joining us."

"Oh, is that a formal invite from the ice princess?"

"I swear to God, Nathaniel." I rolled my eyes. "You have a serious way of ruining the moment."

"Because I called you an ice princess?"

"I have a migraine." I glared at him as I stood. I kissed my dad on the cheek. "I'll be in my cabin."

I walked across the hall and turned the lights off before getting under the covers of the bed. I really did have a migraine, and I really wanted to feel better before we got to Boston. I wasn't lying about that. I closed my eyes and faced the wall beside me, hoping to sleep the rest of the way.

I WAS in and out of consciousness, still knocked out, when the cabin door opened and closed, so I didn't even turn around in the bed. When it sank beside me, I knew it was Nathaniel. He wrapped an arm around me and pulled me to him, kissing my shoulder.

"I'm sorry I called you an ice princess."

"'Sokay."

"It's not." He buried his face in my neck. "I've been wanting to come over here for an hour, but I figured I'd wait a little while. I didn't want my departure from your dad's cabin to seem suspicious."

"Hm."

"Did you book three rooms at the hotel?"

"Hm."

"We might as well cancel one," he said. "I got used to sleeping with you."

I turned in his arms and blinked up at him, still feeling groggy, but somewhat alert as well. I felt the same about sleeping with him. It had been incredible, and I honestly didn't want to stop. But . . . "I have to give back your key."

"Why?" He pushed the hair out of my face, and it was so soothing.

"Because I don't want to keep it. Besides, I finished everything at the brewery."

"I want you to keep it."

"But . . ." I licked my lips, hoping to find my words. This felt important. "You don't give women the key to your place."

He shrugged a shoulder. "What's the key to my place when you have the key to my heart?"

"So cheesy," I whispered, leaning in to kiss him chastely.

"Yet so effective."

I shook my head, smiling. "This is a serious conversation, Nathaniel."

"I know it is, sweetheart. I'm dead serious. Keep the key."

"When should I use it?"

He searched my face. "Whenever you want."

Three words. They were not a declaration in a women's eyes, but I knew Nathaniel. I'd been studying him for many years, and if there was one thing I knew to be true, it was that he didn't mince words. Even if I hadn't wanted to hear the words—which had been nearly every word of criticism received —he'd said them anyway. Like Dad, he rarely wasted superfluous words but spoke candidly with assertiveness. *Like my dad. Which was probably one of the reasons I was drawn to Nathaniel, yet had been equally hurt as well.* His offer to use the key whenever I wanted was much more than an olive branch, which helped me answer succinctly.

"Okay."

TWENTY-SIX

"ADAM MADE THE NEWS AGAIN," Dad said.

I sighed heavily. "I don't want to know."

"It's about the foundation."

"What?" I sat up quickly, taking the phone from his hand. I looked at Nathaniel, who was sitting on Dad's other side. "Did you ever give him money for the foundation?"

"Not yet." He frowned. "My accountant is supposed to transfer it at the end of the month."

"Call it off."

"Why?"

"Just call it off," I plead.

"What the—"

"He's being looked at for embezzlement," Dad said, shaking his head as he took the phone back from me.

Nathaniel's eyes widened on mine. "What?"

"Long story." I closed my eyes. "I can't believe I forgot to tell you not to give him money."

"You shouldn't have let him keep the foundation to begin with."

"I did the right thing. Trust me."

"If you'd kept it, you could've taken his money out and kept what was for the good of those kids."

"If I'd kept it, I would've had many problems on my hands," I said. "It wasn't just his money. It was anyone who gave him money for the foundation. He was basically funneling money for his campaign through there. Why do you think I told him to go fuck himself?"

"You did good." Dad put his hand on my knee, trying to control my response.

"Well, shit," Nathaniel said finally. He took a swig of his beer. "What an asshole."

"I know." I yawned. "This whole leaving our bags with the bellman and coming straight to the game thing is for the birds."

"You slept the whole train ride." Dad shot me a sideways glance.

"I had a migraine. I was restless."

"You still up for dinner?" Nathaniel asked.

"I'm going to pass," Dad said. "I'll let you two youngsters paint the town without me."

"It's just dinner," I said, hopeful. "We can eat at the hotel."

His expression was thoughtful as he looked at me. "Okay, I guess I can eat and then rest."

I smiled so wide my cheeks hurt. I didn't mind going out alone with Nathaniel, but I didn't want to exclude Dad from a trip that was supposed to be father-daughter time in the first place. We went to the hotel and checked in. The three rooms were on the same floor, side by side. As we walked toward the elevator, Dad a couple of steps ahead of us, Nathaniel placed his hand on my lower back and leaned in close.

"I hope you know I'm planning on sharing a bed with you."

My pulse quickened. "I hope you know I'd kick your ass if you didn't."

I'd just finished applying my makeup and getting dressed when I heard a knock on the door. I was walking toward it when I heard the knock again and stopped short, my eyes on the door that separated my room with the one next door. I walked there, unlocked it, and pulled it open, finding Nathaniel standing on the other side. My breath faltered. He looked so handsome in a dark suit, with his arm raised, forearm resting on the top frame of the door as his eyes wandered over my body.

I was wearing a tight little black dress and heels. We were staying at a ritzy hotel, which meant even eating in the lobby meant going to a fancy five-star restaurant. I figured I'd dress the part, and of course I'd thought about what his reaction would be when he saw me. I couldn't lie about that. I'd let my hair down and used my curling iron to create loose waves, a difference from the pin-straight hair I was always rocking.

He dropped his arm, taking a step toward me, not wasting a moment before wrapping an arm around me and pulling me flush against his body, his lips coming down hard, fast, his mouth moving frantically over mine. I kissed him back with the same fierceness, throwing my arms around his neck, my fingers tugging the ends of his hair hard as I pressed into him, getting lost in the lust-filled haze we created. When I was like this in his arms, it was a wonder I'd ever hated him at all. He made me feel more wanted than I'd ever felt before, more alive than I'd ever dreamed. He walked me backward until my knees hit the side of the bed and I fell upon it with a whoosh. He shrugged off his jacket, tossing it aside, his eyes predatory on mine as he knelt in front of me.

I lifted my head so I could see where he was going with this. Surely he wasn't going to . . . I mean, we were due downstairs in five minutes. We had no time for . . . His hands held my ankles, pulling my legs apart as he positioned himself. He brought his mouth to my knees, kissing each one before finding my gaze again.

"So fucking beautiful," he whispered.

I felt those words from the tips of my toes to the top of my head. My hips moved of their own accord. Nathaniel smiled, acknowledging my need, and dropped his head again, dragging his lips up my legs as his hands pushed my dress farther up my waist and his fingers searched for the underwear I wasn't wearing. His eyes flashed with recognition. He groaned against me, his tongue licking from one end to another in a slow, unrushed movement. I jerked against his mouth, my hand flying to the top of his head as if to keep him there.

He chuckled. "Not going anywhere, baby."

I gasped. I'd never let Adam call me that. We both agreed it was a stupid nickname. But I'd never heard it from Nathaniel. Never thought a simple expression could make me feel this intense pressure in my core. His tongue along my folds helped, his gentle suckling on my clit definitely helped. He took his time, working his tongue in all the right places, the sounds I made and pressure of my fingers guiding him. If I tightened, he paid extra close attention, licking me gently there. If I moaned, he sucked on my clit a little longer, but never long enough for me to come. He was dragging this out and the building need was so intense, I felt I would explode if he didn't finish this.

"Please, Nathaniel."

His eyes snapped up to meet mine, but his tongue continued its onslaught. He only paused to ask, "You want to come?"

"Please." I nodded furiously, tugging at his hair, gyrating my hips.

"Maybe I should wait." His tongue slowed, his lips now kissing me chastely, moving to my inner thighs. "Maybe I should make you sit through dinner like this, with this need that only intensifies over time. The way you've been making me feel since the day I met you."

"You're such a liar." I was panting. I tilted my hips up. "Please, Nathaniel. Please."

I couldn't go to dinner like this. I wouldn't survive it. He shook his head, his eyes amused. He set another kiss on my thigh. "I'm not going to make you come right now, baby. I want you to wait."

"But . . ."

He stood, looming above me. "You look so fucking gorgeous right now. You have no idea."

"I'm going to make myself come. The moment you walk out of this room." I spread my legs, bringing my fingers where his tongue had just been. They slipped easily along my folds. I bit my lip, arching my back. "Fuck, Nathaniel."

"Fuck," he hissed, his eyes wild as he watched my hand move.

He walked closer, spreading my legs farther apart, standing between them as he watched me. He wasn't touching me, not really, but with our eyes locked it felt more intimate than the sex we'd had. It felt more intimate than anything I'd ever done. My pulse sped up. My core tightened with an immense pleasure that threatened to explode out of me. I bit down on my lip, keeping my gaze on his as he stroked my knees with his thumbs and watched me find pleasure. As my body shook with the aftermath of the moment, I finally willed myself to close my eyes, but even beneath my lids, all I could see was him and the way he watched me—with a look of awe, as if he couldn't quite believe this was happening.

I made him go downstairs before me. I needed to clean up and sort out what I was feeling. I'd come around to the idea of us potentially dating, and the sex was incredible, so I was okay with that, but love? I wasn't sure I was ready for that. I couldn't fall in love with Nathaniel Bradley. Like seriously couldn't. Yet, I wasn't sure I could stop it either. It seemed like with him, all my emotions were laid bare, raw and unequivocal. It scared me in a way that nothing had scared me before. Not even my relationship with Adam, as publicized as it had been, had scared me this much. With Adam, the entire thing went from a couple of kids in college falling in love to feeling like grownups showing up for a mediocre job. With Nathaniel, things felt electric, like something we could power the world with.

As if he had any right to interrupt my thoughts, Adam called me when I was riding the elevator downstairs. I answered, attitude on hand.

"I read the news."

"And?" He sounded like he was bracing himself.

"And nothing. The very last thing I need in my life is to be associated with your crooked shit."

"I didn't . . . it wasn't supposed to—"

"I don't care. As a matter of fact, I'd rather you not tell me anything at all. I'd rather not be complicit to anything you're doing."

"Well, unfortunately for you that's exactly what it's going to look like." *Is he for real?* No apology, just a statement telling me my name would be dragged through the mud again too. Asshole.

"Do you need a reminder that we're divorced?"

"Do I need to remind you that you're still listed as an agent?"

"I'll have my lawyers handle that and you better believe you're getting the bill for it," I said, exiting the elevator and walking toward the restaurant. I could see Dad and Nathaniel at the table from where I stood outside. "I'm really disappointed in you, Adam."

He exhaled into the phone line. "I don't need—"

"I don't care what you need or don't need. I don't need to be dragged through the mud because you were doing illegal things with a company that we set up in order to help kids in need. And you know what? The world doesn't need it either. It's not fair to those kids.

"Maybe if you get your head out of your campaign manager's skirt long enough, you'd see it too. Or have you already moved on to the senator's wife like I was told a month ago?" I paused. "Oh, that's right. You don't really get your head out of a woman's skirt, do you?"

"Presley." He was silent for a beat. "Are . . . are you dating again? Someone told me they saw you with – "

"How is that any of your business?"

"I just . . . are you? Jesus, Presley. The ink isn't even dry."

"How dare you?" My mouth dropped. "You fucking idiotic, cheating, no-good asshole."

"I'm sorr—"

"Don't call me again. Ever." I hung up the phone and walked to the table. Both of them stopped talking and looked up at me.

"You look beautiful." Dad smiled.

"Thank you, Dad." I sat in the seat between them, setting my phone down. I felt like dropping it in my glass of water, but I wasn't going to pay for a new phone because of Adam's stupidity, and I needed to call Victor. On that note, I picked it up and sent him a text, explaining what I needed done and set it down again.

"You look like you've got a lot on your mind," Nathaniel said, frowning.

"Adam just called." I took a deep breath and let it out. "I don't want to talk about it."

Dad and Nathaniel exchanged a look before looking at me again. Nathaniel spoke first, "Why don't you just have him go through your lawyer for everything?"

"I'm changing my phone number tomorrow. It's the only way."

"You can't just change your phone number every time something happens with a guy," Dad said. "Last time you did that you regretted it and it wasn't even over a guy you were dating."

I glanced away. I could feel Nathaniel staring at me. "Where's the wine?"

"She's bringing it now," Dad said. "Whatever happened with

that guy anyway? I remember you were all riled up about him. Maybe he's single."

"No, I don't think he is."

Jesus Christ, this couldn't get any worse. Thankfully, the wine arrived quickly and served as a distraction, but I knew I wouldn't be able to get away from this. Nathaniel was too smart not to put two and two together. I'd changed my number right when I'd gotten married, right after he'd kissed me. I buried my attention on the menu in front of me.

"Is your mother still in Greece?"

I looked at my father. "Yeah, she's supposed to stay until Christmas."

"You should visit her for Thanksgiving."

"And leave you behind? Nope." I brought the menu back up to my eyes. "Unless you want to come with."

Dad scoffed. "Wouldn't that be rich? Would you go to dinner with Adam and one of his mistresses?"

"I have, actually." I laughed, setting my menu down. "Obviously I didn't know he was fu . . . I mean, sleeping with her."

"He's a bastard." Dad shook his head in disgust.

"Asshole," Nathaniel added. "He didn't deserve you."

I shrugged.

"Nate, I keep forgetting to ask, how's Lisa doing?"

"Last I heard, she was doing well."

I held my breath.

"You haven't spoken to her?" Dad asked.

My stomach coiled. I didn't want to know if he knew how his ex-girlfriend was doing. I set my menu down and looked at Nathaniel anyway. He glanced at me quickly and back at my dad.

"I spoke to her the other day."

"I'm going to give this hiatus two months," Dad said. "I've noticed that's usually how long it takes you two to link up again."

"We run the same circles." Nathaniel laughed. "And I only attend galas every couple of months."

"She's smart to keep showing up to them and getting you back."

"I don't think that'll happen again. I'm done with the back and forth," Nathaniel said.

He wasn't looking at me, so I picked up the wine glass in front of me and looked around the room. I had a knot in the pit of my stomach that I really needed to get rid of if I was going to make room for food. He'd spoken to her recently and knew he'd see her again soon? And apparently even my dad didn't believe he wouldn't get back together with her. I needed to seriously restrain the warring emotions running rampant inside my body.

I couldn't, wouldn't fall for him. Not under these circumstances. Dad and Nathaniel spoke throughout dinner as if I wasn't sitting there. Once in a while, Dad asked a question that I would answer, but for the most part, they spoke about inventions and apps that Nathaniel was trying to launch. I knew damn well I could've contributed to the conversation. It wasn't like they were rudely excluding me. I was excluding myself. Too many things were running through my mind for me to relax and enjoy the moment and that was my biggest regret of all.

TWENTY-SEVEN

NATHANIEL

I COULD SEE her growing distant the longer we sat at the dinner table. When the check was paid, she gathered her phone and the room key she'd brought down with her, said good night, and walked upstairs ahead of us. Winston and I were still finishing up our drinks as we watched her leave.

"She's a good person," he said wistfully. "She didn't deserve what he did to her, how he's screwed her over at every turn."

"Do you think she'd ever go back to him?"

"Honestly?" He glanced over. "I don't know. I hope like hell she wouldn't."

I hated what his admission made me feel. I kept drinking, hoping it would diminish the sudden weight on my chest. It didn't. If anything, it made the jealousy sitting there burn, flourish. It made me want to get up and stomp upstairs, claim her and make her swear she'd never go back to him, that she'd stay with me.

"I think I'm falling for her."

"Presley?" Winston's eyes widened. I nodded. I hadn't meant to say it, but Winston was my go-to. Damn the fact that he happened to be her father. Luckily, I'd worded it in such a way that it didn't make anything suspicious or official. "Presley?" he said again. "You know she's not very fond of you, right?"

"I know." I chuckled. "I think she's coming around. Slowly, but she's being nicer."

His brows pulled together. "How long have you felt this way about her?"

"Not long."

"Well." He drained the rest of his drink. "Good luck with that. She's going through a lot, so you'll have to be patient with her if you decide to pursue anything."

"Noted." I drained my drink and twirled the glass, focusing on that rather than his expression, which wasn't thrilled the way Presley would've imagined it. The way I wanted it to be.

If anything, he looked put off by this idea. We stood up and walked in silence toward the elevators. While we were waiting, he turned to me.

"You know, before Adam came along, I would've loved for you two to get together and make something work," he said. "But then it didn't and she married Adam, and I figured if you hadn't tried up until then, you probably just weren't into her and vice versa. Over the years, I've been glad that it worked out that way because it meant I didn't have to be in the middle of a war between two people I love."

"You don't want me to pursue it," I said.

"I'd rather you give it time." He shrugged. "But who am I to tell you what to do? If you think you can make her truly happy and you won't leave her high and dry when she needs you most, go for it, but be mindful of those things. I don't think my daughter can handle another heartbreak right now."

"I would never break her heart."

"I don't think anyone ever sets out to do that."

We walked into the elevator and rode up in silence. His words echoed in my head. I could never leave her high and dry. I could never break her heart. If anything, I was the one in peril. Winston went to his room, I went to mine, and then headed right to the door between our rooms. It was closed. My heart jumped into my throat at the thought of her shutting me out, but when I pulled mine open all the way I noticed hers wasn't completely shut. There was a sliver of light visible. A heavy weight seemed to lift from my shoulders as I pushed it open. Her room was quiet and dark. It smelled like lavender and tea tree, a mixture of her body wash and hair products. I inhaled deeply as I shrugged off my jacket and toed off my shoes, undressing until I was in my boxer briefs when I hit her bed. Maybe she wouldn't want me tonight. Maybe she wouldn't turn over when I kissed her bare shoulder. Maybe she'd feign sleep. I'd stay either way. Even if it meant just sharing this space with her and not touching her, I'd stay. Having her this close brought me more comfort than I'd ever allowed myself my entire life, and I wasn't willing to part with it.

I kissed her shoulder once. Twice. Lightly, barely touching her. She turned around and faced me without hesitation, wrapping an arm around my neck and pulling me into her. Her lips were a gentle breeze against mine, the kind you crave in the dead of summer, the kind that makes it equally as easy and difficult to breathe when you're in the middle of a run. It embodied the way I felt about her. I matched her gentleness, letting my tongue sweep into her mouth softly, wanting more but waiting for her to take charge.

"You taste like whiskey," she whispered against me.

"I want to taste like you again."

She kissed me harder, deeper, and turned so she was on top of me, her legs straddling me. She pulled her lips from mine and dragged them down my jaw, my neck, my chest, sucking as she made her way to the elastic of my boxers. I lifted to help her take them off and spread my legs to welcome her between them. Her tongue peeked out over the tip of my cock, and I swore under my breath, grabbing a fistful of her hair. She started to tease me the way I'd done her earlier, licking up and down my shaft in a way that made my eyes roll. The difference was that I'd left this room earlier with the biggest hard-on of my life, and the minute I stepped back in here, was in the same predicament. As much as I appreciated foreplay, this teasing would only end with coming all over her face fast, and I needed to be inside her. I tugged her hair so she had no choice but to stop sucking me and look up.

"I want to be inside of you when I come."

She sputtered out a breath. "How do you manage to make that sound so hot?"

I smiled. She moved so she was straddling me again and slipped the T-shirt she was wearing over her head. I cupped her breasts, tweaking her nipples as she positioned herself.

"Is it okay?" she asked. "Without a condom? Are you—"

"I'm clean. Are you—"

"I'm on the pill." She nodded.

"And you want to?" I asked. She nodded again. "Are you sure?"

I pulled her close, so we were nose to nose. She nodded again. My heart felt like it was going to burst. I kissed her again, this time hard and frenzied, as she began to sink down on me ever so slowly, letting me feel the grip she had on my cock. She'd kill me. She'd be the end of me with her attitude and her fight and this magic pussy of hers that I never wanted to fucking leave. I gripped her waist and drove her down on me, my pelvis meeting her each time. Her moans filled the room. I opened my eyes and watched her. Her head was tilted back as she rode me faster, harder, keeping up the pace I had going, chasing this orgasm that was building inside me and I knew was definitely building inside her. I licked my thumb and brought it to her clit. The unexpected move made her gasp loudly. She brought her attention back to me, her eyes on mine. She looked so beautiful, unabashed and dreamlike, as if none of this was real. It was a feeling I was familiar with every time we were together.

It felt like I was in a dream. Surely a woman like Presley Rose could never give me the time of day, but I never wanted to wake up from it. I never wanted to know what it felt like for her to walk out of my life. She kept mewling and moving her hips as I continued to move mine and my fingers. I brought my other hand up to tweak her nipples. She gasped again. Pleasure swelled inside me as she began to tremble, gripping me in a viselike grip I wasn't sure I could handle, but I continued to pound against her, harder and deeper as she moaned.

"Baby, I'm going to come," I whispered.

"Please." Her eyes widened as she nodded. "Please. Please. Please."

It was a chant, a plea that I felt deep inside me, searing through my veins and settling deep in my stomach, and it was with that plea that I emptied myself inside her as she spasmed around me.

TWENTY-EIGHT

MONDAY WAS a busy day for both Nathaniel and me. He'd be at a tech convention all day and I was going to meet with Morgan at the brewery to look at the invitations she was working on for her dating app event. After I finished folding my laundry from the weekend, I headed to Dad's place to make him breakfast. I was almost finished with his omelet when he showed up in the kitchn in a T-shirt and sweats.

"You're not going in today?" I frowned.

He shook his head slowly as he took a seat. I plated our food and served our coffee. We ate in silence. I kept sneaking glances his way because he was being more quiet than usual, even for him, but he seemed fine. I didn't see any outward signs of discomfort, and he was eating, which meant he must have felt decent.

"You should hire a driver again," I said, mainly because he was in a better mood when he was able to use his car. Even though he'd been living in the city for a while, Dad had never gotten used to public transportation. "You can get Edwin to drive you again. I'm sure he won't mind."

"He's taking me to Nate's birthday tomorrow." He looked at me. "Are you going?"

"I guess so." I shrugged, looking back at my plate.

"You can ride with me."

"That would be nice."

"Unless Nathaniel wants to drive you," he said.

I blinked. "Why would he want to drive me? I don't even know if he wants me going tomorrow. I'm going because he was nice enough to ask. And he helped out at the brewery."

Dad laughed. "Trust me, he wants you there."

Oh God. Did he know about us? Did it matter? I decided it didn't. Not that I was going to flat out tell him anything was going on between us, but if he guessed, so be it. I had no reason to hide. I didn't exactly want him rubbing it in my face that I ended up liking Nathaniel after all, but I could deal with it. I thought about that. Did I like him? It felt like more than like. I couldn't stop thinking about him all day. I could barely sleep when I wasn't in his bed. I'd tossed and turned all night last night because I'd come back to my place with Dad to avoid being obvious, and I didn't want to go all the way to Nathaniel's across town in the middle of the night. The thought crossed my mind more than once though. I needed to set boundaries for myself when it came to him, put distance between us.

"Are you getting him a present?" I asked. "I'm not sure what I should get."

"Presents make him uncomfortable," Dad said. "I usually take him a bottle of rare whiskey for his collection."

"Well, that doesn't exactly help me." I started clearing our plates.

What was I supposed to get a man who had everything? A cigar? Socks? Damn it. When I finished cleaning up, I went to look for Dad. He was sitting on a couch on the rooftop looking pensive as he smoked his cigarette. I pushed down the urge to say something about it.

"Dad, I'm heading out. I have a meeting at the brewery in an hour."

"Thanks for breakfast," he said, putting out his cigarette. He winked at me. "We should do it again tomorrow."

"I'll be sure to clear my schedule."

This had been our routine for some time, so being away from him last week, although the nights were incredible with Nathaniel, I'd missed our breakfasts together. He wasn't much of a talker, so his silence earlier really wasn't anything new, but his presence calmed me regardless. I left with a smile on my face and called my mom on my way over to the brewery. I may not have woken up in Nathaniel's bed, but it was shaping up to be a kick-ass day.

I WAS FINISHING up when I looked at my phone and saw a text from Nathaniel.

I miss you.

Simple words, but they made my pulse quicken. I smiled and typed back

I miss you too.

I missed you in my bed this morning. Tell me you're not going to let me wake up alone on my birthday.

Damn him. I smiled even wider as I typed, but then I erased the entire sentence. Birthdays had never been grand affairs in my household growing up. After all, the emphasis had been on what was given not the meaning behind it. When Adam didn't put much effort into my birthday, I hadn't been terribly disappointed. Although, now I wondered if some of his *business trips* around both of our birthdays had been *fucking* trips. God, it was only as each new event arose that I saw how incredibly naïve and blind I'd truly been. Nathaniel actually wanted me to be with him on his birthday, and that bought a moment of peace. Had Lisa made his birthdays something I had no clue how to replicate? *And if I didn't?* When did I become a jealous person? No. Because it wasn't jealousy I'd felt when I found out about Adam. It was anger. So, was it Nathaniel's effect on me?

I turned my phone face down and walked away from it when I saw Morgan walk into the brewery. She was smiling wide.

"Oh my gosh, this is the coolest place ever," she said, beaming with pleasure. "You even set out cornhole? I can't even."

I laughed. "I forgot about your obsession with winning that game."

"It's not obsession. It's a healthy dose of competition."

"You sound like Nathaniel." I rolled my eyes.

She raised an eyebrow. "Not to be like super annoying or anything, but the way you just said that . . . was very suspicious. One may even think you like him."

"Stop." I turned around, biting my lip to keep from smiling, and headed to the table where I had set out two mugs for us.

"Okay, this is my new favorite place." She set down her messenger bag and took a sip of beer, closing her eyes. "Seriously."

"It's one of our new ones."

"It's floral kind of, right?"

"Yup. Infused with lavender."

"That doesn't even seem like it would be good, but somehow it works." She took another sip. "Like totally works."

"Like thank you," I said, laughing at the glare she shot me.

"So, are you and Nate Dog happening?"

I laugh-coughed over my beer. "First of all, never call him that again. That's disturbing. Secondly, I don't know. I guess maybe?"

"You totally are," she squealed.

"We'll see," I said. "It's new. It's really good, but I don't want to set my hopes up and have him crush me."

"Adam didn't crush you."

"He did though." I took a sip of my beer and set it down. "I just bounced back quickly. If Nathaniel breaks my heart? I don't think I'll bounce back as fast. He has this hold on me. I can't explain it. It's scary. Exciting, but scary."

She looked at me for a long moment. "You seem happy."

"I am."

"You no longer hate him," she said, rather than asked.

I laughed. "No."

"So, go with it." She opened up her computer, typed something, and turned it over. "You know this is all digital, so the invites will be emailed and put on the app in two days for the launch, but this is what we have."

I pulled it close to me and read it over. "It's cute. I'd join."

"You should join." She grinned. "But you won't because this thing with Nathaniel is real and serious."

"I'm not going to argue that."

"Man, it feels good to be right. Wait till I tell Jamie about this."

"I hate you guys so much." I shook my head, laughing. "I would spill this beer on you if it wasn't so good."

"And if you didn't have to clean it up." She winked.

"You are just full of knowledge today."

"Always, Big. Always."

TWENTY-NINE

I DIDN'T MAKE it to Nathaniel's apartment last night, so I was scrambling to get there before the crack of dawn. He'd been at the convention later than expected, and I didn't want to show up at his place and hang out without him being there, mainly because I wasn't sure if that was grounds for revoking my key. The upside to not going, aside from keeping my key, was that I was able to get him a present—a fun present for his office and one I was wearing underneath my trench coat. When I reached his apartment, I knocked and waited. He opened the door with a look of confusion on his face.

"Why didn't you use your key?"

"Happy birthday." I handed him the present in my hand quickly and started working on undoing the knot of my coat.

He chuckled. "Get in here."

"Hold on, I'm trying to give you your second present."

He put a hand over mine, covering them and effectively stopping my nerves. I glanced up at him as he pulled me inside the apartment. "You are my present."

"I think yeah, I mean, yeah, but—"

"No, Presley," he said, bringing his hand to my face. "You're my present. You're everything I've ever wanted."

He'd said sweet things to me before, but this felt like a different kind of admission. I wrapped my arms around his neck, pouring myself into the kiss I gave him. I pulled away after a moment and looked at him.

"How much time do we have?"

"Enough."

I smiled wickedly as I continued undoing the knot and showing him what I was wearing under the coat.

MY LEG WOULDN'T STOP BOUNCING the entire time as he drove to his mom's house.

"Nervous?"

I glanced over at him. "No."

"Liar." He chuckled, holding my hand in his. "Relax. She's going to love you."

"How many women have you brought home?"

"Maybe thirty."

"What?" I gaped.

"Just kidding." He squeezed my hand, amusement clear in his eyes. "Two."

"Larissa and Lisa," I provided.

His brows rose. "I'm flattered you know that, princess."

"Shut up."

"Are you jealous that I've taken women home to my mother?" He shot me a sideways glance. "You were married."

"Oh, you're going to point that out? Do you forget how you kissed me on my wedding day?"

"I could never forget that."

I licked my lips. "What was the point of that anyway?"

"The point of giving you your last earth-shattering kiss?"

"Oh, it was earth-shattering for you?"

"Don't play with me, baby, you know it was like that for you too."

"Maybe." I shrugged. "But I still went through with the wedding."

"I guess I shouldn't have expected you to walk out."

"Did you?"

"A part of me did."

"You took a date to my wedding." I laughed. "What were you planning on doing if I decided to call it off and leave with you? Were we going to have a threesome?"

"Are you open to that?"

"Bastard." Laughter bubbled up inside me as I yanked my hand from his and slapped his arm playfully.

"Hey, I think this is definitely something worth discussing."

"Are you open to threesomes?" I raised an eyebrow. I knew I wasn't, but now I was oddly curious.

He shrugged. "If that's what it takes."

"If that's what it takes for what exactly?"

"What it takes to keep you, obviously."

"I have questions." My smile faltered, my heart pounded louder.

"I hope I have answers."

"Did you want to keep Lisa?" I asked. "Or Larissa?"

"Are you asking me if I considered a threesome with them?"

I rolled my eyes. "Be serious, Nathaniel."

"Sweetheart, I know what you're asking. I don't know how to answer the question."

"Truthfully. You answer truthfully."

"Did I want to keep them," he said, as if contemplating it aloud. "I think if I wanted to keep them, I would have."

"What does that mean?" I turned in the passenger seat.

"It means when you want something, you work for it, no matter the cost or sacrifice." He glanced at me. "I didn't work very hard for either one of them."

His mother's house was modest and cute. It had a fence and a pretty little garden that led to the front door of the navy-blue craftsman-style house. Nathaniel let go of my hand as we waited for her to open the door and I instantly questioned why. Did he not want her to know we were together? I shook that thought away. I was the one who'd said I didn't want my father to know about us, but now, as I stood there ready to meet the most important woman in his life, it was important for me to know where I stood with him. Was I just a fling? Was I okay with that? By his own admission, he said he was always on and off with Lisa. When would that end?

The door opened. I held my breath as a woman appeared on the other side. I wasn't sure what I expected his mother to look like, but she was beautiful and younger than I'd imagined. She had the same thick dark brown hair that Nathaniel had, hers styled in huge waves that reached just past her shoulders. Her eyes were the lightest brown, so he must have gotten his deep blue eyes from his father. She had a smile on her face that only spread wider as she took me in.

"Presley. I've heard so much about you," she said, her voice scratchy. I wondered if she was sick or if that was just how she sounded. Either way, it was warm and made me smile.

"I hope nothing too bad." I tore my gaze from hers and raised an eyebrow at Nathaniel.

"Only the truth." He chuckled, draping an arm around my shoulder. He looked at his mom as he spoke. "This is the biggest pain in my ass. The most obnoxious, impossible woman I've ever met."

"That's funny, because you're the biggest pain in the ass I've ever met," she said, throwing her head back in laughter as he dropped his arm from my shoulder, took a step forward, and lifted her into his arms with ease.

He twirled her around as she laughed and honestly, if it wasn't his mother, if it were some other woman, the jealousy singing through me would have killed me. It was adorable to watch him with his mom though. He set her down and when she caught her breath, she walked over to me, wrapping her arms around me and pulling me to her.

"I'm Iris," she said. Ir-is, not eye-ris. I frowned.

"What is your background?"

"Born and raised in Iowa." She smiled at my confusion. "My parents are from Spain."

"Oh wow. I didn't know this." *How did I not know this?* "My mom was born in Venezuela," I said proudly. "She was raised in New York, but she speaks perfect Spanish."

"Do you?"

"Not perfect, but I try." I looked down, feeling as embarrassed as my grandmother would likely feel about that.

"There's no shame in that. You have the rest of your life to perfect it." She was smiling, but she kept looking at me like she was trying to figure me out. How much had Nathaniel actually told her about me? I should've asked before we got here. This was unnerving. She turned around. "Well, make yourself at home. Everyone's out back enjoying the last of these cool, but not too cool nights."

Over the next hour, I was introduced to friends, cousins, aunts, and uncles. My dad was there, talking to a group of men, and he interrupted the conversation to introduce me to them.

"I remember you when you were a little girl," one of them said. I didn't remember him at all, so I smiled and nodded.

"Did you work at the main brewery?" I asked.

"Yep," he said. "Been working there since I was a teenager."

"Wow. And you still wake up every morning and go there willingly," I said.

"Of course I do." The old man howled out a laugh. "I don't know what I would do without it."

"You don't have to lie just because you're in front of my dad. I'm sure he'd forgive you if you told us how much you hate that place." I smiled at him and looked at my father, standing beside me.

Dad chuckled, putting an arm around me and pulling me toward him. "You see why she's my favorite."

"I see," the old man said. "She's a Winston Rose clone."

I laughed. It was something I'd heard throughout my life. Everyone thought I was just like my dad. For a long time, I denied it and got angry when people said that to me, but I'd come to realize that they weren't wrong, and there was nothing bad about it. We kept talking, Dad, the old man, Nathaniel, and me. Everyone was so laid-back and . . . normal. I was so used to having to watch my back at parties and events that I really didn't know how to act in this setting, where no one seemed to want to kiss my ass in order to get to the person I was with and where I wasn't left, even for a second, to go mingle with other people. Wherever Nathaniel walked, he made it a point to bring me along and introduce me and include me in the conversation.

I know I'd said I didn't want to make this official or label it, but standing here in front of all these people including my father, the whole thing seemed dumb. Why shouldn't I be able to hold his hand publicly or let him hold mine? And so, as we stood there talking to my father, the urge to keep him close grew.

"I heard Nate's doing big things with the brewery. Opening up a new bar—brew and all that," the old man said.

"Presley's the one doing that, actually." Nathaniel grinned. "She's the brains behind the whole thing. I came in late as an investor."

"If it weren't for that investment there would be no bar brew to open up," Dad said, raising an eyebrow.

I felt like a child again, where all the men spoke about things in tongues I couldn't understand, except now I understood it. But I didn't know I was supposed to be reading between the lines as I listened.

"I'm sure the investment helped, but we'd been talking about opening the bar for a while," I said, looking at my father.

He glanced away, as did Nathaniel. The old man sipped his beer and looked elsewhere as well. And people wondered why women weren't super comfortable amongst men. One of these men conceived me, raised me, was the first person to hold me when I was born. The other had been inside me countless times now and was possibly hoping to make things official. The third I didn't know, but he'd known me since I was a kid and worked for my mother. And yet they didn't treat me like I belonged in their little circle. How fucking dare they? I took a deep breath and excused myself.

"I need to find a bathroom," I said lamely.

I wasn't going to act like a brat during Nathaniel's birthday party, especially not when it was the first time I'd ever visited his mother's house, but that didn't mean I needed to stand there and feel uncomfortable either. I'd experienced that sensation numerous times over the last five years, not knowing why until Adam's infidelity became a truth rather than an inkling. I knew this wasn't the same thing by any stretch, but that inbuilt insecurity was sending painful tugs to my heart all the same, and I hated the angry heat I felt in my cheeks.

When I got to the kitchen, I found his mother.

"Do you need help?"

She looked up from the cupcakes she was re-arranging. "No, I got this. Did you need anything?"

"I came inside to use the restroom, but I don't know where it is."

"First door to your left." She pointed.

"Thank you." I headed there, taking in the pictures on the walls outside it.

Once I was finished washing my hands, I stepped outside and looked at each picture more carefully. Nathaniel's age ranged from a baby to more recent. Unlike the pictures in my childhood home, these weren't only his big accomplishments, like winning a big game or graduations. They were everyday pictures: him and his parents at the park, him eating a hot dog at a baseball game, graduation, taking communion, fishing with a man I assumed was his father, sitting beside his father on a bench while eating ice cream. I felt him come up beside me but didn't look away from the pictures.

"You look identical," I whispered.

"Yeah, people always say that."

I glanced up at him. "What do you think?"

"I think I look a lot like him." He looked at the wall. "I have better pictures upstairs. If you want to see them."

I nodded and followed him upstairs. The house wasn't very big, but it was cozier than the mansion I lived in growing up. Memories coated the walls and accent tables as we walked to the end of the hall, where Nathaniel opened a door and waited for me to catch up and walk in first. Upon crossing the threshold, I knew it was his childhood room. The walls were navy-blue and adorned with New York Yankees memorabilia. I'd always had a fascination with people who kept their children's rooms untouched once they left for college, as if time would stand still and they'd be able to welcome them back into the same small corners that had kept them safe throughout life. My mother got rid of our house before my high school graduation. She said we'd overstayed our welcome in it anyway, and moved in with her then-boyfriend while I moved into an apartment with my best friend and college roommate.

Memories were just reminders of the past. They weren't

something we held on to at our house. I'd adopted a mentality that we had to walk through life as fast as it would allow and tangible memories didn't really have a place in that. Now that I was here, in this house that was more homey than any other I'd ever known, I was lost for words. I walked around the room in silence, picking up each picture. Most were of him and his father—fishing, ice skating, playing baseball, basketball, at the farm, at the brewery. Those made me smile, though my emotions were marred by the realization that my father would soon be gone and we only had pictures from this last year together.

True to his personality, Dad hadn't even spoken about his health in weeks. He wouldn't let me go to the doctor with him or stand in the room when he was on a call with one. I was going based off his flittering comments—*I won't be here one day. I wonder if you'll miss me when I'm gone. Maybe we should just start watching ball games here and stop traveling to them.* That was the latest one he'd dropped on me, which was consequentially the one that made me freak out. I'd been holding it in because I couldn't talk to anyone about it—not even Nathaniel. I'd given my father my word and I wouldn't break it, but times like these it really hit harder than usual. I set the last one down and blinked away the emotion in my eyes before looking up at him.

"What happened to him?"

"Died in a car accident." He gave me a sad smile. "They said it was quick, hopefully painless."

"I'm sorry," I whispered. "Do you miss him?"

"Every day." He shoved a hand in the front pocket of his jeans and leaned against the doorframe.

"Tell me about him."

He stood tall and walked inside. His presence seemed to fill what was left of the small room as he closed the distance between us. He picked up the frame I'd just put back, the one of them standing by one of the beer tanks.

"He was a great father," he said, speaking to the picture. "Hands-on, hardworking. He picked up a lot of shifts, but never once missed a baseball game. They say time heals wounds, and I guess it does, but most of the time I still feel a hole in my chest when I think about him. Today is normally difficult for me." He set the picture down and glanced at me. "He died on my birthday."

"Oh my God." I gasped, setting my hand on his forearm. "I'm so sorry. I didn't know."

"It was a while ago." He shrugged. "You would think it would get easier to get through the years, but it still sucks. That's why Mom always hosts this huge party. I think it helps her forget about it, you know?"

I nodded even though I didn't know. I stepped closer so I was between his feet and wrapped my arms around his middle, hugging him tightly. I didn't say another word, because I was crying and was hoping to hide my tears as my cheek rested against his black T-shirt. I thought back to when I'd first met him and that whole spiel he'd given me. He was eighteen then, and had probably lost his dad not too long before. I'd been so caught up in my own life that I hadn't even considered what his life must have been like. I hadn't cared. God, how horrible I'd been back then.

"I'm sorry," I whispered.

He pulled back, lifting my face, his brows pulling in. "Don't cry, baby."

"I can't help it." I let out a shuddered laugh, wiping my face. "I'm sorry."

"I wasn't kidding when I said you were my present." He lowered his mouth to mine, kissing me lightly. "Everything I've ever dreamed up wrapped into one beautiful package."

I smiled against his lips. Timing really was everything. Fourteen years ago, I wouldn't have pictured myself standing in this house, let alone this room, kissing him. Today, I couldn't imagine being anywhere else. There had been many frustrating, anger-filled moments that had brought us to this moment, and as much as I hated the bickering with him, feeling judged, believing myself less than him, he hadn't been wrong in how he'd described me. And yet, here we were, and I couldn't be sorry for the tribulation and heartache that had brought us to this time—our time—except the heavy loss he'd experienced.

THIRTY

NATHANIEL

THE THING about falling was that it didn't happen the way everyone imagined it. Sometimes it happened slowly, over time, and other times you found yourself waiting for the other person to catch up. Sometimes I thought I fell for Presley Rose the first time I set eyes on her, this redhead wearing a cheerleading outfit, throwing a fit in the middle of a rainstorm. Other times I tried to see reason and tell myself it was impossible for me to have fallen for her that day, with her poor attitude and outlandish imagination. She was the kind of girl who under normal circumstances would have never given me a second glance. I was a public school nerd disguised as a jock, and she was a fucking princess, draped in designer clothing, with shiny rings on her fingers. She was unattainable and somehow, someway, years later, I'd managed to get her, and even if it was just temporarily, I would bask in it until it was over.

I kept going over it in my head as I walked to my office. If anything, last night had solidified my feelings for her. I wasn't going to tell her that just yet. She needed time to sort out her own feelings and I wasn't in a rush. I'd waited a long time already. Surely, I could deal with waiting a little while longer for her.

THIRTY-ONE

I WAS STANDING outside the conference room, waiting for Victor to come out. It seemed like everyone was in there except for me. For some reason, Dad hadn't invited me in. No. Not *"for some reason."* He hadn't invited me in because he was going to say things he didn't want me present for, though I couldn't imagine what he could possibly say that I didn't already know. I leaned against the wall across from the door and waited like the good girl I was. The door opened. I straightened, waiting. One of the lawyers that wasn't Victor stepped out. He shot me a look that I could only describe as *what the fuck just happened?* My heart sank. What the fuck *had* happened in there? I waited. Two more men walked out with shell-shocked expressions on their faces that didn't help the anxiety rising inside me. Then, Nathaniel stepped out. He looked utterly pissed, his ears were red, his hair looked like he'd ran his fingers through it a million times in there, and unlike his expression before he entered the room—which had been warm and sexy—the one he shot me now was absolutely horrifying. His eyes narrowed at me before he stormed away.

I took a step toward him. "Nath—"

"Not now," he barked.

I froze. Even when he'd been mean to me in the past, he hadn't spoken to me like that. He didn't even turn around to acknowledge me as he stalked away. My phone buzzed. A text from my divorce lawyer that read, *"Congrats! You're divorced. Officially. Docs are in your email."* I couldn't bring myself to be totally excited about it, but I let out a relieved breath. At least one thing was going okay today. I knocked on the door and peeked inside. It was down to my dad and Victor, who looked like he was about to cry, and that was when I knew what had just taken place. It was my father's goodbye, maybe even his will planning, who knew, but he'd definitely told everyone what I'd known for the last eleven months—he was dying. The knot formed in my throat the way it always did when I allowed myself to think about that, as I walked over and took a seat across from Victor, next to Dad.

"You told them." I kept my gaze fixated on the table.

"It was time," he said simply. "I need to discuss some things with Victor."

"Okay." I swallowed again, trying to extinguish the burn of his dismissal right after Nathaniel's. I looked at my father, sitting across the table. "I need to know what you told them before I go."

"I told them things aren't looking promising for me," he said simply.

"What does that mean?" I spoke over the rawness in my throat, fighting a current of tears that threatened.

"It means what you think it means."

"I wish you wouldn't talk about this so matter-of-factly." I swallowed once more and stood up. "I wish you'd take into account that everyone here loves you and news like this hurts."

Dad didn't say a word. He tore his gaze from me and looked at his hands folded in front of him.

"I'll call you later," Victor suggested. "Right now, Winston and I need to settle a few things."

I walked toward the door without another word.

"Come by my place tonight, Pres. I want to talk to you," Dad said as I walked out.

I nodded my agreement and headed to the brewery. The staff had started working a few days ago, though we hadn't had our official opening yet. The dating event on Friday would serve as our start date. The bartenders, servers, and extra hands for the brewery were all eager to be here according to Ezra and from what I'd seen, they were all very well-equipped to handle their jobs. I went to the office in the back and closed the door, hoping to concentrate on the bills I had in front of me, but all I could think about was Nathaniel's anger as he'd walked out of that conference room. Would he want me to go by his place later? *I wasn't sure.* I wasn't sure, but I would go anyway. I wrapped up what I had to do and headed back out, waving at everyone as I left. It was already six thirty, and I knew Nathaniel would be home. He'd been getting home early every day since I'd started staying at his place. I didn't expect today to be any different.

I unlocked the door and walked inside. He was sitting in a barstool in his open kitchen, his shoulders hunched over as he stared at the glass in his hands.

"Hey."

He didn't look up. I licked my lips and walked closer, standing on the other side of where he was.

"So, he's dying," he said after a long bout of silence, still not looking at me.

"Yeah," I whispered.

"He didn't tell me that when he sold me half the company."

"Does . . . do you wish you hadn't invested in it now?"

"It's business." He shrugged a shoulder. "I have plans for it that'll make the investment worth it in the long run."

"You haven't looked at me since I got here," I said. He looked at me then, and I almost wished he hadn't. His eyes were red and anger was still there on the surface, ready to spill out. "You're mad at me."

"That's one way of putting it." He stood up. "I don't want to have this conversation right now."

"What conversation?"

"The one about your father dying and you keeping it from me." He lifted his glass and set it down with such force, I couldn't help my flinch.

"I didn't—"

"You didn't tell me and you could've." He hit the wall beside him with the side of his fist, the drywall splitting beneath his force. "That's the only thing you can say here. You didn't tell me and you could have. You could have saved me from having to find out in that conference room with every other person in there as if I was just some investor or employee."

"I can see how that would hurt, but—"

"But what? There is no excuse for you not telling me, Presley."

"It wasn't for me to tell," I yelled finally. The wild rage in his eyes made me take a step back, though I knew him well enough to know he wouldn't physically lash out at me. "When would I have told you?"

"You had every opportunity to tell me, so don't come to me with that bullshit," he yelled, taking a step toward me. I took one toward him.

"He didn't want me to tell anyone," I yelled back. "I couldn't tell you."

"Couldn't or didn't want to? How long have we been fucking now, princess? Too long to keep a secret like this," he said, answering his own question. "It makes me wonder how many other things you're capable of hiding from me."

What? I gaped wordlessly before I spoke. "Are you calling me a liar?"

"If the shoe fits." He shrugged.

"You're an asshole. I've never lied to you about anything. I couldn't tell you this one thing and you call me a liar?" I closed my fists to keep from shaking as I faced off with him, but it didn't work. If anything, it made me angrier.

"You could've told me when we were at Mom's house or when we were having dinner or breakfast. You had every opportunity and I had every right to know."

"He's not your father. He's mine." The words ripped out from deep within me, leaving a scratch in their wake.

We stood there, scathed yet unmoved. Somewhere throughout our argument we'd drifted physically together yet emotionally apart, the tug and pull of the rope between us wearing thin. I wouldn't budge though, not about this. I wouldn't take the blame for it either.

"He's . . ." He seemed to be holding back as he shook his head and glanced away. "I had a right to know."

"Why? Because he's spent more time with you than me these last few years?"

"Yes." His gaze found mine again. "I never abandoned him. I've been here when you were too busy sorting out your personal shit. I was there when you chose your husband over him."

"Fuck you." I slapped his chest as hard as I could with both my hands, hoping to shake the unyielding. He staggered back slightly.

"Get out."

I blinked. "I . . ."

"Get out." He brought his fingers to the bridge of his nose as if I were a nose bleed he was trying to control. "I don't want to look at you right now."

When he met my gaze again, it was full of distrust. I wanted to tell him to go fuck himself, but the truth was that if I were on the other side of the coin, I'd be upset as well. I grabbed my bag.

"You know what?" I took the key to his apartment off the key ring, where I'd mixed it with mine, and slammed it on his kitchen counter. "Fuck you, Nathaniel."

I cried on the train ride home. I cried on the walk from the station to my apartment. I cried on the elevator ride up. I cried harder when I exited on my floor and not my father's, because someday soon I wouldn't have to go up there for anything at all. When I reached my bed, I threw myself in it and sobbed harder still, my throat, head, and eyes hurting with each tear. I felt like I'd lost today. I'd lost a man I was pretty sure I was in love with. I was losing a man I'd loved my entire life. I'd gained freedom from Adam, but even that felt like a loss. I cried until I felt raw from the inside and my face felt numb. Then, I showered and went upstairs to see my dad.

He took one look at me and wrapped his arms around me. "I'm sorry."

"For what?" I asked, even though it felt good to hear those words. My shoulders started shaking again as fresh tears started. "For dying? For leaving me with a mess I don't know how I can even begin to sort through?"

"There will be no mess." He pulled back and looked at me. "I've taken care of everything so you won't have a mess to deal with."

"How much longer are they giving you? What are they saying?"

"It would've helped if I'd given up cigarettes." He smiled.

"That's not funny. Why are you smiling?"

"I'm already a prisoner of my fate." He shrugged, still smiling. "I'm not going to play by the rules."

"That makes no . . ." I stopped talking. He'd already succumbed to the fact that he wasn't getting any better. I hadn't been put in that position so I didn't know how I would react to it myself. I couldn't judge him for doing what he chose to do, but I could be angry at him for not trying to stick around. "I don't want you to die."

"I don't want to die either, but that's life, Presley. We're born, we live, and then we die. Boring people merely exist. I've lived. I consider myself very fortunate." He hugged me again, putting his chin over my head. "Rosa's going to be coming by every morning before work. I told my physical therapist to stop coming by for a week."

I stiffened. "Dad."

"I want a break for a week." He pulled back. "How 'bout a movie? *The Big Short* is on tonight. We never saw that one."

I sighed heavily and followed him to the living room. Where Dad and I had differed in just about everything else— baseball wasn't my thing, fishing wasn't my thing, and the list went on—we'd found mutual interests in movies and books. We loved horror, crime fiction, and anything that kept us on the edge of our seat. *The Big Short* definitely wasn't horror in the classic sense, but holy shit. We continuously exchanged WTF glances throughout. When it was over, I leaned my head on his shoulder, wishing this never had to end.

"We should watch another movie."

"Which one?" His phone rang as he flipped through channels. "Oh damn it. I have to take this. Rain check?"

"Sure." I stood up, stretching. "I should get some sleep anyway."

I kissed and hugged him goodnight before walking out and checking my own phone, which I'd been checking every ten minutes anyway. Still no calls or texts from Nathaniel. By the time I'd fallen asleep, I'd convinced myself that Nathaniel was done with me. I was the spoiled brat, the unfit princess in his mind that he could easily live without. *I don't want to look at you right now.* Well, as far as I was concerned, he didn't have to.

THIRTY-TWO

I WAS SITTING across from some random guy who was telling me how he made his own dog food. I hadn't signed up to be a part of the event, but Morgan saw me and fed me to the wolves anyway. She said she needed to fill in the space and didn't want it to look dead, so there I was. The buzzer went off, and I waved at dog food guy before going to the next victim. I looked across the room and shot Morgan a glare. She laughed it off. After that guy, I stood up and walked to her.

"I would absolutely love to continue being part of your experiment, but I promised my dad I'd go by his apartment before he goes to bed."

"Oh come on, Pres."

"The deal was that I sit across from one guy for a picture," I whisper-shouted. "I spoke to three."

"How was it?"

"Terrible. Does anyone actually meet their match speed dating?"

She shrugged. "People get married at first sight nowadays. Anything is possible."

"Yeah, but do they stay married?"

"I don't have answers." She shrugged again. "Have you spoken to Nathaniel?"

"No. He hasn't called or tried to reach out to me, and I just can't . . ." I shook my head. "I'm still too angry."

"Give it time." She put an arm around me. "Worst case, you can always sign up for my app."

"Thanks." I laughed and hugged her back. "I'll see you later. I have to go get a liter of Coke for my dad, so I bid you a good night."

"Farewell, Madame."

When I got to his apartment, the lights were mostly off. I set the Coke in the fridge and went in search for him, hope dwindling when he didn't respond every time I called him. Finally, I went to the rooftop and found him sitting there, not smoking a cigarette, though he held one unlit in his hand.

"You know how you're allowed to sell bottles of beer to go?" Dad asked. I didn't know that, but it made sense if the container wasn't open. "You should start filling growlers in your location."

"That's a good idea."

"Maybe half off on Thursdays or something. Give people an incentive to take 'em."

"Dad." I sat beside him and turned my body toward him. "You're slurring your words."

"I'm fine." He waved a hand. Even that looked like slow motion. "Victor was telling me about this new law that was passed that said you could own a brewery and a beer bar."

"Okay?" I didn't even know we weren't supposed to. "Wait, does that mean what we've been doing is illegal?"

"No. Nate owns the brewery."

"Half of the brewery," I reminded him.

"Well, who's to say what half he owns and what half he doesn't?" His eyes glimmered, but only half his mouth moved into a smile.

"I'm going to call the paramedics."

"Give me a minute. Let's go downstairs." He stood up slowly.

I stood quickly to help keep him upright. He hugged me as we walked toward the stairs and I wasn't sure if it was because he wanted to or if he knew he'd fall over if he didn't. Downstairs, I helped him sit on the couch and took my phone out and called nine-one-one. I paced the room, eyeing my father cautiously, as I waited with the dispatcher on the line.

"I'm freaking out," I said.

"Stop freaking out," Dad said.

"It's okay to freak out," the dispatcher said. "But stay calm."

"How the fuck can I freak out and stay calm?" I wailed.

"Presley Rose, please stop," Dad groaned. "You're starting to sound like your mother."

"Oh God." My eyes widened. "That's the meanest thing you've ever said to me."

He laughed, and laughed, his shoulders shaking. "I love you, kid."

And then I started to cry with the dispatcher on the line and my father smiling at me like this was no big deal. Thankfully, the paramedics got there and I hung up the phone and threw my energy in telling them about his past strokes and how he hadn't quit smoking and how he refused to let me go to the doctor with him. In the back of the truck, I continued my rant.

"He's so stubborn and he thinks I'm useless and I'm so done with all of this," I cried.

"You're my most valuable player," Dad said. "My very own MVP. You think I would've made it this far without you? Negative, Ghost Rider."

"Dad, stop making jokes. I'm still freaking out." I looked at the paramedic who was setting up an IV. "Is he going to be okay?"

"He's—" He didn't get to finish his sentence before Dad started shaking uncontrollably.

"Oh my God," I said. "Oh my God."

"He's having a stroke. We need to get his vitals—"

"Oh my God." I kept chanting this over and over.

When we got to the hospital, they shot out of the truck, wheeling Dad into the building faster than I could ask what was happening. I was escorted to a waiting area, and then called to a smaller room inside the emergency unit and told to sit and wait for the doctor. My leg bounced as I waited. I hadn't called anyone. I was too shell-shocked. Who would I call anyway? Mom was sleeping, Nathaniel wasn't speaking to me, Adam and I were divorced, Morgan was on a date, and Jamie was out of town for work again. As time stretched, I felt so alone. I could call Rosa. I could call Victor. I didn't though. I waited. I'd call once I was let into Dad's room. I'd call when I went home for a change of clothes, because surely I'd be spending a night or two at the hospital.

The door opened. A doctor stepped inside. I stood up. It was tiny in there, barely room to move, let alone for two people to stand comfortably, which was probably why he hadn't closed the door behind him.

"I . . ." He started, then stopped. "Are you here by yourself?"

I nodded.

"Do you have anyone who can come keep you company?"

"I'm fine." I shook my head, lifted it all brave and defiant. I didn't need anyone. "How's my dad?"

"We tried to stabilize him. I worked on him for fifteen minutes straight, but there was nothing I could do. I'm sorry."

"Wait." I sat, my knees giving away. "What are you saying?"

"He's gone. I'm so sorry."

I focused on breathing, but even that was shaky. My eyes filled with tears and then spilled over. I blinked rapidly. "But he was okay. He was . . . he was alive."

"He had a stroke and then a seizure, and he became unstable and we couldn't resuscitate him," the doctor said. He continued explaining, but I couldn't hear him over the whooshing in my ears. When he finally stopped talking, I wiped my face and took another deep breath. "I need you to verify that it's him."

"You don't know if it's him?" I shrieked, standing up again.

"I know it is him, but for legal purposes—"

"Oh, for fuck's sake," I screamed. "Fuck your legal purposes. Take me to my father."

He did. I wished I hadn't screamed at him about it. It wasn't his fault that a patient with what seemed like little will to live had been brought in and died. He hadn't been responsible for my father not taking care of himself or the way he'd chain-smoked even after he'd been continuously told not to. He wasn't responsible for the strokes or the seizure and from where he was standing in the side of the room with his head bent down, I knew he felt the immensity of this loss nearly as much as I stood there staring at my shirtless, dead father. Somehow, I kept it together. I looked at the man I'd been talking to hours earlier and swallowed as I nodded and whispered, "That's my dad."

But it wasn't.

My dad was full of life, full of sass and energy and love. He'd never been someone to simply be still, so the man in the bed wasn't . . .

And yet, he was.

With agony in my heart, I approached the bed, not having any clue how I was supposed to absorb this. His skin was cold to touch. I gripped to edge of the bed so I wouldn't fall to my knees as the desolation enveloped me. I vaguely felt the tears as they fell from my eyes to Dad's skin as the doctor walked near the door. *How could you leave me, Dad? I haven't had enough time with you. I'm so sorry for the years apart.* There were so many things I wanted to tell him, but I realized that I was simply too late. But I clung to him regardless, not wanting to leave him alone in this cold, sterile room. I thought back to his words, and even as I sobbed, I was thankful we'd had those moments. *My very own MVP. You think I would've made it this far without you?*

"I wouldn't have been able to make it without you either, Dad." My voice was barely a croak. For the last time, I touched my dad's cheek, somehow feeling the strength that only he could give.

At the sound of a throat clearing, I turned toward the doctor. I thought I heard the words, "It's time. I'm so sorry," but before I could process anything else, I turned and looked at my dad one more time. "I love you, Dad." Before walking toward the doctor, who escorted me out of the room with a hand on my shoulder as he told me they'd transfer the body to the morgue and then to the funeral home of my choosing.

He'd be in touch and again, he was so sorry. I nodded again. I didn't have words. I'd come to the hospital with my father fully expecting to leave with him, maybe not today but in a few days. I hadn't considered I'd be leaving him behind for good.

THIRTY-THREE

I WAS COMPLETELY NUMB. I still hadn't called anyone. Calling Nathaniel crossed my mind, but I resisted. I didn't want to hear his voice right now. He'd turned his back on me, he'd screamed and kicked me out. He hadn't reached out to me again. The more I thought about him, the angrier I became. I knew soon enough I'd get over it, but right now he was the last person on earth I wanted. I thought about calling Victor or Nicole, but I didn't want sympathy right now. I didn't want to have them fly over here and comfort me. I wanted to be alone with my grief for a little while.

I sat on my father's couch the rest of the night, replaying what happened. When the sun rose a few hours later, my eyes were still open, but nothing had become clearer. I heard the door open and saw Rosa as she walked toward me. My eyes met hers, unfocused, hazy with exhaustion and sadness. The reality of what happened just hours ago slamming into me all at once—real and relentless.

"Gone," I whispered, my voice barely audible. "Dad's gone."

"Gone?" She frowned momentarily, and all at once reality hit her too. She propelled forward, wrapping her arms around me as she started to cry. "Oh God. No. Please no."

I sat there. I didn't know why I couldn't feel anything. Rosa helped me get up and go to my apartment. She waited for me to shower and change. She even called my mother for me since I hadn't.

"I don't want to stay here."

"You don't have to."

She helped me pack a bag and told me to go to my mom's apartment. I never went there unless she was in town, but Rosa said she was on her way and would be here by tomorrow morning, so I went willingly. Before I left my apartment, I set my phone on the kitchen counter and left it. I didn't want to talk to anyone. I didn't want to look at anyone. I just wanted to be left alone until my mom got there.

THIRTY-FOUR

NATHANIEL

"WINSTON ROSE PASSED AWAY YESTERDAY," Rosa said, addressing the meeting. She took a breath, as if to steady herself but then started sobbing. "He will be greatly missed. He was our boss for so many years, but also a great friend."

No. *No, it can't be true. He can't be gone.* I'd thrown Presley out because *I* hadn't been told Winston was dying. Thrown. Her. Out. And now he was actually gone. I was a fucking hypocrite. She lost her dad . . . The urge to turn this entire conference table over and scream grew with each passing second, but what good would that do? It wouldn't bring him back. It wouldn't change the course of the last week and—

"Where's Presley?" Victor asked.

Why the fuck had that not been my first question? *Where was she? How did she find out? Was she with him when he—*

"Will there be a funeral?"

"Winston asked for everything to be delayed two weeks. He'll be embalmed and the family will have a private service. When I have more information, I'll let you know."

My heart sank. Fuck. He'd called me right after I'd had my argument with Presley and I'd ignored the call. I'd ignored all of his calls these last few days. It had always been my biggest regret. After losing my father, I'd made a vow to speak to everyone, regardless of how upset I was, and here I was, a fucking hypocrite. How many times had I told Presley to be kinder? To give him a chance? To forgive him when I knew he'd been a little too pushy with her, and I hadn't even answered his phone call. Sadness burned in my chest. I clenched my fist, trying to control it.

"Where's Presley?" Victor asked again, pulling out his phone this time and calling. I banged my fist on the table. He looked at me. "You know where she is?"

"No, I don't know where the fuck she is but even if I did, how is it any of your business? Do you need her to sign something? Read the will to her? What the fuck do you want?"

"I'm her friend." He stood up and headed outside. "I want to be there for her. Something you obviously don't know a thing about."

I blinked. The spare key I'd given her, now in my pocket, burned my thigh. Had she spoken to him about me? I stood up, grabbed my phone before leaving the room. I started calling her. It didn't even ring, went straight to voice mail. I ran over to the elevator, but Victor was already gone. I ran to my office, got my keys.

"Where is she?" I asked Rosa, who was stepping out of the conference room.

She shook her head. "That poor girl."

"Was she with him when it happened?" My chest tightened.

"She called the ambulance and rode with him to the hospital." Rosa wiped her face, unable to fight more sobs. "She was told he was dead and had to identify his body. She was alone. Completely alone."

Alone. The word burned inside my brain. I'd had my mother when my dad died. I'd had Winston and most of Dad's lifelong friends who worked in the brewery. Presley had no one. Her mom was in Greece, I hadn't been on speaking terms with her, her friends obviously hadn't been called according to Victor's reaction. Why would she want to go through this alone? What was she doing? What was she thinking?

I ran to the elevator, hoping to get to her before anyone else did. If anyone knew what she was going through, it was me.

THIRTY-FIVE

PRESLEY

I LEFT to Mikonos with my mom. She'd been home three days before convincing me to leave with her. It's what my father would have wanted, she'd said. I wasn't sure whether or not that was true, but it was what I needed right now. He hadn't been kidding when he said he'd left everything prepared so I wouldn't go through too much while dealing with his death. He'd planned everything down to the exact casket he wanted to be buried in. The funeral wouldn't take place for another two weeks, and I'd definitely be back by then. Mom had Constantine's private jet on standby and was happy when I told her I'd go with her. I'd sent Mom's driver to get me a new phone and called Victor and told him my plans before leaving, and he also told me it was a good idea. Everything would still be here when I got back, he'd said. Nicole also called to give her condolences. I asked them not to give my new number to anyone. I wasn't sure how long I'd be keeping it for. I thought of how often Dad had told me I couldn't keep running away from my problems by changing my number, but it was easier to deal with things in the moment if I started over with a new one.

Constantine's house sat on top of a hill that overlooked

Mikonos. It was the most marvelous thing I'd ever seen in my life, and I'd honeymooned in Croatia, which was gorgeous, so that was saying a lot. The beauty didn't keep me outdoors, though. Not the first few days I was there. I was still too busy crying in the bedroom that had been assigned to me. Mom cried with me most days.

"The guilt is eating away at me," she said. "I apologized to him for everything I put him through, but I never thanked him for everything he did for me."

"Not everything is about you, Mom."

"Presley," she gasped. "I have a right to mourn as well."

"I know." I shook my head and took a breath. "I'm sorry. I'm just . . . I want to go home. I know I said I'd stay here, but I miss my bed. I miss . . ." I sniffled. I missed making breakfast for Dad. I missed setting tickets on top of his desk for our next adventure. I missed talking to him and watching movies with him. I missed him—period. I must have said some of this aloud because Mom wrapped her arms around me and held me tight.

"I'm sorry, sweetheart, but he's not there." She pulled away, setting a hand on my head. "He's here." She took the same hand and put it on my chest. "And here." She wiped my face. "And what's in our hearts never dies."

I stayed. I was glad I did because three days later, I felt a little more like myself and even went out to eat with Mom and Constantine. The following night, he invited his nephew Alexander out with us. I could totally see why Mom was constantly trying to push him off on me. He was tall and handsome, with blond hair and blue eyes and a perfect angular jaw. He looked like a well-shaven Viking. He was also very polite and kind and attentive, but as we sat in the restaurant and every single woman seemed to have something to say to him or about him, I thought of Adam and the way that turned out. Even if I didn't like Nathaniel as much as I did, I would never put myself in that situation again. I said this to my mother later that night, who thought it was the most amusing thing I'd ever said.

"You don't have to marry the guy, Presley." She eyed me carefully. "Are you in love with Nate?"

"You call him Nate too?"

"Well, your father always did. What do you call him?"

"Nathaniel." I frowned, then smiled. "Other things when we're . . . you know."

She laughed. "Well, in that case, I'll stop trying to make you and Alexander happen."

"Thank you," I breathed out. "I think I'm ready to go home."

"Because of Nathaniel?"

"No. Hell no. I'm never talking to him again."

She blinked. "But you just—"

"I know, but that doesn't mean I want to speak to him. He's an asshole, and I hate him."

Mom shook her head but agreed to go back home with me.

THIRTY-SIX

THE HARDEST PART about losing someone close to you was that you felt their absence in the simplest things. I'd never cared to go to any baseball games, but even as I continued receiving the two tickets I'd purchased from my connection at the stadium, I felt the need to call my dad and tell him about it. Then I realized there was no one to call and became sad all over again.

"Do you want to just cancel the tickets?" Mom asked, coming to the couch and sitting beside me. I'd been staying at her apartment since we got back.

"Tickets can't be canceled. I can re-sell them, but that feels weird." I rested my head back and closed my eyes. "We only have tickets to five home games left anyway. I was supposed to buy one for another stadium once we were done with these. I guess he didn't feel well enough to travel but didn't want to tell me."

"You don't even like baseball. Why not cancel the whole thing?" Mom shook her head. "Damn Winston. So stubborn."

"Yeah." I smiled.

"When is the next game?"

"Tonight."

"Well, we're not going to let the tickets go to waste, are we?" She stood up. I smiled and followed her to her room. She walked into the closet and back out with a huge jersey. "This is too big on me, right? I can't even wear it as a dress?"

"Is that signed?" I walked forward and picked up the fabric. "Mom. This is signed by one of the best baseball players ever. Constantine would kill you if he found out you even touched this. Put it back."

"Damn it." She walked back into the closet.

I sat on the corner of her bed. It felt weird to sit in here. Before Dad died, I'd never been in this room longer than a minute. I was always afraid he'd find out I was hanging out here and would think I was betraying him the way she had. Mom hadn't cheated on Dad with Constantine. She met him years after the divorce. He was nice though, and Dad had treated it all like water under the bridge anytime he spoke about it, so I was getting used to sitting here. I shimmied and got a little more comfortable.

"You don't have to make a big deal about it, Mom," I said. "We're not meeting the players or anything. I'm wearing what I'm wearing now."

"Yeah, but you always look cute. You have youth on your side," she said from the closet. "Besides, how do you know a player won't see you sitting there and want to talk to you after the game?"

I snorted. "Have you ever been to a major league game?"

"No. I've been to college games though," she said. "That's where I met your dad."

"At a college baseball game?"

"Football."

"Okay, entirely different sport." I frowned. "Were you dating a player?"

"No."

"So I'm seriously not understanding what this has anything to do with the fact that a major league player isn't going to see me and fall in love with me from the field."

"Yeah, me either. I'm just trying to keep you entertained so you'll let me change and do my makeup."

I laughed and fell back onto the bed, closing my eyes.

"Have you spoken to Nate?"

"No."

"You're not going to call?"

"Nope."

"How is he supposed to try to win you back if he can't get hold of you?"

"I don't know and don't care. I can't even stand the thought of seeing him right now."

"Fair enough," she said. "What about the brewery? When will you go back there?"

"Thursday night."

"After the funeral?" she asked. "So basically you're going when everyone else is going."

"I'll probably go by in the morning to make sure everything will be ready for after the funeral."

"Okay." She sounded closer now, so I opened my eyes and pushed myself onto my elbows.

"Did you even change?"

"Yeah, these jeans are the ones I don't mind getting dirty."

"How would you . . ." I shook my head as I stood up. "Mom, this isn't a little league game."

"Let's go. The driver's waiting for us by the front door."

I followed her out without saying another word. This was surely going to be an interesting experience.

THIRTY-SEVEN

NATHANIEL

I'D BEEN GOING to the brewery every day in hopes to catch Presley there, and every day they'd told me the same thing: not yet. Not yet. Not yet. I understood her need to take a break from this. I was sure it wasn't easy to be reminded of her father when she came here, or home for that matter, but she couldn't avoid those things forever. And so, here I was, once again, knowing they'd tell me not yet. Except this time, they didn't.

"She's around here somewhere," Maya, one of the bartenders said. "She wanted to be here personally to help set things up for her father's . . . for tonight."

For tonight. It had been thirteen days since Winston's passing, and it still felt so wrong.

I nodded and thanked her as I walked away, in search of Presley. Her key was still in my pocket. I didn't know why she'd given it back. *That's a lie.* I'd been an asshole. That was why she gave it back, but I didn't want it. I wanted her. I wanted her to keep this key forever and use it every day. I wanted her with me forever. The thought was jarring, but only for a second, because I knew that deep down I'd been wanting this for too long to be afraid of it. I needed to convince her that I was worthy of her. I was walking toward the back when a woman, walking backward, bumped into me. She turned around, ready to apologize, until she saw my face.

"Nate."

"Elena." I smiled.

I hadn't seen her in years, but somehow she still looked the same. She'd always looked more like Presley's older sister than her mother, though I knew from Winston that their resemblance started and ended there.

"I told her you'd come looking." She didn't seem pleased about this. My heart skipped. I'd really fucked up.

"Where is she?"

"She doesn't want to see you," she said. "I'm just warning you right now. She's really upset with you."

"I know. I messed up."

Elena's brows rose. "That's one way of putting it."

"I came to apologize."

"Good luck." She brushed past me. "She's out back talking to Ezra."

"Thanks." I started walking until she called my name, then turned around and faced her.

"Don't think that just because you've grown up to be this hunk of a guy she's going to take you back easily."

"I would never think that." I felt myself smile as I turned and kept walking.

I found her talking to Ezra, just as her mom had said she'd be. They seemed to be having a serious conversation, so I waited by the door a while, watching her. She was wearing black pants and a black coat, her soft waves looked like fire in contrast to her apparel. She looked beautiful and tender and I felt like kicking myself all over again. After a moment, I couldn't take it anymore and started walking toward them. She glanced up, her eyes widening in alarm when she saw me. There was no elation in her expression. She looked tired and wary and

I hated being the cause of the latter. Ezra seemed to take a hint and left quietly as I reached them. I thought she'd slap me. Instead, she threw her arms around my neck and hugged me. The relief I felt threatened to take us both down, but I managed to put my arms around her.

"I'm so sorry, baby," I whispered against her head.

"I just can't believe he's gone." Her small body shook against my chest.

"I'm sorry." I held her tighter. "I'm sorry he's gone, and I'm sorry I wasn't there for you."

She pulled away, wiping the tears from her face. "I heard you've been coming by here."

"Every day. Your apartment too but you never come to the door."

"I haven't been staying there."

"I realized it after the sixth day." I half-smiled, half-laughed. "Well, I hoped that was the case after the sixth day."

"I haven't been really up for visitors," she said.

"I understand." I shoved my hands in my pockets to remind myself not to reach for her. I gripped the key in my fingers. "I really messed up, Presley." I reached for her hand despite myself. "I shouldn't have gone off on you like I did. I shouldn't have—"

"No, it's fine." She shook her head. "Well, it's not fine, but I have other things on my mind right now."

I reached for the key in my pocket, but just as I was about to drop it in her hand, she yanked it away. My gaze shot to hers.

"I don't want it," she said.

"I want you to have it."

"Thank you." Her smile was forced. "But I don't want it."

I took a step back, feeling as though she'd physically pushed me. I deserved it. I knew I did, but accepting it was still diffi-cult. I searched her face, hoping to find more than that placating smile on it. I stopped myself from saying anything else. She was mourning. I was mourning. Winston had been like a father to me. He'd been the strongest male figure in my life these last fourteen years. Of course Presley knew that. It was why she was being so kind to me. It was why despite the fact that she probably wanted to slap me, she'd hugged me instead. It was why I knew without a shadow of a doubt that I'd royally fucked up with her and she was taking it in stride, because I did what she was used to from every other man in her life.

"Please." I tried to hand it to her again. She put her palms up in defense, so there was no way for me to place it in her hands. "Presley."

"Thanks for stopping by. I made a spreadsheet of our expenses while I've been gone. I'll email it to you in five minutes." She took a step back and turned around, walking away. "I'm sure I'll see you around."

I dropped my hand. My chest felt like it was being ripped up from the inside as I watched her walk away from me, but I let her because I knew she needed time. Ezra stepped back into the room shortly after. I probably looked like a sucker, standing there in the middle of all of those containers of beer, salivating over something I couldn't have.

"Do right by her," Ezra said as he neared me.

I blinked. "What?"

"Do right by her. Winston told me you were in love with her." He raised an eyebrow. "Was he right?"

"I . . ." My heart hammered. I felt caught off guard. "Yes, I guess I am." I frowned. "What else did he say? About me being in love with his daughter. What else did he say?"

"He seemed happy about it." Ezra smiled, shrugging again. "He loved you, you know? The way a man can only love a son."

I swallowed, nodding as I patted him on the shoulder and left. I wasn't against grown men crying, but I definitely wasn't about to do it in front of fucking Ezra. He was too old-school to let that fly.

I TOOK his advice and slept for two hours. By the time I showered, shaved, and got dressed again, I was cutting it close on making it to the church where Presley and her mom had arranged for a service. I took the train and managed to get there on time. As I walked into the church, I searched for Presley. Her mother wore a huge black hat, and Presley was beside her. They were leaning down speaking to an elderly woman in a wheelchair. Beside her on the other side was Adam. He had an arm around her, holding her by the elbow. I felt my temperature rise as I took a seat. I inhaled and exhaled a few times, hoping it would help calm me down. I'd seen them together a countless number of times—in college, at their wedding, occasionally at a gala, and I'd felt annoyed each and every time, but nothing compared to the suffocation I felt now. I let it go for Winston, but I vowed to get her back in my arms as soon as possible.

I was shocked when I saw her walk to the podium. Even in her grief, she looked stunning. She wore a black dress and no jewelry. Her hair was down, pin-straight. She looked sleek and fierce, but when she opened her mouth, that soft voice filled the room and held my heart in its grasp as she'd done from the moment I first saw her.

"My dad was a hardworking man." She licked her lips, offering a small smile. "I know a lot of you worked with in some capacity. I used to think that the only thing I got from him was his tenacity, but these last two weeks, as I've dealt with his absence, I realized I got a lot more from him than only that. Some good traits, and some bad, but all are things that make me who I am and make me feel closer to him." She paused again, swallowing and exhaling a shaky breath.

"What I valued most about him was his ability to love. He didn't care if you were poor or rich. If he felt you needed him, he was there." She smiled. "It used to bother me a lot when I was younger. I hated having to share him with others. I am an only child, you know." She chuckled lightly, as did the rest of us. "As I grew up though, I realized how fortunate I was to have someone in my life who cared so deeply about what others were going through that he'd spend time with me, go to work, and then make it a point to be there for someone else. So, I guess what I'm trying to say is that we can all learn a thing or two from Winston Rose. Sure, he was successful. Sure, there was a time when he had a beautiful house and fancy cars and all the things money could buy, but in the end, he'd traded all of that in. Money, having it or not having it, didn't change who he was. He was always selfless and giving and his time was worth more to him than any dollar bill or any company opportunities. And for that, I thank him. I'm going to miss him so much." Her voice broke as tears cascaded down her face. I squeezed my hands to remind me to keep sitting. "But I'm going to do right by him and make sure White Oak continues to grow and thrive, because it's what he would have wanted. Thank you for coming."

THIRTY-EIGHT

I WAS SHAKING as I stepped off the little stage, thankful for Adam helping me back to my seat. I was shocked to see him there. Shocked because he'd come completely alone. This wasn't one of the publicity stunts I'd gotten used to from him. Shocked because he didn't get along well with my father, but still chose to come to pay his respects. Shocked because I liked that he was there, even though I knew as well as anyone that this was a fleeting moment of kindness. The service was a blur. I spoke, but even that was a splotchy memory. Thankfully I didn't think I took too long. I glanced at Adam.

"Did I blabber a lot?"

He patted my knee. "You did great."

"I hate public speaking. I don't know how you to it."

"Practice." He smiled. "You used to hate how I hogged up the mirror to practice my speeches."

"It was highly annoying." I smiled, grateful for the repose from the grief that had taken me hostage. "I hope your new girlfriend doesn't like to wear makeup."

"I'm seeing a therapist. Not dating one, actually seeing one." He swallowed as he looked at me. "I know I didn't do right by you and I can see now that it was 100% me. I hope you can forgive me."

"I already forgave you, Adam."

"You deserve to be treated right."

"I'm not putting my future in anyone's hands or anything."

"I'm sorry for everything." He squeezed my knee again. "By the way, your name is completely gone from everything having to do with the foundation. I'm in the process of having it looked at and doing right by it."

I raised an eyebrow. "Your therapist must be a miracle worker."

He chuckled. I excused myself and walked to the back, where I was due to thank everyone for coming and reminded them to head to the brewery for beers and hot dogs—that was Dad's wish.

Nicole and Victor each gave me a huge hug and held me tight longer than the others before them had.

"I love you," Nic said. "You know we're always here for you."

"I know. Thank you for being here now."

"Always, Pres." She pulled back, wiping the tears leaking down my cheeks. "Always."

I smiled because I couldn't say anything else. Victor pulled me into another hug, squeezing the life out of me. I had to laugh.

"Babe, you're going to make her throw up," Nicole said.

"Sorry, not sorry." He let go. "I haven't wanted to call you about the will and all that because I don't want to be the asshole lawyer who doesn't give you time to mourn, but whenever you're ready to discuss it . . ." He tilted his head.

"We can discuss it. I'm good. Seriously. I mean, I cry randomly and stuff, but I'm good most of the time. Let's talk about it at the brewery."

"Tonight?"

"Well, you can explain the gist of it to me."

"Okay." They walked away.

Morgan and Jamie walked over next. I gasped when I saw Jamie. "I didn't know you were in town."

"I wasn't." She threw her arms around me. "I came for tonight. I have to go back tomorrow night, but if you want to do brunch, please let me know."

"Of course." I had no idea what to say next. I'd missed Jamie very much, and there were so many holes in our lives to fill. I pulled away and hugged Morgan next. "Thanks for coming."

"You know it, Big. Papa Winston was a father to us all," she said, smiling through the tears she tried to blink away.

"He really was," Jamie said. "We were all lucky to have him."

I smiled even though I couldn't seem to stop crying. "I'll see you guys at the brewery."

"See you there." They waved as they walked away.

I took a deep breath and let it out when I realized that was the last of them. Or so I thought, until Nathaniel approached. Unlike this morning, when he looked like a complete mess, he was wearing a black suit and tie. His hair was slicked back, and he'd shaved his messy beard down to a sexy scruff. His blue eyes found mine and held them as he closed the distance between us. His cologne infiltrated my senses as he brought his hand down to cup my face.

"You did great up there."

"Thanks." I swallowed. "I was nervous."

He leaned in, resting his forehead against mine and exhaling. "I miss you, princess."

My heart pounded. I missed him too, but I didn't want to admit that to him. He'd yelled at me. He'd shut me out when I'd needed him most. I knew he'd done it out of pain because he was hurting, but it didn't lessen the blow. I took a step back, putting distance between us.

"Are you going to the brewery?"

"Want to go together?" He looked around. "Where's your mom?"

"Waiting for me in the car with Constantine." I paused. "Do you want to come with us? He has a limo." I rolled my eyes. "So extra, I know."

Nathaniel smiled. "I'll ride with you."

"Adam's riding with us too. Mom invited him," I said. Not that I owed him an explanation. "He came to pay his respects."

"Is she a fan of his?"

"Who knows?" I shrugged, glancing up at him. "Doesn't really matter to me."

His jaw was twitching. "She doesn't like me much."

"She's . . . difficult," I said. "I'm not sure she likes anyone much at all."

He pulled the door open and slid in behind me. Mom, Constantine, and Adam were settled in their seats, looking at us.

"Hey, man." Adam walked over in a crouch, careful not to hit his head on the roof and extended his hand for Nathaniel to shake. He did. "I'm sorry for your loss. I know you and Winston were close."

"Thanks." Nathaniel shook his hand and scooted closer to me, his thigh pressed against mine, his arm draped over the back of the seat.

He might as well have draped himself around me, he was obviously trying to make a point. I shot him a glare. He shot me a grin. I rolled my eyes and looked forward, not missing the shock on Adam's face. Mom seemed to be stifling a smile as she focused out the window, and Constantine was typing away on his phone, so he wasn't really paying attention, but somehow it felt like all eyes were on us anyway. Tonight, there was no small talk amongst Nathaniel and Adam like they were buddies. Tonight the air was crackling with intensity. Emotions were already high, but whatever unspoken thing was happening between Adam and Nathaniel was threatening to suffocate us. The second the limo pulled up to the brewery, I shot out of the car without waiting for the driver to come open the door.

Inside, I busied myself saying hi to the people that hadn't made it to the service. One of them was Nathaniel's mom. She was wearing scrubs and I was so surprised by that and her being here that I almost walked right past her.

"Iris. Oh my God." I stood in front of her, holding her arm. "I'm so sorry. I barely recognized you."

"Is it the messy bun, the no makeup, or the fact that I'm running on zero hours of sleep?" she joked. "I just got off work, but I wanted to pass by and extend my condolences personally. Your father was a gift to the world. I'm so sorry he left us so soon."

For a moment, I simply stood there, trying to swallow past the knot in my throat, but it was no use. I threw my arms around her and breathed out when she hugged me back. People had been so kind to me, but only some of them knew what Dad was really like and even fewer of them spent as much time with him as Iris and Nathaniel, so I knew she didn't say those words in vain. I felt embarrassed as I pulled away and wiped my face. This lady was going to think I was crazy.

"Nathaniel should be making his way here shortly," I said. "I have to go check on the catering, but thank you so much for coming."

She grabbed my hand, sandwiching it between two of hers, and held my eyes. "If you need anything, even if it's to get away. Anything at all. Please come see me. My door is always open to you."

"Thank you." I hugged her again, a little lighter this time before walking away.

I wasn't lying, I really was checking on the catering, but as soon as I did that, I slipped into my office in the back and sat there catching my breath. I'd go out there shortly, but for now, I needed to be alone to process. I felt like since that night at the hospital things had been nonstop. As I sat there, massaging my temples, I felt gratitude not only for the many people who'd come to pay their respects to my father but also for the time I'd had with him. Nathaniel had lost his at eighteen. I had friends who'd never met theirs. And mine was larger than life. Impossible to deal with sometimes, yes, but amazing nonetheless. I just wished I'd had more time with him. It was selfish, I knew, but I felt what I felt. I lowered my hands when I heard the knock on my door and looked up to find Victor standing there.

"You okay?" He walked in and took a seat across from me. I nodded. How could I explain that amongst everything else going on inside me, the numbness returning was the biggest threat?

I cleared my throat. "Just taking a little break from people."

"It's a miracle you were ever married to a politician." He smiled.

"Ah well, you know politicians and their wives are good pretenders."

"I gathered that." He chuckled. "Adam's out there making his rounds."

"I'm surprised he didn't bring a camera crew with him."

"Give him time."

I smiled, shaking my head. "So, what's up?"

"The will. As you know, your father sold half of the company to Nathaniel. It was a merge, of sorts. White Oak was bleeding and Nathaniel wanted to step in to help."

"Right."

"This brewery was fully funded by Nathaniel," Victor said cautiously. He obviously knew I didn't know this.

"What?" My mouth dropped momentarily. "Does this mean . . . what does this mean?"

"I want to preface this next part by saying this doesn't mean anything for you. This is yours and it's safe."

"Safe from what?" I put a hand on my pounding heart. "Is Nathaniel selling?"

"No. No." Victor took a deep breath. "I probably shouldn't have even mentioned the fact that Nathaniel funded this whole thing, but I never thought it was right to withhold that information from you to begin with."

"I don't understand," I whispered. I thought about the very first day I saw him and the way I flipped out on him and told him the brewery was mine. "Oh my God. I feel so stupid."

"I was afraid you might. Anyway, during our meeting, your dad said that once he passed away, Nathaniel should keep the brewery and give you money for it in exchange for more ownership in White Oak."

"Makes sense." I licked my lips.

"Nate turned him down."

I blinked. "When did you start calling him Nate?"

Victor rolled his eyes. "Can we stick to the task at hand?"

"Yes, bossy." I sighed. "So *Nate* wants what? To buy the rest of the company so he can have it all?" A loud knock on the door interrupted the tirade I was just beginning to go off on. Nathaniel peeked his head in. "Oh, fun. Come join the party, Nate. Pull up a chair. Get cozy. After all, this is your office, isn't it?"

"Presley," Victor said.

"I'll take it from here, Victor," Nathaniel said.

Victor stood, eyeing me cautiously. "We'll continue this later. Maybe I can bring you the papers tomorrow." He walked toward the door and mouthed something that looked like "Be nice". I flipped him the finger just in case I'd read his lips correctly. Judging by the sound he made, I was probably right.

"Oh, I'm sorry." I looked at Nathaniel, who still hadn't sat. I stood up and waved a hand to the chair I'd vacated. "Would you like this chair, boss?"

"What are you doing?"

"What am I doing? What are you doing? You paid for all of this. You funded it," I said, using air-quotes. "You—" He walked toward me until he was looming over me. I lost my train of thought. "You—"

"I what, princess? I saved your ass? I saved this company from oblivion? What exactly do you want to blame me for?"

I pushed his chest. "I hate you."

"I think what you feel for me is the complete opposite of hate and that scares the shit out of you." He grabbed my wrist. "You know how I know? I feel it too. And it's not going anywhere."

"That's a lie." I shook my head, yanking my arm from him. "You're a liar. You kicked me out of your apartment and called me a liar. Well, you're a fucking liar, Nathaniel Bradley. You think you can just waltz in here and take over my life because you feel like it? Because you felt a connection to my father and you thought a good way to stay in his good graces was to become one with his company? Fine. That's fine. But you don't own me. I'm not yours. Just because—"

His mouth crashed down on mine before I could finish my sentence. My heart soared, pounding so hard I was sure it would leap out as his tongue slid inside my mouth. He lifted me, pressing me onto the concrete wall behind me, caging me there with his mouth, his hands, his muscular legs that parted mine leaving me no choice but to wrap them around his waist. The need for him was greater than every single sense I had that was previously telling me I hated him, because he was right. I didn't hate him and I was afraid to admit what it was I actually felt. This was safe though, this grinding and teasing. The physical we had down. I made quick work of his belt and zipper as he lifted me higher up the wall, hoisting me with one arm as the other pulled the dress I wore over my hips.

"Please," I hissed against his lips.

"Fuck," he growled against mine as he thrust inside me—hard—in a swift motion that made me throw my head back.

Fuck was right. He brought his mouth to the side of my neck, raining hot kisses on it as he thrust into me, his fingers grabbing my ass, spreading me open wider.

"You don't want to tell me how much you hate me now?" he grunted.

"Shut up." My eyes rolled back. "You're going to ruin the moment."

He chuckled darkly and continued to fuck me like that—hard, fast, relentless—as if taking everything out on my body, and I returned the tempo as I pulled his hair and moaned his name. My legs started shaking. I swore I was seeing stars every time my eyelids slammed shut and reopened. He brought a hand between us and started rubbing his thumb against my clit in circular motions.

"So close," I whimpered. His hand moved faster, his thrusts got harder. "Oh my God. So close."

"Yes, baby." He buried his face in my neck and bit me.

I yelped, holding on to this shoulders as the coil that was building and tightening inside me finally snapped and I convulsed around him as he pulsated and shivered, emptying himself inside me.

"This doesn't mean anything."

"I'm still inside you, princess. Can you give it a rest one more second?" He raised an eyebrow.

I inhaled and exhaled as he set me on shaky feet. "This was a mistake."

"No." He stopped messing with his pants and grabbed my chin so I'd look in his eyes. "I'll let you say whatever the fuck you want. I'll let you blame me for whatever crazy things you think I've done to screw you over, but I will not let you call this a mistake."

I adjusted my dress and lifted my panties, which were in

shambles. *What was I supposed to do with these?* Nathaniel snatched them from my hand and shoved them in his pocket. The fact that he seemed to have an answer for everything only further pissed me off.

"Why didn't you tell me we were using your money for this place all along?" I crossed my arms. "Did you enjoy playing me for a fool?"

"It didn't matter." He exhaled, throwing his head back as if asking for help from above. Knowing my dad, he'd part the heavens and actually come to help him. I rolled my eyes. He looked at me again. "The brewery is yours. I guess I interrupted the conversation a little early, but I signed it over to you. I don't want it. Just like I never set out to keep White Oak. I wanted to help someone who helped me without a second thought throughout the last fourteen years of my life. I didn't do it because I expected anything in return."

I blinked, biting my lip. "What do you mean it's mine? I don't want it. I don't want a freebie."

"It's not a freebie. Jesus Christ, Presley." He shook his head. "You worked for this. You did everything to make sure you opened this space. How is that a freebie?"

"You giving it to me without me paying you is a freebie."

"I'm not . . ." He glanced away.

"You are. You're giving it to me and I don't want it. I'm sick of being in debt to men who—"

"Do not finish that sentence." His eyes were thunderous. "I do not want you to box me with any of those men. I messed up and I'm sorry, but I don't think it's fair that you crucify me for lashing out on you one time."

"One time?" My brows rose.

"Oh please. Don't act like you're a fucking saint in all of this."

"I never said I was. But I don't want to be used. I don't want to feel like you're tossing this on my lap because my dad died and you feel sorry for me."

"I signed the papers to hand it over to you before he died."

"Because you knew he was dying."

"Because it was what I'd planned on doing all along." He threw his arms up with his shout, then shook his head. "This is going all wrong. This is not the way I planned to win you back."

"When you think of a way, let me know, because so far the odds are definitely against you." I brushed past him. "Now, if you'll excuse me, I have people to go thank for being here."

THIRTY-NINE

"I JUST DON'T UNDERSTAND why you wouldn't be on your own app if you don't have a boyfriend yourself," Jamie said, frowning.

"Well, funny you should say that because I got on it last week." Morgan stuck her tongue out. "Anyway, I matched with this really hot guy, right? He seems well-put together. Works in investment banking, divorced, which means baggage, right?" She shot me a look. "No offense, Big, but divorce often means baggage."

"None taken, but in my defense, I think I had baggage before I got married."

"I'm not talking Daddy and Mommy issue-type baggage, I mean love baggage, like you're afraid to let go and be."

"I am not afraid to let go and be," I argued. Jamie and Morgan exchanged a look. "Oh, fuck both of you. You're supposed to be cheering me up after my father's death, not sitting here further depressing me."

"You're right. I'm sorry." Morgan put her hands up. She looked over at Jamie who was working on her second Bloody Mary. "What about you?"

"What about me?"

"Any wise words from you about dating?"

Jamie scoffed. "Please. I'm so hung up on Travis that I've officially reached a new low. My stalking went from social media to the Netflix account we share, and since I saw that he's dating some bitch and also watching the *Haunting of Hill House*, I waited until he'd watched the semi-final episode and then I changed the password."

I blinked. Morgan let out a laugh. We both asked, "Wait, you're serious?"

"Dead-ass serious," Jamie said, nodding her head proudly. "Fuck him and the new slut he's with. She looks like Barbie's dream and she has a fucking pink Corvette to boot. Who owns a pink Corvette?"

I felt my eyebrows raise. "Is she Russian? Maybe her family is the Russian mob and she's Daddy's little girl and gets whatever she wants."

"Oh my God. Are you back to conspiracies?" Jamie asked. "Because for the longest time in high school you thought you were going to get kidnapped and it never happened, and I swear I thought you wished it had."

"Well, duh." I scoffed. "Did you not know my parents? I would've done anything to get out of that house."

"That's so insensitive, Big." Morgan slapped my hand playfully.

"I'm just playing. I love my parents." I smiled, until I didn't because the realization that my father was no longer here hit me again. "I miss him so much."

Jamie held my other hand and squeezed it. Neither one of them said a word. They simply held my hands as I breathed. When I was sure I wasn't going to start crying, I slid my hands back to the mimosa I was drinking.

"You know who's an asshole? Nathaniel or *Nate* as everyone and their mother is apparently calling him these days."

They laughed.

"Let's hear it," Morgan said. "What'd he do this time?"

"He owned the brewery this entire time."

"What do you mean?"

"He owned it on paper and was the one funding the whole thing. Meanwhile, I was over here acting like an idiot and saying all these mean things to him about it and he never once said a word about owning it. He just kept it from me and made me think I was the owner all along."

"And now he's just keeping it and kicking you out?" Jamie asked, wide-eyed. "You're the rightful owner."

"Oh my God. What a jerk," Morgan said.

"Well, no." I took a big gulp of the mimosa. "He signed it over to me." They both blinked, like fucking puppets. "The point is he lied to me and then he kicked me out of his house that day for lying to him about my dad being really ill. It's fucked up."

The silence stretched. I lifted the jug and poured myself another mimosa, looking at the two of them impatiently.

"I mean, I would've been mad too," Jamie said. "But he still did right by you in the end."

"I'm with her on this." Morgan shrugged. "But I still wanna build you a dating profile. Come on, it'll be fun. You don't even have to go on any dates. I'm dying for you to see what's out there, and also I really need someone to go on this group date with me for New Year's."

"New Year's Eve?" Jamie and I both said rather loudly.

"I can't go on a date on New Year's Eve," I said.

"Why the hell not?" Morgan asked. "Besides, this would be on the thirty-first during the day, so it's technically not the eve. Unless you think you'll be exclusive with Nate Dogg by then."

"Oh my God, would you stop?" I covered my laughter with my hands. "I most likely won't be exclusive with anyone by then, so okay. Whatever. I'll check out the app but only because it's yours and you want feedback."

"Thank you." Morgan smiled wide. She slid her attention to Jamie, who shook her head.

"Uh-uh. I can't join that. I'm still emotionally involved with my ex."

"I can't believe you changed his Netflix password."

She smiled wide. "Sometimes you have to fight dirty."

HER WORDS STAYED WITH ME. Nathaniel had once said he'd fight for whatever he wanted to keep in his life, but he hadn't even called. . . . *when you want something, you work for it, no matter the cost or sacrifice.* It seemed that even though he'd implied he'd wanted me, I hadn't been worth the effort after all, either. I hadn't given him my new number, but it didn't mean he couldn't get it from someone and call anyway. I headed to my building and took the elevator to Dad's penthouse. Tonight would be the first night I wouldn't be staying at my mom's apartment. I felt like it was time.

As I walked down the short hall and unlocked the door, I held my breath. How many times had I done this and called out for my dad? I went to the kitchen and opened the fridge, taking out the eggs and setting toast to make. I'd bought the food and dropped it off yesterday out of habit. My mom had been with me and hadn't said a word when I said it was for Dad's fridge. Everyone mourned differently. Some people played out their grief emotionally while others acted it out in their daily routine.

I heard footsteps approach as I stirred the eggs with the spatula. My heart stopped beating for a moment before speeding way up. I turned around and saw Nathaniel standing there, wearing jeans and a black hoodie.

"Jesus, Nathaniel." I dropped the spatula and placed my

hand on my heart. "What the fuck are you trying to do? Kill me?"

"I'm sorry. I . . ." He looked around slowly, as if in a daze. When he glanced back at me, he raised a key. "I've always had a key. I didn't break in or anything."

"Okay." I frowned, looking back at my eggs. "Do you want breakfast?"

"It's eight o'clock at night."

I shrugged. "You want eggs or not?"

"Sure." I heard him sit down on one of the stools. The squeaky one. Of course. I swear he did it to annoy me.

I ignored him as I plated our food and set out utensils for us. We ate in silence, but it wasn't awkward. It was comfortable, and lately the only thing I craved was utter silence, so I was glad for it now.

"What are you doing here anyway?" I asked after a while.

"I went by your apartment and you weren't home. I figured you were out, so I came up here to just . . . hang out." He was looking at his glass of orange juice as he spoke, twirling it in circles. "I miss him."

"So do I." I swallowed. "I'm sorry I didn't tell you he was sick."

He met my gaze. "No, Presley. You were right. It wasn't your job to tell me. It wasn't my right to know. I was so wrong to say that to you."

"I had wanted to tell you, and I still feel I should have."

"I was so angry at him. I took it out on your because I thought I was angry at you, but when I heard he'd died . . . I was so angry at him for not telling me. For not giving me a chance to grieve properly." He swallowed and licked his lips. "He knew how losing my dad unexpectedly tore me up. He knew, so why wouldn't he tell me?"

I stood slowly and wrapped my arms around him. I didn't have an answer for him. I had no idea why my father did what he did. I had no idea why he was so adamant in keeping his health struggles to himself and not letting us carry some of his burden. But he was gone now and there was nothing either of us could do about that. I held Nathaniel tighter. After a moment, he wrapped his arms around me and we held each other, two souls in mourning, but not alone.

FORTY

I DIDN'T ARGUE about keeping the brewery. The way Victor had put it, which was the way Nathaniel had said it during the meeting was, "It was always supposed to end up in your hands." So I took it. Did it go against my whole not letting a man help me anymore? Possibly. The difference was that this man wasn't helping me conditionally. Things between Nathaniel and I had been . . . weird. He'd been coming to my dad's apartment every morning, and I'd gone there and made breakfast for us as if nothing had changed and Dad was going to waltz out of his bedroom any minute. Maybe it was dumb. Maybe it was useless. It seemed as though in our case, pretending was a coping mechanism we needed to make us feel like everything would be okay.

Today, I waltzed into the office, smiled at Rosa, and set the envelope of tickets on top of Dad's desk, top left corner just like he always asked. When I walked out, closing the door behind me, I felt a sense of panic creep up inside me knowing full well he wouldn't come to the game. I'd go, though. I'd go and sit in our seats and not type away on my phone the whole time. I'd go and actually watch the game, even though I had little interest in it. I'd go because even that made me feel a little closer to him. I'd go because it lessened the blow, and even if it was just for a couple of hours, it dulled the numbness. I went into my office and closed the door. I'd been coming in here on Mondays and working out of the brewery the rest of the days. Mostly, I was working on getting the word out there and setting up specials for each day. So far, I had Ezra going to a morning news station with two of the bartenders, and other people handing out flyers with two-for-one specials.

That night, as I sat in the stadium, watching the baseball game, I couldn't stop thinking about life. Dad's favorite player hit a home run at the end of the game with bases loaded, and as I stood up and cheered along with the rest of the crowd, the seat beside me didn't feel as empty as it looked. My smiling and cheering quickly turned into crying and then sobbing because it was empty. It really was empty, but I felt his presence. That made me laugh as I cried. I definitely looked like a lunatic, but I didn't care. Tomorrow was the last home game and the last of our baseball tickets and I'd come back and sit here again. Alone, emotional, but present.

AT THE BREWERY, I went over the schedule for the week as Ezra leaned against the doorframe sipping on his coffee.

"You need to hire a manager."

I blinked. "I'm here all the time. Why would I need a manager?"

"For things like this." He shot a pointed look to the clipboard in my hand.

"I'm just trying to run it by someone because they're starting to sound stupid. Thirsty Thursday, Wacky Wednesday . . ."

"They sound stupid, but it works." He shrugged. "Ask Nate."

"I don't want to ask Nate."

"You're still not talking to him?"

I shrugged. "Nothing to talk about."

"He keeps asking for your phone number," he said. I shrugged. His brows rose. "He keeps showing up at your house and not finding you there."

"We hang out sometimes." I didn't mention that it had been at Dad's apartment and while we'd shared a meal, we hadn't exactly spoken much.

Ezra shook his head. "Well then, why is he asking me for your number?"

"Because I won't give it to him."

He gave me a bemused look. "But you're hanging out with him."

"Sometimes." I set my clipboard and pen down with a sigh. "We're both mourning."

"Want to know what I think?" Ezra walked into the office and took a seat across from me, not waiting for my response. *God, so much like what Dad would do.* He set his mug down on the desk. "I think you're mad that he got to spend so much time with your father."

"You're not wrong." I felt tears build despite my effort to hold them back. "I should've been there more."

"You were there when it mattered."

"It always mattered," I whispered. "I was just too busy being mad for wanting him to treat me like his equal and not just his dumb daughter that didn't know anything about business or beer or baseball or whatever. I was too blinded by my anger to realize that he wasn't treating me like that because he didn't like me, but because that's exactly what I am."

"You're not dumb, Presley. You never were. He never thought that." Ezra shook his head, letting out a sigh. "As someone with a daughter about your age, I'll tell you this. We're old-school. We look at these women right's movements and are proud that someone is speaking out for our daughters, but we're too stupid to see that we're part of the problem." He shrugged. "Cassidy is heavily involved in marches and protests, but when she comes home for the holidays, she lets me speak to her like she's four and that's on me, not her. I'm proud as hell of that girl. I don't know how to tell her and it scares me. The world scares me. I'm afraid my little girl is going to get eaten out there, and so, I'd rather her conform."

"That's bullshit." I wiped my tears. "If you're proud of her, you should tell her. You should show her."

"I'm trying." He smiled sadly. "And your father was trying with you. I know because we spoke about it often. You taking it out on Nate isn't going to do anything but make you angrier, and you don't deserve to live with all that anger."

"So what do you suggest I do?"

"Let it go."

I blinked. "Let it go?"

"You can't control how things make you feel, but you can control what you do with those emotions. You can choose to let it go or stay angry. I learned the hard way that it's best not to harness negative emotions." He shrugged. "Let it go."

He stood up without saying another word. Not that he needed to say any more than he'd already said. When he left the office and shut the door, I let myself openly cry. A few hours later, I took a cab to the game. I rarely did so, but I didn't feel like dealing with too many people right now, and I needed time to reapply my makeup and fix my hair, so a cab was the easiest way. On the way there, I kept thinking about my conversation with Ezra and wondered if he was right about the manager thing. I wasn't going to ask Nathaniel.

Me: Should I hire a manager?

Morgan: *What exactly is your position right now?*

Jamie: ^^

Me: Idk. Owner, I guess? Manager? Managing owner?

Morgan: I don't think you need one yet. When you feel like you may be getting overwhelmed or don't want to deal with certain things—hire one then.

Jamie: I think you should hire one now. Make life easier.

Morgan: Another salary though.

Jamie: True. Can you squeeze one into your budget?

Me: Idk.

Fuck. I really didn't know. I put my phone away and got my ticket and credit card out as the car slowed in front of the stadium. As I walked toward it, I was engulfed by the excitement of everyone walking along with me and I forgot about the brewery, forgot about my dad and Nathaniel, and stepped in with the same pumped-up feeling as everyone else did. Inside, I went to my usual vendor, grabbed a beer and a pretzel and walked down to my seat in the third row behind home plate. I stood up for the anthem and when I sat back down, instead of taking out my phone and using it, I set it on airplane mode and sat back to watch the game. *Actually* watch the game. When Dad's favorite player got hit with the ball, I gasped. And when the next player on the lineup was purposely walked, I shook my head and shouted, "Come on, Ump!"

I blinked and sank down into my seat. *Had I said that aloud?* Oh my God. During the fourth inning, I brought my legs in to let someone pass, but when I inhaled the familiar scent, I froze and gaped to see Nathaniel take the seat beside me. The empty seat. Dad's empty seat. I blinked over at him.

"What are you doing?"

"I was in your dad's office looking for something and saw the envelope." He shrugged, then reached for my beer. My mouth dropped even more. Was he kidding me right now? "I figured Winston wouldn't like the thought of the ticket going unused."

I snatched my beer from his hand. "First of all, he would be highly offended by you just coming over here and taking my beer."

"Would he?" Nathaniel smiled.

"Yes. That's like the rudest of rude." I took a sip. "And I'm sure he'd be totally okay with me saving the seat for his ghost."

"For his ghost?" His smile widened. "Is that what you're doing?"

"I was." I shot him a death glare. "Now you're sitting on him."

He chuckled, a loud, vivid laugh that made me look away because I wanted to kiss him and slap him at the same time. I felt myself smile though.

"He would've enjoyed this game," he said after a long silent moment.

"Yeah, it's been crazy so far."

"Oh, you've been watching?" He had a twinkle in his eyes that made my heart skip a beat.

"Yes."

"And you understand what's happening?"

"Yes." I rolled my eyes. He always ruined it. I fought a smile, and then I paid attention to the field again and lifted my arm in protest. "This is the same stupid umpire that made us lose the last series we played at home against them and he's still making stupid calls."

"He's probably a Boston fan."

"Definitely a Boston fan," I scoffed. The beer guy came around. Nathaniel bought two bottles and set them on the floor between his legs. My eyebrows shot up. "Double fisting? Seriously?"

"One is for you." He lifted one and handed it to me. "But you have to finish yours first."

"Thanks." I set the bottle down on the floor between my legs and picked up the cup I'd been drinking. "I'm so disappointed in you for getting bottles, by the way. They have taps inside."

"Not our taps." He lifted his bottle. "I'm supporting our company."

Our company. I took a deep breath and let it out, focusing on the game again. *Our company.* I'd expected to feel anger at those words, so the content feeling that formed in my belly was jarring.

"You still haven't given me your phone number," he said after a moment.

"Yet you keep asking."

He huffed out a breath and took a sip of his beer. We ignored each other the rest of the game. When it was time to leave, we kind of waited around outside.

"Do you want to—"

"No," I rushed out. "I just want to go home." Alone.

I didn't add that word, but it was implied. I wasn't even looking at him as I said it. And so, he hailed me a cab and shut the door behind me. I cried the entire ride home. I didn't know why. I hadn't wanted him to join me. I hadn't wanted him to join me at the game either, yet the longer he sat there, the more grateful I became for his presence. I couldn't figure anything out with him, least of all my feelings. On one hand, I felt like I could breathe, and on the other, everything felt stifling, like his very presence took up too much of the air around us. Yet, I wanted him there. I wanted to feel like I was gasping for breath every time he made me laugh or shot me a sexy grin. *What the hell was wrong with me?*

I walked to my apartment feeling like a moping teenager as I got ready for bed. I switched on the television as I got under my comforter. There was nothing I particularly wanted to watch, but having it on would help drown out my thoughts. It didn't work. I replayed tonight over and over. I replayed all the days I'd had breakfast with him. He hadn't tried to kiss me or hold my hand. He'd asked for my phone number, big freaking deal. If he hadn't been inside me countless times, I would've thought more of it. All roads led to his disinterest in me and for some reason that hurt more than I wanted to allow. I'd wanted casual dating. I'd wanted sex but not attachments. With him, I felt like I'd gotten more than what I bargained for, and everything I never knew I wanted. And now I'd lost it. No, I'd purposely pushed it away, and for some reason I wanted him to fight for me anyway. Maybe it was better this way. The ringing of my phone interrupted my thoughts. I shot up in bed, heart racing as I reached for it. Please dear God, don't give me any more bad news. When I looked at the screen and saw Nathaniel's name, I frowned as I answered.

"How'd you get my number?"

"Finally wore someone down," he said, then added, "Rosa gave it to me."

"Oh."

"I had to bribe her."

"Oh." My frown deepened. I'd literally just seen him, why was he calling? "What's up?"

"Do you want to have a threesome with me?"

I blinked. "What?"

"Do you want to have a threesome with me?" he repeated.

The question felt like a knife to my heart. Was he having sex with other women? Already? Had he ever stopped? I licked my lips. "No."

"Why not?"

"Because I'm not into that sort of thing," I said. "Because I thought . . . I thought I was the only one you were having sex with to begin with, not that we're having much of anything right now. Because I let you come inside me without second thought because I thought I could trust you. Because—"

There was a loud bang on my door. My head snapped up in that direction. I stood up and walked over, the phone still in my ear, but I was no longer talking. He stood on the other side, looking like he'd walked all the way here from the stadium, though I knew that couldn't have been the case. He was in shape, but he wasn't The Flash. I hung up the phone and opened it, peering into the hallway, wondering if he'd brought whatever bitch he was fucking with him. Maybe he looked winded because he'd just come from her place. Who knows? He smiled. I didn't.

"What do you want?" I crossed my arms. "Did you come here to tell me that you've already moved on? Because that's totally fine. I'm totally over you anyway."

He grinned. "I wasn't aware you were ever into me. You never told me."

"Well, I was. Fleeting moment. Totally short-lived."

"Tell me more about this fleeting moment." He stepped inside, closing the door behind him with the side of his boot. "When did you realize things weren't working the way you wanted them to?"

"When you tried to steal my beer earlier tonight." I licked my lips as I stepped back. "But you asking me about a three-some definitely solidified the notion."

"Hm." He stepped forward, closer to me. I had to crane my neck to look at his face. "How'd you feel when I asked that?"

"Like I wanted to murder you and the bitch you're fucking."

He threw his head back and howled out a laugh. I held my arms tighter, my fingers digging into my biceps.

"This isn't funny, Nathaniel."

"I think it's hilarious."

"You're a jerk." My eyes narrowed. "Of course you think it's hilarious."

"So you were exclusively fucking me during your whole little *'I'm only going to casually date people and casually sleep with people'* phase?" he asked. "That's what you're telling me?"

"Obviously, dipshit. Get out."

"You know what I've always enjoyed?" he asked, stepping closer still, his chest almost touching mine. "When you get angry, really angry, you start name-calling. I don't even think you notice it."

"I . . . why would you enjoy that?"

"I don't know." He let out a huffed laugh. "It turns me on like nothing else though, to see your eyes flashing like that, the way those cute little claws of yours come out."

"Is that what you came here for? To get your fix before you go back to whoever . . . Lisa or Larissa or whoever you choose to get back together with?"

"There was never anyone else, baby." He brought a hand to my cheek, bringing his lips down to brush lightly against my mouth. "I think you're smart enough to know that."

"Did you forget why I got a divorce?" I leaned into his touch. "The last man I was with slept with other women like it was his job."

His eyes flashed. "Don't compare me to him."

"I'm sorry. I know it's not fair, but the fact still remains." I brought my hand up to his, pulling it away from my face. He threaded his fingers through mine. "I have no reason to believe you're here for anything else but a lay."

"Well, you're wrong, princess." He pressed his lips against mine. "You're so wrong."

It was a gentle kiss. He grabbed my other hand and threaded his fingers through it so that both of our hands were linked as he slid his tongue into my mouth, slowly, cautiously, taking his time with the kiss. I felt out of breath, my chest rising and falling with each movement. What the hell was he doing to me? I pulled back, panting.

"Tell me," I said. "Tell me how I'm wrong."

"I once told your father that I thought I was falling for you," he said. "That was a lie. I fell for you the day I picked you up outside of your snotty private school. I fell for you as you kicked and screamed and gave your dad a piece of your mind."

I licked my lips. "No, you didn't."

"I fell for you when you asked me to kiss you in college." He grinned. "Every time you asked me to kiss you in college."

"You're such a liar," I whispered, but I wasn't so sure he was. He looked like he was telling the truth. He let go of one of my hands and brought it to my face.

"I wouldn't lie to you, Presley. I mean, yeah, maybe I could've reworded the way I said some things to you in the past, but everything I've ever said and done has been with the best intentions. I loved you, but I didn't deserve you. I wanted you, but I wasn't your type. I wasn't rich or preppy. I didn't have political inclinations. I didn't want to be a lawyer. I wasn't an heir to anything but my dad's debts." He kissed the tip of my nose. "But I loved you."

I blinked. Maybe it was because I was emotional from everything else happening in my life, but his admission crawled into my throat and stayed there. All those years I thought he was keeping me at arm's distance because he didn't like me . . . all the times he told me I wasn't his type . . . he'd been lying?

"So what you're saying is, you're a liar," I whispered, finally.

He rolled his eyes. "Sometimes I lie."

"You know I wanted you with or without money, right? You know I didn't care about that."

"You say that now that you've lived and lost and experienced a bad relationship, but back then? I think you would've accepted me, married me even, and then wished you would've married someone else. Someone richer." He shrugged.

"You're so dumb sometimes, Nathaniel." I shook my head. "I would've accepted anything you had to offer."

"You slapped me when I finally kissed you."

"Because you kissed me the day I was marrying someone

else," I argued. "What would you do if we were about to get married and Adam showed up and kissed me?"

"I'd probably kill him and throw him into the Hudson," he said, totally nonchalantly.

I laughed. "I almost believe you would."

"I really think I actually would." His brows pulled together slightly as if he was picturing it in his head. "Yeah, I would."

"So, I have questions."

"I hope I have answers." He kissed me lightly.

I sat down, pulling him onto the couch with me. "Are you just saying all of this because you're emotional right now with my father's passing and all that?"

"I'm saying it because I should've said it months ago. Years ago. And I don't want to let more time pass by without putting it out there. I know that trusting me is hard, that secrets slay you. But I'm fighting now, princess. And I won't stop, just like I won't ever stop loving you."

"You haven't kissed me in weeks."

"I was letting you mourn." He let out a laugh. "Hell, I was letting myself mourn."

"When did you tell my dad how you felt about me?"

"In Boston."

"Wow. Sneaky." I raised an eyebrow. "He didn't even mention it to me."

"I knew he wouldn't. He was a good confidant, you know."

I smiled. "I know."

"Any more questions?" He looked like he was ready to pounce me.

"Why now?"

"If not now, when?"

The answer was good as any, and when he came toward me again, I let him pounce.

FORTY-ONE

"YOU NEED to think about what you want to do with the apartment," Victor said.

"Victor," Nicole warned. "No talking business over brunch."

"It's okay. I mean, I do have to think about it." I shrugged.

"Man, it feels good to have a childless-date," Jensen said across the table.

Mia did a little raise-the-roof motion. "With alcohol."

"You're going to regret that the minute you get home and you're still drunk and your kids expect you to actually parent," Nicole said, raising an eyebrow. "Trust me, I've been there."

"You always ruin everything," Mia sighed. "Damn it, how long is Krista going to watch them for?"

"She said the whole day." Jensen shrugged.

"Is Krista the babysitter?" I asked. "You should pay her double and tell her to stay longer. My mom used to do it all the time when I was a kid. I never minded."

"Krista's his ex-wife," Mia answered, laughing at the expression I surely made. "I know. Trust me, I know."

"Ex-wife?" My brows rose. "She's watching your kids?"

"Yep. She's amazing," Mia said.

I scoffed. "I can't even get past the fact that my boyfriend sometimes talks to his ex-girlfriend and you guys have this whole modern family down to a science." I took a sip of my mimosa. "That's impressive."

"Trust me, it took a while." Mia shrugged. "But it's worked out wonderfully."

"How's Estelle doing?" I looked at Victor. "Is she still making those hearts? I've been asking for one for years now."

"Oh my God," Mia said. "You want one? The last person on earth to place that task upon should be Victor. I'll get you one."

"She's making ornaments of them now," Nicole said. "She's slowed down though. It's hard to work with shattered glass when you have a baby crawling around."

"I saw pictures of him the other day. He looks like a Gerber baby." I smiled. "I bet it's easy for them since Oliver's a pediatrician."

All of them looked amongst each other and lost it laughing.

"That man won't do anything medical to that kid," Jensen said.

"He's so fucking scared he's going to break him," Victor added, laughing.

"It's the cutest thing to witness," Mia said.

"It's hilarious," Nicole added.

I found myself laughing along with them. "We need to hang out more often. I know we only hang out when Victor's in town, but seriously."

"You can call us anytime," Mia said. "But you know we're homebodies. It's either the house or the park or whatever else we can take the kids to."

"You can bring them to the brewery." I shrugged. "We can set up a section for them to play while you guys hang out."

She gaped. "Seriously?"

"Yeah, why not? Kids come all the time."

"New favorite person." She lifted her glass to clink it against mine. "Officially new favorite person." She looked behind me as she sipped. "Hot dude at twelve o'clock and he's headed this way. Act natural."

I laughed because I knew without turning that it had to be Nathaniel.

"This is what you do when you brunch with friends?" Jensen asked, raising an eyebrow.

"With my single friends? Obviously," she said. "I need everyone to get their happily ever after."

Jensen wrapped an arm around her and whispered something in her ear. I wasn't sure what it was, but it made her blush hard and made me look away because I felt like an intruder. I finally pivoted around, wondering what was taking Nathaniel so long to get to me. When I saw him, my breath caught in my throat. He hadn't been wearing suits lately, but today he was. He was dressed in a navy-blue suit, no tie, his top button undone. His eyes stayed on mine as he walked over, my heart pounding with each step he took.

"That one's yours?" Mia asked behind me.

I nodded, still looking at him. "He's mine."

Nathaniel grinned. When he reached me, he lowered his head and kissed me deeply, not caring that we were in a restaurant full of people. "Missed you, baby."

"I saw you this morning."

"Missed you anyway." He took the empty seat I'd been saving beside me and looked up, introducing himself to Jensen and Mia, and saying hi to Victor and Nicole.

We spent the rest of the day amongst friends, laughing at stories from their childhoods and talking about our hopes for the future. I'd agreed to come to breakfast to discuss impending decisions about Dad's apartment and mine, but I was happy to put all of that on the backburner at least for now. One thing I'd learned this past year was that life was too long to settle on things that made you unhappy and too short to let it pass you by.

FORTY-TWO

NEW YEAR'S EVE

"I CAN'T BELIEVE you'd signed up for a dating app while you were dating me," Nathaniel said. He was grouchier than usual tonight.

"I didn't sign up." I rolled my eyes. "I can't believe you continuously answer the phone for your ex-girlfriend."

"Does it really bother you?" He held his vibrating phone in his hand. Lisa had been calling him for who knows how long, surely thinking they were due to get back together, and it was definitely bothering me.

"Obviously. She wants you back and I hate knowing that it's a possibility."

"It's not even remotely a possibility." He frowned, looking at me. He answered the call. "Lisa, hey, I'm going to need to ask you to stop calling me. The love of my life doesn't like it." My mouth dropped. He was silent for a beat. "Thank you for understanding. I wish you the best as well." He hung up and slid the phone into his pocket.

"Let me see your phone." I put my hand out. He took it out and handed it to me. I looked at the minutes on the call, then looked at the rest of the log. He really hadn't spoken to her as often as I thought. Still. "Can I delete her number?"

He chuckled. "Would you like me to get a new number while I'm at it?"

"Actually, that's not a terrible idea."

He laughed harder. "Delete her number if you want. I'll get a new number. Whatever. I don't care as long as you stop being paranoid about something so insignificant."

"It's not insignificant to me." I knew I was pouting, but I didn't care. It really wasn't insignificant to me. I wasn't even trying to compare Nathaniel to Adam because they were entirely different people, but it didn't change the fact that I'd been cheated on and I didn't want to go through that again. So yeah, maybe I was paranoid.

"What if she calls you and tells you she's pregnant with your baby?" I asked.

"That would require me to have fucked her during the last few months, and I haven't even seen her since we broke up."

"What if she tells you she can't live without you and tells you she doesn't need to move in with you yet? Or that a key to your place isn't necessary now, but when she does move in with you, she won't even take over half of your closet?"

"I would still say hell no." He looked amused as he brought his hand to my face. "You're the only one who will ever get a key to my apartment because I want to make it ours. You're the only one I would ever let take over half of my closet, and you're the only person I would ever want to put a baby inside of. What will it take for you to believe me?"

I shrugged, taking a breath. "Time. I guess."

"Okay." He kissed me gently. "Are you ready to go upstairs now?"

"Not really, but Morgan would kill me if we didn't show up." I shrugged. "It's like twenty minutes to midnight anyway."

When we got inside, we said hi to the people we knew and

stood by one of the windows. The fireworks hadn't started, but this was definitely a good place to see them from. Morgan came up beside us, looking like she had some big secret.

"Spill it, Little," I said after a moment.

"You know how I came up with the dating at work app and the singles in my office have been using it?"

"Uh, yeah." I looked at Nathaniel. "It's not the same app I'd signed up for. For feedback."

"Okay." He raised an eyebrow but looked back at Morgan with interest. Anything that had to do with a new invention, he was all over. "So what is the work app? It's only for people in specific offices?"

"Yeah, well, that's the gist of it, yes. Why go meet someone at a bar when in some situations, rules permitting, you can hook up with someone at work." She was talking really fast, the way she does when she's really nervous, and in turn, it was making me nervous.

"What did you do? Did you hook up with someone you weren't supposed to?"

"No." She shook her head. "That's the thing. This is supposed to be an intellectual app. No physical hookups. It's very . . . new."

"Not that new," Nathaniel said under his breath. He shrugged when I shot him a look. "What? That's essentially what Match is, or was before social media."

"Okay, what's your point? Why are you freaking out?"

"I think I've been talking to my boss," she whisper-shouted, pulling out her phone. "And he wants to meet me. Tonight."

"So go," Nathaniel said. "What's the problem?" He looked around. "I mean, aside from bailing out on the party you made us all come to."

My mouth dropped, but I couldn't help but laugh. "Why not wait until tomorrow?"

"I'm going to tell him we need to break things off. Honestly, this app was a stupid idea. Doomed from the start. I'm trying to look for a new job."

"Because of this?" I gasped.

"No." She frowned. "No. I just really want to branch out and find something that leaves me with more me time so I can develop more apps on my own."

"You're working there because you need a steady income," Nathaniel said, "But I thought the dating app was yours?"

"It is, but it hasn't made any money yet. I need to give it a year and until then I'm stuck working in this company and my freaking boss now knows about my app and is on it, and if he finds out I made it and that I'm the one he's most likely been talking to he'll fire me anyway."

"I thought your boss was Devon's best friend?"

"He is Devon's best friend," she said, wide-eyed. "Oh my God, Devon is going to kill me."

"Devon, your brother? The one in the NFL?" Nathaniel asked, shaking his head. "Yeah, that's not a situation I'd want to be in."

"Right," she said, chewing on her fingernail. "I need to think about this and I need another drink."

We watched her walk away. Nathaniel chuckled. "Well, shit. I thought I was in a bad situation falling for my friend slash business partner's daughter."

"You are in a bad situation." I smiled up at him as he put his arms around me.

"Do you find yourself going over the same scenarios over and over lately?" he asked.

"Sometimes," I whispered. "Like baseball with Dad."

"I keep thinking about that meeting, when he told us all his health was declining rapidly." He exhaled. "He was watching me cautiously the entire time, as if asking for forgiveness for not telling me beforehand. I just can't understand why he wouldn't tell me beforehand."

I squeezed him in a tight hug. "I don't think he wanted you to worry. You know how he was. He never wanted to talk about anything negative."

"Death is invitable," he said, pulling back and holding my gaze. "We're the ones who make it a negative thing because we're selfish. Because we don't want to say goodbye. We don't want to let go."

"Yeah." It was true, but really, how could you not make it negative when you know you're not going to see the person you love at a moment's notice? "Hey, Nate," I said after a beat.

He chuckled. "What?"

"You wanna have a threesome with me?"

He raised an eyebrow. "Sounds tempting."

"Only tempting?"

"I don't know how I feel about sharing you," he said. "Actually, that's a lie, I know I hate the idea of sharing you." He pressed his forehead against mine. "I know I wanted to rip Adam apart for touching your damn elbow at the funeral. Imagine how I'd feel about sharing you completely?"

I kissed him softly. "Hey, Nate?"

"Stop calling me that, sweetheart," he grumbled against my lips.

"Why? Everyone else does."

"You're not everyone else." He pulled back. "You're the *only* one."

"What does that mean?" I whispered.

"It means I'm in love with you. It means I have been since the moment I met you. It means I want to stop playing these games where you're not spending every single night in my bed, and before you start with your hating on men bullshit, if it makes you feel better, I'll move in with you instead. Whatever it takes as long as we're never apart." He searched my eyes. "I know it's too soon to ask you to marry me. I don't even know if that's something you want, but I never want to let you go, and it's the only way I know I can keep you. Forever."

"What if you want me to give your key back?"

"I never wanted my key back." He cupped both sides of my face. "I would never in a million years want my key back. Come home with me and stay forever."

"Forever ever?"

"Forever ever."

And that was how, at midnight, with fireworks going off outside, we ended up with our arms wrapped around each other, kissing like tomorrow may never come, because you could never be too sure, and I was done wasting time. But, that was the consequence of falling in love. The best consequence.

EPILOGUE

I'D BEEN DEPRESSED all week and had run out of things to blame it on—the weather, the second brew bar I was scheduled to open not passing the building inspection for the second time in a row, the fact that my dad's birthday had been looming all week and now that it was here I was even more upset than I imagined I'd be. On a whim, I'd called my ticket contact and was amazed to find out that one of the seats she'd sold me before was available. I called it kismet and bought it right away. Now that I was sitting there though, I felt different. The seat beside me was empty, but according to her, the person who bought it purchased four only to end up reselling the one I got, which meant I got lucky and I'd soon have three neighbors beside me. I looked at my phone for the fourth time, expecting Nathaniel to call me back at any minute. He'd been out of town the entire week, checking out a tech company in Seattle.

Apparently they needed more start-up money, and since he and Ryan had it and they went gaga over anything tech, they stayed a few more days to work out a deal. His flight was supposed to land any minute and I'd sent him a text letting him know I was trying to get a ticket for the game, but he was in the air, so I wasn't expecting a response any time soon.

I sat down after the pledge and started fighting a box of Cracker Jacks. You would think after years of opening them, I'd be a pro, but my fingers slipping on the box proved otherwise. Unlike the last time I'd been there, I checked my phone every five seconds. Dad wouldn't have been pleased. He would've made fun of me and shook his head in between shouting at the umpire. The thought alone made me smile, but it soon faltered. I missed him more than I ever imagined I would. I missed badgering him about his smoking habits and I missed going over for breakfast in the morning. Victor and Nathaniel helped me put his apartment and mine on the market at the same time. I thought about staying in the building, but I couldn't. Every time I rode the elevator or there was something as simple as a knock on my door, I just about lost it. Nathaniel asked me to move in with him before it was even listed. Of course, I'd made that difficult as well. I didn't want to be the woman who once again let a man take care of her, but he made it feel different. He made it feel like he wanted to take care of me and he'd asked me to take care of him as well. The rest of the row started filling in and a sense of sadness hit me again. I put my phone away and focused on the game, determined not to let myself start crying. I'd cried enough in this seat.

I rattled my box of candy popcorn and popped another one in my mouth. The kiss camera came on, then a dance camera, then birthdays. My chest squeezed as those scrolled on. Then, I saw, "In Celebration of Winston Rose's life". I gasped, dropping the little box in my hand as I brought my hand to my mouth and looked around. Nathaniel was standing in the aisle, watching me. His hair was in disarray, he wore navy blue dress pants and a white button-down that looked slightly wrinkled. I felt like I was frozen as I stared at him, like the scene was a picture and not a moment I was actually living. His mouth tugged slightly as he excused himself and took the seat beside me.

"Surprised?"

"But you . . . " I blinked. "You . . . " I shook my head. "How did . . ."

He smiled. "You may want to wait until you find your words, princess. I don't think I've ever seen you speechless before."

"You were supposed to be on an airplane right now," I finally managed to get out, rushed and rather loudly. "When did you plan to get that on the screen? How did you even get in here?"

"You think I don't know you?" He raised an eyebrow. "I asked you a month ago if you wanted to come to this game—"

"And I said no. It would be too painful."

"But you live for pain, so I knew you'd come anyway."

"I don't live for pain." I frowned. "This was a last-minute decision. My girl didn't even think she'd be able to get me a seat."

"Brittney is good at keeping secrets." He chuckled at my obvious confusion. "I bought these seats a month ago."

"But . . ."

"I'm a good liar. What can I say?"

"I don't think that's a good trait to have or one you should boast about to your girlfriend."

His gaze flickered to the screen. Mine followed. *Presley Rose, you are a royal pain in my butt. Will you marry me?* was written on the screen now. My mouth dropped. It switched and the same thing was written again. And again. And again. And again. And then the announcer said, *"For God's sake, Presley Rose, say yes already."* I covered my face, hoping to hide my embarrassment, but I was sure it showed even through them.

"Has she said yes already?" the other announcer asked.

"Let's pan in on them. Where are they sitting?" the other said.

"Oh my God, Nathaniel Bradley. Of all the annoying,

stupid, crazy things you've done, this one takes the cake," I said through my hands, still hiding. "I'm going to kill you for this."

He laughed, bringing my hands down. I felt like my face was glowing red. I was sure it was. My body temperature would never reach normal numbers after this. I stared at him, hoping it looked more like a glare than a dumb stare.

"Presley Rose, I want to bicker and argue with you, kiss and make up with you, take care of you even when you remind me you don't need me, I want to grow old with you, have kids with you, and more importantly, I want to love you like you've never imagined being loved before. You're my dream girl, my ultimate crush, the unattainable love of my life that I somehow managed to reel in. I think I've been in love with you forever. Let me keep you for just as long. Please?"

I blinked, but this time the tears did trickle down my face and they weren't sad. This time, I wasn't thinking about how much this place reminded me of things I could no longer have, but how this man before me has made every effort to make me find happiness everywhere. I nodded, brushing the tears off my cheeks and when my brain caught up with my heart, I threw my arms around his neck and kissed him.

"You couldn't possibly have been in love with me forever," I whispered against his mouth.

"I was."

I shook my head, smiling.

He smiled back. "I was just waiting for you to catch up."

"And that, ladies and gentleman, is what we call a happily ever after," the announcer said as the camera actually zoomed in on us.

The people around us cheered, and when Nathaniel took out a ring and slipped it onto my finger, I felt like I could soar. When everyone settled, I turned to him.

"How long have you been planning this?"

"My entire life." His eyes glinted with amusement when I shoved him playfully. "A while."

"Does anyone know?" I asked. "Morgan? Jamie?"

"Are you crazy? They would've probably made me get them tickets and I'd already spent a fortune making sure that screen kept replaying the same message continuously."

"People were probably pissed you took up all the slots."

He shrugged a shoulder. "Oh well."

"Not nice, Nathaniel." I shoved him playfully again and stretched my hand to admire my ring. "It's so beautiful."

On our way home, I stared some more. He wrapped an arm around my shoulder and pulled me to him.

"You know you haven't said yes."

I looked up at him. "What do you mean?"

"I mean, you haven't said yes." He chuckled. "You've been staring at the ring, staring at me, kissing me, but you haven't agreed to marry me."

"Ask me again."

"What?" His eyes widened. "I bared my soul to you back there. What do you mean, ask you again?"

"Ask me again and be nice, otherwise I'm not sure what answer you'll get." I raised an eyebrow.

"Is that so?" He mimicked me, raising an eyebrow back. "I'm not sure I want to ask someone so bossy to spend the rest of my life with me."

"Your life?" I laughed, holding his hand as we reached our building. "What about my life?"

"Good point." He tilted his head as we waited for the elevator.

He didn't say a word as we stepped inside and rode it up to our floor. He didn't say a word as we walked down the hall or as we unlocked the door and opened it. He didn't say a word as we took our jackets off and hooked them on the hangers. Once we were in the kitchen, he faced me again, bringing his hand to my face.

"You are the bossiest, craziest person I've ever met."

"This doesn't sound like a nice proposal," I whispered.

"I told you, I used up all my sentimental lines already." He smiled slightly, caressing my face. "I love you, princess. I will love you forever, whether you accept my proposal or not, but I really would love it if you stand by my side through this relentless, crazy life we live. Will you marry me?"

"Yes." I nodded. "Forever and ever yes."

He grinned and it was the most blinding, gorgeous smile. "You make me the happiest man alive."

As we kissed, I remembered the announcers' last words to us, and held him tighter, because this was the happily ever after I'd always dreamed of.

UNTITLED

Do you want to read Victor and Nicole's story free? Get it here:
Elastic Hearts

FUCK MARRIAGE BY TARRYN FISHER

CHAPTER ONE

The salon is warm with all west-facing windows. I stare out at the parking lot wishing for a fan, a breeze—anything to cool my skin. A mother chases her toddler across the cracked asphalt. He falls. Rolling onto his back, he screams, arms and legs flailing. When she picks him up, I see that her hair is stuck to her face in wet clumps. The entire state of Washington is being strangled by stagnant heat.

I want a cigarette so bad I'm jittery. The bell to the door jingles, and one of the stylists walks in carrying two tabletop fans under her arms. She purses her lips to blow her bangs off her forehead, but they stay put.

"It's all they had left," she says to a different stylist.

They confer about where to put the fans and settle on a central location. If I lean to the left I can catch some of the breeze they're causing.

"Can you sit up straight?" my stylist asks, tapping me on the shoulder. "I thought you wanted to cut it." She stands over me, hands suspended, mid-action.

I can see the damp on her blouse where she's sweating through her clothes. She opens and closes her scissors for emphasis, drawing my eyes back to her face. I think of comparing her to Edward Scissorhands, but she's freshly twenty-five and I doubt she'd know who he is.

"Change of plans," I say. "I'm going home next week."

The word *home* is a sour word in my mouth. Even as I say it, my tongue curls back in protest. Home to me is a city, not a house, or a husband, or a family. Maybe because I don't really have those things anymore, or maybe because I'm not cut out to have those things.

"No one there has ever seen me with long hair," I explain, as if that's a good enough reason.

It's not entirely the truth. There's no one left to see me. My friends are gone. In my exodus from the city two years ago, I made the decision for them. For a while they'd tried to stay in touch, but in my grief I sent their efforts to voicemail. And just like that, they stopped trying. My ex was the one who stayed so he inherited custody of our friends. It sounds silly to think that, but it's true. When there's a divorce, lines are drawn, sides taken. I reach up, running my fingers through the length of it. It's past the middle of my back, hanging in sleek mermaid waves, thanks to Tina's grooming. I like the idea of them seeing me in my new body, with my new hair. I am thinner, longer, wiser...more jaded. If Woods met me now, there'd be no way he'd think me trusting.

"Home, huh? I thought you grew up here in Port Townsend," Tina says.

She likes to make fun of my divided loyalty; though, if you put a gun to my head I'd choose New York every time.

"Do you have a cigarette?" I ask.

"Nice try. You told me not to give you one no matter how much you beg."

"I just want to put it in my mouth."

"That's what she said," Tina jokes.

She rummages around in her bag and pulls one out: Marlboro. *Ew.* I stick it between my lips and close my eyes in pleasure.

"You're pathetic," she says when I hand it back to her.

"I know."

"—but beautiful."

"In New York I'm Billie, and here I'm plain ol' Wendy."

"Oh my dear," she says, spinning my seat around to face the mirror. "You're anything but plain."

I smile at my reflection. A lot has changed since I arrived home two years ago, my tail tucked between my legs. And Tina is right, partially right: I am no longer the plain girl I once was. Rejection is a fine motivator.

"When do you leave?" She unclips the robe from my neck and I unfold myself from her chair. The breeze from the fan finds me and I close my eyes in pleasure.

"Tomorrow." I turn to face her.

"Will you see Woods?"

Tina's stylist chair doubled as a therapy chair my first year home. She probably knows more about my failed marriage than my own family.

"That's the plan," I say.

She frowns. "I hope you know what you're doing, Wendy. Be careful, okay?"

Careful? That's what I will not be this time. Careful is what got me into this mess in the first place.

"Sure," I say, and Tina frowns. "Wish me luck?"

"Luck? You don't need luck for revenge. You just need balls."

ALSO BY CLAIRE

Also in Kindle Unlimited:

Then There Was You - sexy, angsty duet

Kaleidoscope Hearts - brother's best friend romance

Paper Hearts - ultimate second-chance romance

Elastic Hearts - forbidden second-chance romance

Complete Hearts Series - all three bundled up in one

Prefer a standalone?

The Player - sports romance (Kindle Unlimited)

The Wilde One - music industry romance (Kindle Unlimited)

Want a little suspense with your romance?

There is No Light in Darkness - a little mystery, a lot of love.

Because You're Mine - sexy mafia romance